My Journey Into The Oncoming Holocaust

Larry Lee Farmer

This is a work of fiction. Names, characters, places, and incidents are either the product of the author's imagination or are used fictitiously, and any resemblance to actual persons living or dead, business establishments, events, or locales, is entirely coincidental.

My Journey Into The Oncoming Holocaust

ISBN-13: 9780997683714
ISBN-10: 0997683716
Digital ISBN: 978-0-9976837-0-7
Library of Congress Control Number: **XXXX (If applicable)**
Published in the United States of America

It's a long way from Texas to the Middle East.
But when Olivia's husband Max sees his American
Dream flounder in the post-911 world, she follows
him back to his home in Lebanon. Just in time for
the Arab Spring.

For months rockets hit the areas where I lived.
Daesh bombed Christian villages, as well as Shia,
because they wanted to create an Islamic country just
like the Taliban had done before in Afghanistan,
the country that harbored Bin Laden and inspired
911. Some of the rockets were a mere three miles from
our house. We heard them daily. We heard them in
our sleep. Once, a rocket came so close, the
repercussion knocked me out of bed as I slept.

Dedication

To Betty and to Nan
And to the memory of Luz Long

CHAPTER 1

I heard footsteps, but wanted to finish the last of my typing. I knew it had to be the client my boss was sending. His case was lucrative for our law firm with the chance of success promising. That meant I must handle him with care. Yet here I was, right off the bat in my new job, keeping him waiting, if only a few seconds.

Instinctively, with one fluid motion, I hit the return key to finish my brief, then turned towards him with a warm smile on my face. A smile that turned to a gasp when I saw him. All tall, dark, and gorgeous hunk of him. My girlish reaction embarrassed me, though he relaxed my angst with an ever so slight and reassuring grin. As if he had caused women before me a heart skipping gasp. I was sure that was so.

"Are you Max?" I asked after regaining my composure. "I was told you were on your way. I have your file in front of me on my computer screen."

"Yes, I'm Max," he affirmed.

I waited for him to say more, but his straightforward answer was it. The strong, silent type perhaps. I studied him quickly. With his olive skin and dark black hair he looked Hispanic. In contrast to my blonde hair, blue eyes, and white Anglo skin. He seemed tall for a Hispanic. My older brother stood six foot three. Max seemed that height looking at him. A foot taller than me I was sure. His build was solid with well-defined muscles. Every bit the physique of an athlete. Looking at the crows feet around his eyes and slight line creases near his mouth, I guessed him to be in his forties. Like me. *Why does all this matter to me*, I wondered? But I knew why. I glanced at his left hand quickly. No ring. I hoped he noticed no rings on my fingers likewise.

"I've read parts of your profile, Max." I looked at him apologetically. "I know we haven't been introduced," I said. "I didn't mean to be so informal as to call you by your first name."

"You can call me Max," he said with his smile now friendlier.

"Good," I replied. "It makes it more comfortable to work informally if you don't mind. My name is Olivia." I held out my hand to shake his in greeting, to break what was left of any ice. And hopefully for him to notice my bare, single fingers. "Your case is given a high priority. I have a lot of forms for us to fill out."

"Yes," Max replied. "I don't live in San Antonio anymore. I had to take leave from my job and only have a few days to be here. There are claims to file."

His lack of an accent of any kind had me baffled. All the Hispanics I knew had either a Texas drawl or a Spanish accent. His speech and delivery seemed so refined. As a matter of fact, there was something dignified in his bearing overall, as if he were a college professor or lawyer. Perhaps even an attaché for President George W. Bush or for Texas Governor Rick Perry for all I knew. Instead he was in marketing and finance with a Master's degree in economics. Going by the gist of his essay, he was one of these managerial types hired to turn corporate situations around.

"I understand," I said. "You're my highest priority. We can work into the evening if need be and however long tomorrow. We'll just see how it goes."

Being with Max didn't seem like work. Dealing with forms, essays, and questionnaires felt more like shopping online together. We worked through the afternoon without taking a break.

"It's seven o'clock," I mentioned as we finished yet another form. "I'm reaching a diminishing returns situation here," I said with a laugh. "We can start early in the morning if it's all right with you."

"That's fine," he said. "When do you arrive at work?"

"Eight o'clock."

"I'll see you then," he said as he got up from his chair to walk out.

I grimaced slightly as he dashed any fantasy I had that we might have dinner together.

I hated working late, if for no other reason than our office was near a bad neighborhood. My boss owned the building where our law firm was located and rented it out to two other law firms as well. The building was located across the street from the County Courthouse, but just a couple of blocks away a rather volatile area began. I rented a parking space in this poorer part of town to save money. It worked out fine during the day, but once it got past twilight it seemed the seedy elements began to get obnoxious. In fact, some of the criminal cases our lawyers handled were for inhabitants in this part of town. Criminals requiring our lawyers walked in and out of our building often. Many did their mischief nearby, right in this area where I was parked. Another reason to be asked on a date by Max. That would have made me feel much safer.

Even the walk past the courthouse made me ill at ease. I felt so alone and vulnerable. I could feel lusting eyes staring at me as I entered the parking lot, but assured myself it was only paranoia. As I neared my car, however, I saw a shadowy figure approach me. *Why isn't this parking lot better lit*, I wondered?

"Do you have some pocket change?" the shadow turned solicitor asked me. "I need to catch the bus home."

"Sorry," I said meekly as I shook my head no.

"Listen, lady, I really need to get home. I got a wife waiting for me. Can't you check your purse for a couple of dollars? I sure would appreciate it."

"I'm serious," I lied. "I have no money left. I'm just a secretary and I spent what little I had on a bottle of water and a sandwich from our machine at the office."

"I know you have to have a couple of dollars on you, lady. Why don't you loosen up and check? I sure would appreciate it."

"I have to go," I said as I walked past him towards my car.

He grabbed me by the arm gruffly and scowled menacingly.

A car pulled into the lot from the street. I looked towards it expectantly, hoping my tormentor would think I knew someone and back off, but he gripped my arm all the harder.

"Are you okay, Olivia?" I heard a voice from the car say. I focused and saw it was Max. Just like the US cavalry. "Is this nice man causing problems?" Max asked further.

My tormentor sneered at me, then turned to face off against Max. The car door opened with athletic and muscular Max getting out and walking our way. I saw the look of concern on my tormentor's face. He loosened his grip as I jerked my arm away and mocked him with a smirk.

"I really do need to get home," I said to him. "Can't say it wasn't nice meeting you. Tell your wife hello."

The man readied to say something but then walked away.

"I should have walked you to your car at the office," Max apologized. "I had no idea you parked this far away."

"I'm newly divorced," I explained. "I just moved from New Mexico to be near my parents. The parking lot at work is small and there was no room for me with the lawyers and clientele, so I chose a cheap lot to rent from. I should have asked you to escort me. I was even nervous since it's dark out, but I was afraid you'd think me forward or something."

"It was irresponsible of me not to ask," Max said showing guilt. "Can I make it up to you?" I looked at him with longing, in hopes it was an offer to take me out. "There's a Mediterranean grill nearby," he said. "That's where I was headed when I saw you here. They serve lamb there. Would you like to join me?"

I wasn't much for lamb, but wasn't going to tell him.

"Sure," I answered with a chirp as we walked to his car.

"I'll bring you back after we're finished," he offered.

He walked me to the passenger side where he opened the door for me. Once I was in, he closed the door behind me. I was never so charmed in my life. A real Southern gentleman. I had almost forgotten. I decided it was worth my unsavory encounter with the antagonist as I now had my hoped for date with Max. I wanted to believe it was all some cosmic plan.

"It's good," he said while driving, "that I stopped at that convenience store back there to pick up a quart of milk. I left the office before you and would have never seen you in the parking lot if I hadn't stopped at a store first."

"Makes you believe in fate." I replied with a smile.

It was a greasy spoon type restaurant where he took me. I never fancied a Mediterranean grill in the middle of San Antonio, but it was Texas' second largest city. It made sense somehow there would be some diversification. *What kind of cuisine is Mediterranean,* I wondered as I studied the pictures of dishes alongside the menus hung from the walls by the counter where we ordered? I recognized nothing except rice, lamb, and kebab. This could be scary, especially since I hated lamb.

"Khalil," a voice from behind the counter bellowed. "You are back, my friend."

A short, brown skinned, mustachioed man was looking at Max as he spoke.

"I arrived yesterday," Max answered him with a warm smile. "I am in town for a week on business. I have much to do, then must hurry back to Kuwait."

"It is good to see you again," the man said. He turned to a woman at the cash register to the side of the counter. "Look who came to see us. It's Khalil."

"Don't tease me," she scolded while reading a piece of paper. "That's not nice."

"No, I'm serious. Look up for a moment. Right here ready to order."

The woman burst into an exuberant smile as she did so. Quickly, she rushed from behind the cash register over to us, then pushed me aside to hug Max affectionately.

"You couldn't stay away, Khalil," she said. "I knew it." Max glowed as he hugged her back. She looked over at the man behind the counter. "It's on us. Anything he wants."

"Of course, of course," the man replied. "Our long lost comrade has returned. Everything is on the house in celebration."

"And so who is this?" the woman asked as she turned to look at me. "You didn't pick her up and bring her from Kuwait. I can be sure of that."

"This is the legal secretary I am working with," Max answered with a smile. "She is helping me with my case. I filed a lawsuit here before I moved away and we worked late because of my time constraint. I am rewarding her for all her efforts."

"She's very lovely, Max," the woman said as she scoped me out. "You still have good taste. It looks to me like you are rewarding yourself. So, my dear, take good care of Khalil and we will take good care of you. Enjoy our feast tonight and come back anytime."

I looked quizzically at Max, as if to ask what all this was about. I could understand seeing old friends again, but something else was going on here. Especially with all this about him being Khalil to these people and living in Kuwait.

"So, my friend," the man behind the counter asked, "what will it be?"

"The lamb with *basmati* rice," Max answered. "I assume everything is still *halal*."

"That is all we serve, of course."

Max looked at me to see what I wanted.

"I haven't a clue what to order. I just know I hate lamb."

"Americans always like kebab," Max suggested. "They have both lamb and beef." I nodded my head to approve the choice of beef. "It's the smell, isn't it? You're problem with lamb, I mean."

"Absolutely. It is wretched. I don't know how you handle it."

We walked to a small wooden table in the corner. There would be no need to look for conversation. I had a million things I was dying to find out.

CHAPTER 2

What possessed a middle-aged American woman, namely me, to up and start a new life in a country half a world away? A country even further away culturally. A Middle Eastern Muslim country. I'm not a feminist, but I certainly am not into being dominated like I heard time and again happened in Muslim countries.

This was just a few years removed from the turmoil and aftermath of the suicide airliners that killed over three thousand innocent people in New York's twin towers on September 11, 2001. A horrific incident that became a pseudonym known as 9/11. It has since been labelled 911, like the emergency telephone number. Soon came the wars incurred from it. 911 changed the national consciousness. 911, in fact, changed everything.

I'm a rural Texas girl. That may explain part of why I ventured off to places far removed. Texas women have a reputation for being rugged and independent. We fought Santa Anna and the Comanche, and worked the fields with our men. My parents survived the Dust Bowl on their farms in West Texas during the depression while they were growing up, then the Second World War just as they reached adulthood. I, myself, grew up on a cotton farm in southern Texas and I suppose I've got some of that cultural DNA in me. But that doesn't really explain it to me, now that I look back and bother to wonder why I pulled up stakes for a new challenge.

I should blame my brother probably. He outdid every folk tale I ever heard. He is ten years older than me anyway, and seemed bigger than life while I was growing up. Through the years I got letters from every corner of the globe. He was even in a Hollywood movie as a stuntman. Just walked onto the set, auditioned, and got the part. He also got stranded on a Greek island when the war with Turkey broke out over Cyprus. He had to stow away on a boat to get back to Athens, just in time to see the military dictatorship there fall. I remember the letters he wrote me as he trekked overland through Iran just before the Shah abdicated. From there, on through the then Soviet satellite of Afghanistan, then through the Khyber Pass, down to India, and eventually the Far East. Years later he sang Country music in Switzerland for several years, if you can believe.

I suppose his example spurred my impulse for adventure more than anything. I was bored with my life and always envied him. I felt I hadn't done much to show anybody. I made a good middle class living. I had a happy marriage once, but that was over and I was on a rebound. That probably was part of the restlessness in me too. But actually, nothing fully explains why I married Khalil in 2006 and followed him back to his home in Lebanon by way of the Persian Gulf states.

"Khalil means true and intimate relationship," he explained to me that first night at the Mediterranean grill when we first met and got to know one another.

Though Khalil was well travelled and well educated, I was as leery of an Arab as anyone when I met him. It wasn't engrained in me to be so, but after 911 we all were. That's why he left America, in fact. He had had it with post-911 attitudes about Arabs everywhere he went. He came from a good family, but they were Shia. The worst of Muslims in many people's minds. Al-Qaeda, which is Sunni, seemed more evil anymore, but between the mullahs in Iran and Hezbollah in Lebanon, the Shia seemed like out of the Dark Ages to Americans. If an American even knew what a Shia or Sunni was.

Max, which is what he called himself now in hopes to pass as Hispanic, seemed the epitome of sophistication to me. I was intrigued and fascinated. Just who was this new guy in my life?

As I listened to his stories, I tried keeping my feet on the ground, so as to not be taken in by an Arab charlatan like the suckers I heard about on the news constantly. I studied him skeptically. I even watched the movie, *Not Without My Daughter*. The doctor in that movie was a Shiite from Iran. He was happy here while chasing the American dream. Until he was mistreated, got bitter, then went home and became a monster.

I began to trust Max the more I got to know him. His stories sounded real and he seemed sincere and authentic. A good man.

"I had high hopes to join the Drug Enforcement Agency," he told me in one of our many talks each night after we worked on his case the week I first met him. "Also the Central Intelligence Agency, or the Federal Bureau of Investigation. I was recruited by all of them because I have talent with languages. However, the security checks revealed I was from Lebanon and was Shiite, which dashed any of these hopes. I have a Master's in economics and excel in finance. I found work as a top manager in business. But nothing seemed possible after awhile because of my sensitivity. That's an Arab trait. We're so sensitive. I tried to hang in there, knowing of this characteristic about myself. Maybe I would grow and become an even better manager from this. But even the slightest look or comment regarding Muslims and the Middle East, in general, made the anger seethe in me. I am just too thin skinned. I had to come to grips with that. I knew my chances of a good job here were limited in spite of my overall competence."

I liked his honesty about his flaws. He called himself thin skinned, which is true, but it wasn't just thin skin that caused him trouble. In spite of how far I've seen America come concerning race, religion, and ethnicity in my lifetime, there are many intolerant people here. I think we're probably the most caring and tolerant people on earth, which isn't saying much, but intolerance seems to be a human trait and probably for good reasons. That's the best I can do in making excuses for how he was treated. I don't blame him a bit for being angry.

"I came to America just after the Iranian crisis happened with the Ayatollah Khomeini," he related to me on our last day together working on the case. "Many thought I was Iranian and would literally spit on me on college campuses I attended."

"My brother had this problem as a Marine," I told Max, thinking back to when Cotton came home in the early seventies after serving. "Liberals did this to him. It may well be rednecks that spit on you, but you said it was educated, supposedly open minded people. Judging others and distrust seem to be a human trait. No group has a monopoly. I've detested people too. We're geared to this reaction probably to protect ourselves. But it's also easily an overreaction."

"I had an athletic scholarship for soccer and thrived playing," Max continued. "I love competition. I need challenges in my life. I am talented, big, and strong as well. I made our national team back home. I was so excited for the opportunities it presented me in America. But being Arab was a constant battle in every university I went to and I was always verbal in defending myself. This competitive spirit in me. There is a fight inside me. Arab blood. Especially Shia. We're the most hot-blooded of all. But I don't mean as part of any jihadist attitude. I am indeed religious. I love and respect Islam, but my views and lifestyle are modern and moderate. There is much to love about Islam, in spite of things not so lovable about some Muslim I have met. I will not make excuses for my culture or my religion. There is much to love and admire, but excesses too. But I admire the ethics and rituals of Islam. I just resent fanatics."

"We all have our baggage," I replied to him. "I love Texas and the South. The old South even. But boy are there Neanderthals in the mix. Maybe rock apes is a better word. There are people I can't stand. I want to crawl behind a couch sometimes. But I don't feel like smoking dope because of it, or being cool and hip either, and go around bashing the culture that nurtured me quite successfully. My culture did a lot right for me. We're our own managers, Max. There's a saying how everyone is his own priest. That's not just about religion, it's about everything we do. We are responsible for our own behavior and our own results. Our religion, our family, our country, and our culture provide the framework, but also stick us with baggage. The rest is up to us."

"I appreciate that, Olivia. You are level headed. I like talking to you."

I smiled, even blushed, at the compliment.

"I'm homesick for the Persian Gulf," he said point blank. "I spent much of my youth living in Kuwait. I'm going back there tomorrow. It's where I belong. But I tell you; my departure is America's loss as far as I'm concerned. I became an American citizen years ago chasing the American dream. If I could have stayed here in peace it would have been to America's benefit. Consider me arrogant, but I tell you this."

I assumed we would never meet again. Then a few weeks later, from out of nowhere, he returned to settle a car accident case with his lawyer, the one for whom I worked. But my boss screwed up so badly that what looked like a million dollar settlement turned into a total loss with Max only getting a few thousand dollars. He had left everything behind in Kuwait thinking he would be in

America for a protracted stay, then go back with a large settlement. But not to be.

My intrigue over him had not diminished. I constantly thought about him with fondness while he was gone. Then suddenly, here he was in my life again. He was as handsome as I remembered, and with incredible charisma and demeanor. His presence held swagger and command as it mixed with his intelligence and worldly knowledge. I was nervous as hell about this man with Arab origins, but couldn't resist. We dated for a month upon his return when he proposed. He was even more bugged with America after being deprived of a fortune now, and more determined than ever to be rid of his adopted homeland. So, I had to make up my mind on the spot if I should marry him. Believe me, I didn't want to do it. That's when I watched the film, *Not Without My Daughter*. I wanted to come to grips with what I might be getting myself into. So again in my head, I went over the stories I heard about Arab hustlers because these stories haunted me. But when push came to shove, I took the plunge. I trusted him. He had so much I admired. I was game. We quickly got married, just before his departure back to Kuwait.

Now to tell my parents. And my brother. And his sons, my nephews, who worshipped the ground I stood on. But I was going to follow Max come hell or high water. I expected them to be understanding. These rural Texans had been around and were not the stereotypes so called open minded people hung on their ilk. But I was going anyway like I said, no matter how they took it.

CHAPTER 3

I heard a knock and knew who it was. As I opened the door I saw intense looks directed my way.

"Well, look whose here," I said, smiling broadly to lighten things up while letting my family in. "Come on, come on," I said to shoo them. My oldest nephew Bucky was the first one to enter and I gave him a big hug. "How's my wrestler?" I greeted him, loving how manly he hugged me back. "You're getting as big as your dad. I can feel those muscles. I feel sorry for those guys in other schools who have to wrestle you."

"Hello, Aunt Olivia," he greeted back, wearing a scowl in spite of my compliment. "But I'm just a freshman. I'm still learning. I just hope to survive my first year."

"He's big for his age," my brother Cotton said. "He was good enough to make varsity right off. But a lot of kids in the big cities like Houston, Dallas, and San Antonio have been wrestling since elementary school. He's liable to get his butt kicked for awhile by older kids that grew into what's his size already."

"Dad already told me that stuff," Bucky said with a tired moan. "He gave a big speech about it. How I'm gonna get my butt kicked my first year, but it will be the best year of my life."

"You're such a bad father," I teased my brother as I walked Bucky to my couch in the living room.

"I'm just doing my job," Cotton replied as he and the others followed us. "First off, it's a warning to him. It ain't no picnic. I have to admit, I'm glad of that."

"Come," I beckoned everyone. "Come sit. Some of y'all can sit on the couch, the rest will have to sit on the chairs at the dining table. I'm down to a few sticks of furniture. It's a small apartment as you can see, with the living room joined as one room with the dining room. It'll be okay. It's just for this afternoon. Then y'all will be going home to Corpus Christi."

I then turned back to Cotton to admonish him further.

"He's your oldest kid, big brother. You can get off this macho crap and encourage him."

"He encourages me a lot," Bucky explained defensively for his dad. "He always has. But he likes the facts of life stuff too. So I won't be a wimp."

"Once a Marine always a Marine," I laughed. "Is that how it is?"

Cotton grinned. Finally, some life in his demeanor.

"He's old enough for that stuff, the so called facts of life," Cotton answered. "The infamous road of hard knocks. It's time even. He wants to be a Marine. This will prepare him."

"You were born with Marine DNA, Bucky," I said in sympathy as I smiled his way. "You never had a chance. You wanted to be a Marine at the youngest age. As soon as you knew there was such a thing as a Marine Corps."

"I want him to win," Cotton said to get back to the subject of Bucky being a wrestler. "I hope he goes undefeated. But mostly, I want him to grow. To toughen. He's big for his age with no experience. Losing's part of life and you have to know how to handle adversity. Common sense says his wrestling career ain't going to start off easy. Like I say, he'll be up against some older kids that have grown physically to his size while wrestling. They'll be juniors and seniors with experience and maturity. So, I don't want a self-fulfilled prophecy with him and get him to lose before he even starts, but I want him to not quit too, when the going gets rough. And it will. So, here we go. The rubber hits the road. It's going to be the best year of his life. He'll hate every minute of it. But learn how to win and how to not ever quit. To want to quit so badly, but not quit anyway. To learn what it takes to win. To know firsthand just how much losing sucks. He's gonna love it. Just hate every breathing minute of it like you're supposed to do about losing."

"That's how you used to write me when you were in boot camp," I said nostalgically while looking at him with affection. I then looked back at Bucky. "I loved his letters from San Diego Marine Corps Recruit Depot. Everyday, it seemed like stories about Drill Instructors and how they screamed at him. All the push ups and squat hoopies, whatever those were. The miles of runs and forced marches. Even the thumpings, where they physically assaulted the privates in training. Practiced karate on him just like in the movie, *An Officer And A Gentleman*. I then looked at Bucky's little brother, my youngest nephew, also called Cotton like his dad, as if to share the memories. "My brother, your dad, seemed to love every sadistic minute of it and now passed it down to his oldest son, Bucky, your older brother. I loved growing up with him as my big brother and inspiration. Bucky will be there for you too."

"Dad already hits me with the facts of life stuff too," Cotton Jr sneered. "We practice baseball everyday."

I looked back at my brother.

"He's just twelve, brother of mine. Ease up a bit with this hard knocks crap."

"You love it, Cotton," my brother moaned to his youngest son. "You know that. You want to be a New York Yankee. You live for baseball. You're in Pony League now, or whatever it is they call it these days. We've got a long way to go."

He then looked at me showing frustration.

"He hit over four hundred last year and didn't make All-Stars. He's so shy and the coaches have their own kids. They act like mine doesn't exist. He's not a power hitter, but gets on over half the time. But it's like with Bucky. Adversity like this only means hang in there and try harder. Life lesson stuff, free of charge."

I smiled at all three of them.

"I'm going to miss all of this," I said while shaking my head in dismay at the thought.

"So why are you leaving us then?" Bucky and Cotton Jr asked in unison with the scowls returning that I saw on them at the doorway when they arrived.

For a second I didn't have an answer. How could I leave them indeed? I watched them grow up. They were the children I couldn't have. All of a sudden, I didn't want to go away from my home, just looking at them again.

"I'm married now," I tried to explain. "My husband lives far away. I didn't mean it to be this way, but it's what happened. He's a very good man. I'm happy to be with him and excited to see another part of life. But I'll come back now and then. We'll keep in contact."

Their scowls remained. They weren't convinced.

"Let's go somewhere," my sister-in-law Connie said to break the stalemate.

"Sure," I answered, glad for her intervention. "Let's go to the Riverwalk one last time. Eat Mexican food."

"The Alamo," Bucky exuded.

"Yes," I seconded, "we'll eat at a restaurant on the Riverwalk right next to the Alamo."

Connie looked at my brother Cotton, her husband, intensely.

"But we are not, understand me, *not* visiting the Alamo," she ordered. "The Riverwalk is as close as we get. We'll spend the entire afternoon at this Alamo place if we let my crazy husband on the grounds. He still, even yet, reads every single plaque and stares in reverence at every single picture there. Sometimes I think he's ready to cry. Absolutely crazy and raising our kids to be just as crazy."

"Crazy enough to marry a Filipina," Cotton sneered back in defiance.

"Let's set the record straight," Connie returned, "*I* married *you*."

"That's right," my mother said on her behalf. "Best thing that ever happened to him. And to me too for that matter."

Connie smiled broadly.

"Thank you, Mother," she said, oozing with affection.

"Are you coming with us or are we splitting up into two vehicles?" my father asked while looking at me. "I brought the van. It'll fit all of us. I'll have to detach the trailer though. It'll only take me a minute. If I can get Bucky and Cotton Jr to help me."

"If you don't mind, let's go in one vehicle so we can chat on the way," I suggested.

We made small talk as we drove, but I knew that once we got settled at the outdoor Riverwalk restaurant, the conversation would get heavy.

San Antonio is the most beautiful city on earth. I know that's not literally true, but true enough. It's an old city. One of the first capitals of Spanish Texas. It's not old like cities in the rest of the world, but old for America and for Texas, and has an antique feel about it. It's hallowed soil to Texans. Not just because of the Alamo, though mostly for that reason, but it's one of the first settlements of New Spain when it was part of Mexico as a Spanish colony. There are beautiful missions of which the Alamo is but one. The memory of the glorious defenders of Texas freedom confronting the tyrant Santa Anna at the Alamo made the whole town seem like a shrine, however. There is a pride, like no other, from just being in the city, much less visiting the site itself.

But the Riverwalk is as peaceful and tranquil as the Alamo and the other missions are majestic and sacred. The San Antonio River originates in the city itself, formed from a cluster of springs that cuts through the heart of the city. There are shops and restaurants on both sides of the banks cluttering it. The view is gorgeous. It was a fitting place to relate about my new, expected life, and to say good-bye.

"Max was named after the famous Lebanese writer Khalil Gibran," I explained as we munched on picante sauce and chips while we waited for our orders. "That's the perfect name for him too.

Max is the name he chose once he decided to pass as a Hispanic. But in Lebanon, he grew up being called Khalil and that probably was an inspiration for him to read so much. I never met anyone that knew so much from studying his books, or from all he's done." I then looked at my brother. "Except maybe for you, Cotton. I wish y'all could have met. He doesn't respect Americans much. They're so shallow and insular to him. Naïve. I have to agree, but I know I'm not one that gets to judge. He thinks me smart, one of the reasons he likes me, but naïve. Ignorant. I'm three years older than him, but it's like I'm three years younger. So, I can't argue with that in comparison to all he knows and has done. But you could, Cotton. You're in his class. I'd love to just sit and listen to y'all exchange stories and information. He even has a Master's degree in economics like you do. Anyway. One of these days y'all will meet."

"He sounds like a very nice man," my mother said.

She said it in a reserved way and I wondered how much she meant it. But I knew she was trying and I appreciated it. The fact that my brother already married a dark skinned foreigner helped pave the way for me, but my parents have come a long way on their own. Texas, like the rest of the South, was segregated while they were growing up. It was while I was growing up also, but that's the only life they knew. They, like much of America, made genuine efforts to expand their outlooks. What was left of racial and cultural bigotry inside of them, I didn't know. But they made their efforts through the years to open up and I think my mother was more worried about the turmoil in the areas where I was going than in any ethnic differences.

"After going through all of Cotton's shenanigans," my mother said, "I guess I can handle you going away with someone that can take care of himself."

Cotton's expression turned to one portraying guilt as he glanced down awkwardly at the table. He nodded his head as if in agreement with what our mother said.

"There's a God," he moaned. "Cause it's payback time these days."

I laughed and asked him what he meant by that.

"I still remember when I joined the Marines to go to Vietnam," he began his explanation. My mother grimaced and looked away towards the peace of the San Antonio River. "Y'all threw a fit."

"I didn't," I said defensively. "Daddy didn't."

Cotton chewed on his lip for a moment then cocked his head slightly to the side.

"Mother sure did," he said.

Everyone looked at Mother who continued her gaze at the river.

"It hurt me," he continued. "I don't know why it did. It even shocked me how much it hurt me the way Mother threw a fit about it. I was so determined about joining. The rest of the country was burning the flag and I was so determined to go fight the bad guys. I even intended for my joining to make a statement of defiance to my dope smoking generation. Then I watched my mother throw a fit. I thought she believed in all I did."

"Do you remember what you said to me?" Mother asked just above a whisper. "To hear that my son quits college to join the Marines to go off to a war no one wanted. To be the last one killed there perhaps. You even told me, 'You can't love me and not want me to do this'. I watched him grow up. Had all these dreams for him. Then not only had to let him go, but go to the abyss for all I knew and never come back. Then he questioned if I loved him."

My brother's look of guilt increased.

"That's why God's paying me back big time," he said. "Now my son wants to be a Marine. Everyday I blame myself. I thought I would be proud and I am. But I wonder if I killed him. Are they going to bring him back in a body bag someday? Because of me." He looked up at me. "Now you, Olivia. If I'd graduated back then from college like everyone else and worked in a bank or taken over the farm, maybe you wouldn't be traipsing off to the Middle Ages."

"If I hadn't met Max," I answered, "I'd be wasting the rest of my life thinking I'm supposed to be watching TV or buying a new car. Pretending life is fulfilling doing so. Don't take credit for me wanting to see something more in life, big brother. I do envy all you've done, and the family you've raised to boot, but whatever it is that made you restless has been haunting me all of my life. Now I met a man that can show me more than I've ever dreamed. I'm grateful for it."

Cotton nodded his head, as if wanting to believe me, and allow himself to have a clean conscience.

"Let me tell you about Max's family," I said, hoping it would emphasize my point.

"Yes," Mother said. "We want to hear about him."

"Not only is Max's real name Khalil, but his last name means lion in Arabic. I'm not sure, after all his explanation about it, if it's like the African lion, or Asian lion, or what they call the Canaanite lion like Samson slew in the Bible. But still, that's a neat last name and garnered of respect about his family. He has lineage. Nothing that we would care about in the West, but he has regional lineage. But there is turmoil in the family too. Related to all that's happened in Lebanon. It was part of Syria for so long. They needed a homeland for all the Middle Eastern Christians. Syria had a past, Lebanon had a Phoenician past. After Constantine, the Middle East was mostly Christian. Then came Muhammed and suddenly it was Muslim. But still with so many Christians and even Jews. So, Lebanon became a refuge for some of those Christians, but with so many Muslims still. They paid a price for this cultural conglomeration. What's going on in the great melting pot of

America is nothing in comparison. Max's family was so involved in all the strife going on we've heard about for decades now. At least for those listening. His mother is Sunni Muslim, his father Shiite. There is nobility-type respect for his family and insanity too. Maybe even literally insanity."

Everyone was staring at me. This wasn't reassuring them at all.

"Max's dad," I continued, "was a professional fighter when he was young and became famous for that. That family is born with genetics any athlete would kill for. At birth they are rock solid muscle. Including the women, which is not a good thing. Although the men are handsome by Arab standards, the women look like men because they are built like solid steel. Anyway, his clan, and there are a slew of them he says, are very pro-government and as far away from Hezbollah, these Shiite fanatics trained by mullah-ruled Iran, as you can get. His clan is a mixture of beliefs, as are all the big tribes in Lebanon. Everybody marries, Sunni, Shia, and Christian intermixed. This has created a very strong tribal existence, in some ways at least, encompassing all the factions in Lebanon. This is how they coexisted for centuries with all the other indigenous people. Max's mother derived from a Bedouin Sunni tribe, a very big tribe, whose relatives were also in government, far removed from Hezbollah. Max's grandfather on his mother's side was a famous tribal chief back in the day."

I studied them now. I had them going. These are things of which Texans can relate in our own tribal, melting pot ways.

"Max has several uncles that were generals in the army and as high up as police chief in Beirut back in the pre-civil war days. Back when Lebanon was rich even without oil. Rich the old fashioned way. The Switzerland of the Middle East days. His father was police chief and moving up in the world when he met Max's mother. They married and lived in Beirut. There was a huge family scandal because he was a lot older than her and the families opposed each other. I truly don't know why that was since Max didn't explain, but the families hated each other. So Max's dad kidnapped his mother and they moved to Beirut and the scandal basically ruined his career."

"You know," my mother broke in to say, "that happened out in West Texas where I grew up. Your great Aunt Rose, you know, maybe you remember her from the family reunions back in Snyder, was kidnapped by the big rancher from that area when she was thirteen years old. She was a pretty thing. I can see why the local thug hotshot rancher would want her. But hotshot or not, no self-respecting Christian family out in West Texas is going to allow a thirty-something year old man, I don't care how well off, go and marry their thirteen year old daughter. So, he had his cowboy, rogue army go and get her. My great Aunt Olivia, from where you get your name, was weak and in bed from just giving child birth when those punks came and kidnapped Auntie Rose."

"I didn't know that," I said in conjunction with my brother. Bucky and Cotton Jr sat upright with that pronouncement.

"Max's dad," I continued on, as if unfazed by the interruption, "also was a big gambler and lost everything. His family's property, everything, and was in ruin. So he migrated to Kuwait, opened a restaurant, and was successful. Max spent much of his youth in Kuwait because of it. As time went on, Max's mother developed mental illness. She actually tried to kill his father several times. So he divorced her and remarried an equally evil Shiite woman, who went on to have several children herself. Max's father died in a car accident, I don't know when, but Max's mother met and married again with someone, also a Shiite, while they were in Kuwait. A lot happened that I don't really understand the chronology of. It's impossible to keep up for me, but somehow Max's mother was in Kuwait, when for some reason the Kuwaiti's expelled all the Shia because they were trying to overthrow the Emir of Kuwait. Funny how that works. So Max's Sunni mother took her Shiite children back to his father's tribe in Lebanon."

I could see that I was losing them on all this scandal. I'm sure they liked the story as much as when I heard it from Max. But this was the world taking me away now and it brought out concerned looks once more.

"The admirable part," I continued, "is where Max's father was considered one of the most revered police chiefs Beirut ever had. He's still remembered by his generation. Max gets his way with them when they see his name."

I almost smirked. I had them going now. Even my parents seemed mesmerized by this story of Max's family.

And there was more.

"Max's uncle was revered even more. He was a general with the secret police and a personal bodyguard to one of the Presidents of Lebanon. The Arabic names escape me because it's too much information to retain. But this uncle was the most revered of the clan and well loved. He even saved the life of whatever President he was working under at the time. However, the uncle was later murdered by a big, local tribe when he arrested several members of this family for murder and drug dealing. These vendettas happen a lot in Lebanon, Max told me. The uncle knew that when he arrested these people that the family would come after him. He knew he would die, but Max's clan is so stubborn and he accepted his fate. He sent his family away and carried on. That criminal family hired assassins. The uncle was at home and looked out the window and saw them coming. He made a last stand because no one was going to tell him what to do."

I saw Cotton ready to smile in spite of himself. Bucky and Cotton Jr yelped with glee at the story. Maybe all the gore I just told worked and was worth it. This, after all, was the life I had in store for me. I couldn't sugar coat it if I tried.

CHAPTER 4

By the time I left Texas to join Max, he had moved from Kuwait to Dubai to look for work. It was no big deal to me at this point. I had no idea where I wanted to live anyway. One place was as good as another for all I knew.

But Max did not prepare me at all for what to expect in my new life in the Middle East. He let me find out everything for myself. That's the way he thinks. He's so independent and such a doer, he expects it of everyone even though hardly anyone is like that. And somehow, it was all part of a giant sales pitch to get me to leave everything behind and move to Dubai. I also didn't realize how little money we had to start our new life. He was so confident he could find a job immediately, and that I would too, that he miscalculated how much it would take to start our life there. We would live happily ever after somehow. Just the two of us. And naïve me was game.

He made a great living in Kuwait before I met him, and was highly regarded for his talent and education. He just assumed someone would snap him right up wherever he went. It had always been this way for him up until now. He had lived in Dubai before and been very successful there. He loved the Persian Gulf area, their social atmosphere and culture, so that's where he wanted his new life with me to start. And just assumed, as is normal for him, that things would just fall into place.

But things did not start out well at all. My flight from Frankfurt to Dubai was very stressful to begin with. The minute I boarded the plane and settled into my seat, the man next to me started getting drunk. He was in his twenties, from Mumbai, India, formerly called Bombay, and was on his way back to work in Dubai after an annual vacation.

Somehow, I decided from the way he looked at me, *this young man thinks I'm a prostitute.* I had on a wedding ring, jewelry, and a blazer with jeans. This was my version of being conservative. Even though it was hot, I thought a blouse with a nice blazer looked conservative. I wore high heels, however.

"I work in a casino," my abrupt, obnoxious airplane companion told me, even as I was trying to take a nap. "You should come see me." He grinned wickedly as he said it. As if it would be this big treat for me. I wondered if he ever watched a John Wayne movie. *Would John Wayne or Maureen O'Hara care about going to a stupid casino,* I huffed inside? I knew I never did. "I can show you around," he smirked. "You will enjoy yourself."

I smiled as politely as I could.

"Thanks," I returned, "but I'm supposed to meet my husband. He has a job in Dubai and I'm not sure we'll have time. It's been a while since we've seen one another. Thanks though."

"Never mind," he replied unfazed. "We can still meet each other. I work for a big casino. Very nice. You will really enjoy it. I can show you around."

"I start work as a secretary tomorrow," I lied, "and I really have to get my bearings."

"Oh, secretary, never mind that. I can get you much better than that. You are a very attractive woman. You should work at my casino. I gamble there professionally. I do very well. Come with me. I can get you much better. Trust me."

"My husband is a Shiite though," I said, hoping it would strike fear into his heart and plans. The Shia sect of Islam don't like you messing with their women.

He still wore that wicked grin. I wanted to slap it off his face.

"Never mind," he said. "You come see me at my casino." His stare intensified and all of a sudden he leaned over to me. **"It is so hot," he said. "Let me take your garment off. You have a beautiful body. I'd like to see it."** He then grabbed my blazer and began to pull up on it as if to take it off of me. "You look uncomfortable in that," he said further as he tugged. "Let me help you get more comfortable. The flight is several hours. You will be too hot. I will help you."

"Listen to me!" I shrieked at him. "Get your stupid hands off of me or you won't have to worry about my Shiite husband. I'll kill you myself. Do you understand me? I'll scratch your stupid eyes out of your ugly face. I'm a Texas girl and we hate dung like you. And don't even pretend you work in a casino. You're just a coolie on a work gang. Maybe you finally got a little money and think you're hot stuff. I know your type."

I wanted to add a racial slur for affect to make it personal to him. Better he hate me as a bigot, which I'm not, than for me to put up with more of this.

He looked at me in shock.

"How did you know I work with laboring?" he asked in disbelief. "But I am a foreman now. I have many laborers under my supervision. And I promise you this. I will be a gambler in a casino someday. Take off your bitching smile of arrogance. A whore has no pride. No rights."

I refused to answer him or change my expression. Let him squirm.

And it worked. Sort of. He leaned back into his chair, then took another sip of wine. Soon he was asleep, but leaned his head onto my shoulder as he did so. *Welcome to the Middle East*, I thought. I leaned away from him in my chair as far as I could, but never got his head completely off of me. I thought about shoving it off, but decided not to do so with what little there was left of my Texan, Christian charity.

He awoke as we landed and I mentioned once again about my Shiite husband. This time he listened. He was the first one off of the plane.

My ordeals on the plane weren't over, however.

"Get off, you prostitute," a sneering man in Arab head gear said to me as he shoved me aside just before I could grab my purse from the luggage rack over my chair.

This was my first encounter with what is called a *Salafist*. These are the puritanically strict fundamentalist Muslims. Some call them *Wahhabis*. The kind that would shoot an adulteress, legally, in the head. The kind that won't let a woman drive. He was old and looked at me with such contempt as he cursed me in Arabic.

I was totally confused as to why he hated me so much and didn't know what to do. I thought he was going to hit me. There were some American oil workers near me who put their bodies in front of me and said something to the old man, who reluctantly moved away. They looked at me apologetically, but also coldly, as if I was a prostitute to them also. The only thing they said to me was, "It's okay," then returned back to their cold stares.

I could barely breathe with the plane so full of passengers. I stared back at them hoping for a sign of life towards me somewhere among them. But nothing. Finally, I broke off my stare at the oil workers and looked around the cabin from curiosity. I noticed not a single covered lady on the entire plane. I had expected many.

After retrieving my luggage at the baggage claim I started looking for Max. I had emailed him on what plane I arrived so he could meet me at the airport. I was disappointed he wasn't at the baggage claim for me, especially after my encounters up to this point. I wanted immediate relief from further insanity or mischief.

But then there he was. All six foot two of him with his black hair and stoic look. He stood at the exit of the terminal near the street outside. There were those beautiful athletic muscles to ensure I was safe and sound. And respected. My heart leapt. I wanted to Bogart him smack dab on the lips Texas style, my hero, and throw my arms around his neck. But this wasn't Texas. As much not Texas as I could imagine. So, I settled for honey eyes thrown at him. They couldn't sue me for that. Or could they?

"Hi, sweetie," I said with a smile I couldn't exaggerate. Max was all man and all my man.

"How was your flight?" he asked easing into a slight, controlled smile.

"Worst experience of my life," I replied.

He waited for an explanation. And I damn sure explained. Every gory detail. He nodded his head after I finished telling him. It somehow made sense to him.

"Yes," he said while nodding his head. "They think you are a prostitute. You are blonde haired, you have blue eyes, you are wearing high heels and jewelry. This is the Middle East. An oil rich

40

Middle Eastern country. With so many tourists, so many wealthy, and so very many estranged workers. Loose women are a hot, excuse my American pun, commodity. They flock here. They advertise themselves with jewelry and high heels. Even your blazer in the hot sun says to them that you are here as a hot commodity. I should have warned you. Blonde haired Russian women especially come here. But even if they knew you were American, they watch American television and see Hollywood movies. Even if you are a tourist, you are a whore to them."

I looked at him ready to spit. Why had he not warned me? But actually, the more I stared at him, the more I wanted to kiss him for being the most hunk of man I'd ever seen.

"To them you are a special whore," Max continued, his lessons of preparation to me not yet complete. "You would be abused, but not as badly as a Filipina. There are so many Filipina prostitutes here. Arab men like them a great deal. So they can abuse them. Even beat them up."

He quit talking and motioned for me to follow him. We caught a bus to our apartment with him saying barely a word. He thought it better for us to be in privacy before he unloaded the rest of the story. The story regarding the attitudes of so many men in my new demography.

As we arrived at our first ever home together, I was taken aback at how similar it was to an American apartment. I expected Persian rugs, smells of incense, exotic colors, maybe even water pipes on the tables. But the Middle East of the emirates was used to Americans and other Westerners by now and Max wanted me to feel at home. So, bland, blasé home I got. But all ours.

"The rumor is," he said as he handed me a cup of freshly brewed coffee while I sat on the couch in our living room, "that among the Filipina office workers there are those who sometimes get beaten. Not just the prostitutes get beaten, you see. I have never witnessed this myself," he related. "Not in the UAE anyway." He studied me for a moment as if wanting to tell me something. "The UAE stands for United Arab Emirates, I assume you know," he finally related as if hoping he hadn't insulted my intelligence.

"I know that," I replied, which I did. But I would have pretended I did anyway.

"The normal thing for the entire Gulf region," he continued, "which includes the UAE, Qatar, and Kuwait, is that they get these fresh young females who are eager to please and look forward to sending money back to their families. Ultimately, it comes down to sex with the owner or their immediate supervisor. This especially happens in Kuwait. It is by far the worst abuser of female workers in the Gulf. It is just taken for granted. Arab men love Filipinas because they are very subservient and they work for much less than any Western expat. These Filipinas get benefits for their friends too. They are usually very capable and educated workers. Filipinas all know English very well and learn Arabic rapidly. In general, they are very skilled and intelligent, and will put up with anything. The office workers have the prize jobs. The housemaids are a different story. Kuwait is a nightmare for them, but not so much the UAE. I personally witnessed abuse of housemaids in Kuwait and constantly there are stories of some Filipina housemaid's body found in the desert after being gang raped and left to die. I also witnessed in an internet café in Kuwait where three young Filipina sales girls were monitoring the computers. They were threatened and demeaned constantly by some of the Kuwaiti men that would come to use the internet."

Max sipped on his coffee while studying my expression. I could not contain my look of shock. What had I gotten myself into? Even married to Max, I suddenly felt so vulnerable.

He went on. Somehow there was more to the story.

"Once I was at a computer in one of these internet cafés and a black Kuwaiti walked in wearing his *dishdasha*, which is the robe you see in pictures that an Arab man wears as part of traditional attire. He was with two of his friends. They tried to leave without paying. They also printed several pages off the internet and refused to pay for that as well. When the girls that ran the shop protested and tried to get them to pay, the Kuwaiti men physically shoved one girl. I thought one of the men was going to hit her. I was furious, but I had to back off because this was Kuwait and their country. If I interfered it would be an international incident. Such brutality against women is legal and the police would haul the girls off, not the Kuwaitis. This is a common occurrence there. You do not see so much of this here in the UAE. But even here, I can't tell you how many times I've seen housemaids yelled at and pushed. Even by Arab women and children. They call them stupid and show such contempt. This happens to Ethiopian housemaids as well."

I couldn't take anymore, but Max was on a roll. I had complained about him not preparing me for hazards here. Boy was he telling me now.

"Once when I was with a Kuwaiti household, the teenage son of the family pushed their Ethiopian housemaid down on the couch and started yelling at her. She began to cry and I jumped up ready to kick the kid's ass, but controlled myself. I knew better, but sometimes it overwhelms me. If I interfered they would deport the maid and punish her. So I sat there and watched her cry. When I got up to leave, she begged me to take her with me, an Arab man she could trust. But I couldn't do that. I heard later that she ran away. I hope she made it back to Ethiopia."

Max's stories helped adjust me to my new setting. But nothing prepared me more than just living it.

CHAPTER 5

Before I could dwell on any regrets building up inside of me, Max took me to a restaurant just outside of Abu Dhabi that sat on a glorious beach of the Persian Gulf. I love the ocean. Just seeing one again, just breathing the fresh salty air again, just wading barefoot in the soft waves and sand, perked me right back up. I grew up on the white beaches of Padre Island in South Texas and part of me shrivels if I stay away from God's most glorious wonder, the ocean, for very long.

At last, the stories Max told me of the Persian Gulf were real to me. Mixed with my own first impression now. I was glad to be here after all.

"How I missed oysters on the half shell," I swooned as I gulped one after the other at this small, open air restaurant on the beach he took me to. "There was this place just outside of Houston, where Texas won its independence way back from Mexico. A place called San Jacinto. I don't know what you know of Texas history, but never mind. In San Jacinto, near the battlefield where Sam Houston and his Texan army defeated Santa Anna for independence, there was this restaurant called the San Jacinto Inn. Oyster to die for. How could their raw oysters be better than anyone else's in history is beyond me? Maybe they put lemon and garlic or whatever spices and they really were the best. I don't care. I was in heaven. I am again. Thank you, sweets, for bringing me here. And the Gulf is so beautiful. I adore the clouds. Sand castles in the air clouds."

His smile of appreciation was intoxicating. I made his day and that made mine.

"The Persian Gulf used to be the center of the world in the pearl trade," Max explained. "It still is, I heard, but I'm not convinced it still is. Bahrain was the epicenter, but all along these shores my ancestors used to make their living diving for the highest quality pearls."

"What a romantic concept to go with my meal," I replied.

"But, Olivia, I don't want to spoil your happiness. I must temper it a bit with our reality now. I still haven't found work and we can't do this often. I just wanted to give you a welcome. Especially after your first gloomy experiences. We'll have to live cheaply for awhile."

"I understand, Max. It's okay. I've been down and out before."

"Let's enjoy ourselves then," he said. "We can be happy. This is just an example. Welcome to your new home."

I leaned over to give him a peck on the lips. At first he resisted since it is considered vulgar for such displays of romantic affection to be made openly. But after considering, he relented and we kissed. It was hard to not hold his hand, another gaudy display to the Arab world, but we sat side by side staring out into the ocean until the sun went down. Then returned to our home.

Before we started out the next morning, Max returned to his explanation of some of the local facts of life in the Gulf.

"The United Arab Emirates has a high rate of unskilled and semi-skilled immigrant workers from third world countries such as India, Pakistan, and the Philippines," he said over our first breakfast together in our apartment. Instead of a dining table in the kitchen, we dipped pita bread into *hummus,* a dip made from garbanzo beans, from our coffee table as we sat on the couch in the living room. "The UAE treats these immigrant workers horribly and it is tantamount to slavery by Western standards. They often get told whatever it takes to get them here, and once here, find it is nothing at all like what they were told. They are stuck, however, because once here on a work visa, the contracted laborer can't leave without the company's permission. And they never have the money to sneak out."

Is the honeymoon over before it ever started, I wondered, as I sat listening to his serious discourse on conditions here?

"A contract for an unskilled or semi-skilled worker is much different, than say, for a Petroleum Engineer from Texas," he continued. "Many times the poor laborer isn't given permission to go home because the company knows they won't come back. This means no vacation for them, no special benefits, and often they are not paid for months at a time to make sure they can't leave. These workers send much of their low scale salary to their families back home. With such a poor arrangement they are forced to sleep five or more to a room. Food and nutrition are very poor. Very few of these workers renew their contracts because of their bleak conditions. It seems that no one in the UAE cares."

"I know I'm naïve," I said solemnly, "and I just got here. But how do they get away with all this?"

"There are human rights organizations in the UAE," he explained, "but they seem helpless to deal with the onslaught of naïve, desperate immigrants in constant flux between the departing and the renewed. As a result, the laborers stick together and form their own little cliques. While some do come back and improve their lot, the majority live in slums, have no education, and are at the mercy of the merciless. Even skilled computer geeks and office workers don't fare well. They are treated worse than any illegal alien back in Texas that I heard of. A skilled office worker in the UAE also accepts their bleak existence because the poverty and desperation back in India or the Philippines seems hopeless. All the Arab oil countries put together hire fewer than the colossus of America does. There is so much poverty in the home countries of these unskilled immigrants and with very few places for them to go for opportunity. So, the few thousand Gulf jobs available become highly sought after. These immigrant workers also have an inherent, subservient mindset due to their colonial period past."

"It's these thousands of laborers who build all the fancy skyscrapers we see on TV and travel brochures, isn't it?" I sighed. "They don't seem so glamorous to me now."

Max nodded his head in agreement.

"The Emir of Dubai prides himself on trying to recreate a second Hong Kong and advertises his country as the pearl of the Persian Gulf," Max explained further. "And these feudal Arab oil sheiks lord over the immigrant serfs from afar. Horrific poverty for the poor immigrant laborer is the result."

"So, what does that mean for me?" I asked nervously.

"There are many expats," he explained, "but even they are not treated particularly well. Nor do they treat each other very well."

"You'd think everyone would stick together and help one another," I whined as I thought about it with fear hitting me."

"Competition is fierce for jobs," Max said bluntly. "Money is God."

Though I am speaking as a rural Texas girl with simple values, I really don't know why anyone decides to come to the emirates as a tourist, much less stays for any length of time. With all the preconceived hype about the place that I brought with me for my first impression of the Gulf region, I expected to see in Dubai some desert paradise. A Palm Springs, California, except with oil wealth too. But that was not at all what I thought now after hearing all of this. And then living some of it. The congestion proved to be unmanageable, the government corrupt, and there was little natural beauty to look at. Nothing to do that a country girl would care about.

The more I stayed the more this attitude was reinforced inside of me. I constantly saw on TV where American celebrities came to Dubai to shop, then rave on how fabulous the place is. *Sorry, but I just don't get it*, I thought every time. It made me glad I wasn't a rock star to be honest, if that is what it takes to appreciate this kind of lifestyle. I'd rather go fishing at a cattle tank on our farm back home. Or skinny dipping in one when no one is looking. But I'm sure the celebrities that choose Dubai over my daddy's cattle tank get in a round of golf too and it just seems the ultimate to them somehow. Or perhaps they dine in one of a seemingly million restaurants. That must explain it somehow, and more power to them, I suppose. If there for only a short period of time the UAE must indeed seem glamorous.

Soon came my second encounter with a Salafist. This happened in nearby Sharjah, the capital city of one of the emirates. Max and I couldn't afford to live in Abu Dhabi anymore because of limited funds, but in Sharjah there are cheaper places to live. The hotel room home of ours was as plain as our apartment had been, but was shabbier. The complex was made up of mostly Indian workers, all of whom were convinced, seemingly, that I was a prostitute.

Daily, Max and I walked to the local internet cafe, which was next door to us. There was an old, white British man in Arab headgear wearing the long Arab style robe called dishdasha that Max described to me when I got here. It was filthy. This man always sat at one of the computers. I noticed that when I walked by he would glare at me with much hatred. Max picked up on his attitude and was very rude to him if they encountered each other. I did my best to tolerate this man's attitude. Still, it baffled me.

Everyday, as Max and I entered the internet café, this man would have long conversations with people, including a covered Somali woman who was the manager. He was always glaring at me.

"What is your problem, old man?" Max finally asked him one day in disgust.

The Britisher was a convert to Islam and a fundamentalist.

"How can you stand being married to a *kuffar*?" the British Muslim asked Max in disdain. A kuffar is used like a racial slur, but in this case is more related to an impure infidel that prepares or touches food. The handling of food by an infidel makes the food non-halal. Halal is the Muslim version of kosher. "How can you eat food from her hands? Both of you are going to hell."

"It is not of your concern, old man," Max huffed. "Mind your own business."

"I have noticed you are Shia," the old man mocked. "No wonder you have no shame. You are godless. Eat your filthy food from your whoring kuffar. It is fit for a Shia."

"Does eating halal fill your need for pride?" Max sneered at him. "Your clothes are filthy, your mind is filthy, but your heart is the filthiest of all. Nothing about you is worth camel dung, but you live this pathetic life in the illusion food has cleansed you somehow. Or perhaps by quoting from the Quran, as if you are worthy of it. Nothing about you is halal except the food you eat. Go to hell and leave my wife alone. Pretend she is not worthy so you can live with the worm that you are. It's your business. But I will have no more to do with you."

"Salafists can go to hell," I said hatefully to Max as we left the internet cafe.

"Olivia, let me warn you. You better worry about what such as he thinks because these are the dangerous ones. These guys, especially the converts, will be the ones to hurt me if they can."

CHAPTER 6

The Middle East that Max remembered from his youth, as well as the one to which he returned from the States after finishing his degrees, was gone. After 911 everything changed. There was now a backlash of feelings against the Western world mixed with a new surge of Arab nationalistic pride. With it came a demand on Arab governments to take care of their own people. Resentments were already bubbling beneath the surface regarding Westerners coming in and taking over jobs during the pre-911 days. This meant that even though Max was Arab, and even though his American passport was coveted by all, the need to fill job quotas by locals now took priority in order to restore the idea that Arabs should revel in who they are.

This was very inconvenient to my husband and myself, but I could understand it. It did not excuse all that happened to us, but in my calmer moments, I understood that life could be unfair in ways against you, not just for you. We had to work with the hand dealt us. As it was, expats were still in demand to some degree, if even to boost Arab confidence by having expats around to successfully compete against.

The harsh reality we found for ourselves, however, was that there was little for us in the Persian Gulf.

"You are very good at what you do," the executive with whom Max interviewed said. "In fact, you are just what we are looking for. Your acumen for business development is perfect for us. You have a good history with sales and marketing. But I will be blunt. We are facing hard times. Your timing is a problem. Though we would love to have someone like you, and the Emir doesn't like to talk about it, we have problems facing us. The real estate market is crumbling. Good people are leaving. Everyone is unsure. Hiring is at a minimum. The country may be facing bankruptcy. I am sorry."

"I have always been able to turn bad situations into good ones," Max replied to him.

"You do have such a history. This indeed makes you very attractive to us. But I'm sorry. There is just too much unsureness these days. I wish you well."

My interviews for jobs were jokes. Even if a company hired a foreign secretary, I had no chance against immigrants from India or the Philippines. They were a dime a dozen, plus they would also act as housemaids, and as an added bonus, the young ones could make extra money as prostitutes for Arab CEOs and General Managers.

In pre-911 days, Western expats of both genders came from their native countries and made huge salaries with fantastic benefits. This was because big companies in the Gulf region wanted the prestige of these professional Europeans. It presented a desired face to the European community, how they were equal to whatever Western company with which they were doing business. In the 1970s and 1980s, Western executives, even secretaries, made more money than their counterparts in the States.

The downside of this was that locals were knocked out of the running for such jobs and felt discriminated against, which they were, and by their own people. Unemployment was high for locals, and when hired, their salaries were minimal. This created a backlash of resentment for any Westerner that now came. Which included me. Just in-the-nick-of-time you might say. What made the resentment worse was how many of these pre-911 Europeans developed an arrogant attitude and lorded their superiority over the indigenous population. The worst of the lot, I was told, were the British. Many of them were totally unqualified in their own countries, could not make it there, and so moved to the Gulf to become big fish in a little pond. Until now, Westerners were taking Arab jobs and could not be trusted. On top of that, the women coming to the Gulf countries were taking Arab men from the local women.

All these realities made Max and me nervous. There was just no place to unwind or forget our woes. Every facet of everything we faced seemed to be an ominous sign of bleakness.

"Let's get Mexican food," I said after each of us failed in interviews yet again. "I not only miss the food, but I need to get away in my mind. Crawl into my mama's womb psychologically. Some home loving through home cooking. I'm sick of the greasy spoon restaurants anyway. I need some uplifting quick."

"You don't like my cooking or something?" Max asked me. "It's cheaper too."

"Yours is about the only food I've liked since I've been here," I answered truthfully. "But I need to get away. I'm having an anxiety attack. Humor me, Maxie."

"You haven't tried camel meat," Max replied as we walked the sidewalks of the Jumeirah Beach district where the tourists hang out. "I could make it where you would like it. An exotic Arab dish, as you call them. Why must we spend money we don't have? Let's try some dishes that may be fun for you. That would cheer you up."

I kept walking silently. A cold, loud silence. Camel meat was out. End of story.

"Olivia, give me a break," he said in exasperation.

"I'm sorry, but I'm still not up to it," I sighed. "I love the hummus and falafels we've had. The *couscous*. But I can't stand lamb. Somehow camel is worse than lamb. I just need a sure thing now. I know you love lamb and probably adore camel, but I can't get past the smell of the lamb. It's horrendous. Cotton and the boys had lamb all the time when I visited them and I hated it there too. And I don't know what you did differently back in Texas, Max, but I don't enjoy the meat here so much when we buy in the market or when we order it in dishes in restaurants. It's too bland or something. There's too much rice in the menus too. I'm a potato girl, I guess. But even potatoes in these recipes here don't do anything for me. I'm not trying to be a drag. I keep hoping I'll get used to all this. But so far I haven't. And I'm just not in the mood yet to try camel. Sorry. Let me try Mexican here. We've never been to a Mexican food restaurant yet and now is the time. Even if it's not like back home. I just need something to reassure me in my life right now. Mother's milk of Mexican food. To assure me all this is a bad dream up to now. That there really is a Texas somewhere out there for me. I know it doesn't make sense."

"You love the Indian food we've had," Max suggested. "It's cheaper too. We're running out of money, Olivia. I'm not sure you'll like Mexican here anyway. I've never had the Mexican food here so I can't recommend it one way or the other."

"Let's just try," I said with an appealing, give me a break look.

As if a sign from God, right up ahead of us was a famous Mexican restaurant chain. I loved the food this chain served back home.

"A burrito, please," I said to the Filipina waitress. "One for me and one for my husband. And a taco for each of us too."

"It comes with beans and rice," she said.

"That will be fine," I answered, picturing Spanish rice and refried beans like back home.

The waitress smiled and took down the order. That was the best sign of all. As if she understood what civilization was.

"Did you bother to look at the prices?" Max asked me, showing concern.

"I don't know how to translate into US dollars," I said. "I always let you do the shopping and the ordering in restaurants."

"Well, you're going to have to learn," he whined. "If we're going to live out anymore of your fantasies, you're going to have to understand the cost of that fantasy."

I looked at him prepared for the worst. After his speech, I knew it had to be expensive. But how much could a burrito and taco cost? Even with beans and rice in an expensive Mexican chain.

"It will come to seventy-five dollars," he said with a groan.

I nearly died. There was no peace at all anywhere. It was like we were being machine gunned with bad elements.

"I hope you enjoy, Olivia, but we have to go back to our Indian restaurants again. The one good cuisine and at low prices. This night is for you, but no more."

"I love the Indian food here anyway," I said meekly, exposing every ounce of guilt I felt.

I don't know if the price destroyed any hope of me enjoying the food, but this was the worst burrito and taco I ever had in my life. I was afraid Max would never try again, even if we went back to this same chain in Texas.

"The Gulf has changed the most, I think, of any part of the Middle East," Max said to me as we chewed disdainfully at the tacos we hated and couldn't afford. He looked at me apologetically. As if sorry he drug me here. His new wife from America who had a happy home once. "Prices are so much higher now. We're running out of money faster than I could ever imagine. And there are all these new university branches here. More competition everyday from Arabs being educated in them. Good universities with high standards. From Texas A&M to Cornell, Northwestern, Georgetown, and Carnegie-Mellon. The competition with Arabs even for jobs at the new American Air Base is so much more than when I was here before. The Salafists are taking over the country now, too. They are Sunni. Staunchly Sunni. Many are vocal for al-Qaeda. I am a Shiite. They openly insult me. Worse than in America. I am called soulless and godless."

He looked now at me with the sympathy in his eyes even more pronounced.

"And you, Olivia. Before, you would have been one of many expats. A perfect fit. But now to be an expat is a curse. When I worked here and in Kuwait, each company I worked for I doubled sales. Performance doesn't matter now. I am missing my new homeland. The one I took you from. America. I had problems there because of distrust for Arabs after 911, but it wasn't personal otherwise. I could prove myself to Americans and they appreciated me. They got to know me, opened up with me, and trusted me. But not here. No matter what I do. In your case, as a woman, to them you are old. We are cursed no matter what. Not for anything we've done, but for being from the wrong tribe, you might say."

I nodded my head at all Max said. I looked at him as I readied to relate my earlier experience today.

"The manager told me I was worthless this morning in my interview," I explained in contempt of the memory. "That's what got me in this mood in the first place. 'You are outdated and too old', I was told. And this guy said that with a smirk right to my face. 'And your previous experience as a court reporter is a joke', he went on to say. 'It was a government job. That shows lack of ambition'. He told me to go home to America. That there was nothing for me here. Talk about being depressed. This very depression led me craving Mexican food which ended up depressing me even more."

In America I never had to deal with the age issue. I looked younger than my age and often dated younger men. Though I am three years older than Max, people thought we were the same age. I had normal aging fears about wrinkles. I would dab on makeup, color my hair, and tried to feel as young as I could. But I never felt hindered or worried about it. I assumed I would age gracefully and happily, accept social security when it came time, and live to a ripe old age. The shock I faced now in the UAE horrified me and made me feel as worthless as the locals intended. They seemed to love putting me in my place.

"In an Arab country," Max explained to me, "if you are female, you work until you are thirty-five." This stunned my American sensibilities as I listened. "All of the Arab countries," he continued, "the Gulf countries especially, deport you when you reach age sixty. Whether you are male or female. When my father turned sixty in Kuwait, even though he lived there many years and had children born there, they were going to deport him back to Lebanon. It will be hard for you, Olivia. Be brave."

I not only was old, but American. A blonde haired, blue eyed one. So, I constantly faced contempt for marrying an Arab man. It exhausted me and seemed hateful to me. Much of this was from the resentments I mentioned earlier. From Arab women having been lorded over by Westerners until recently. It didn't make me feel better, nor did I feel very forgiving about it. I wanted to get along. In my eyes I tried hard to get along. But the hate expressed for me being in their country was strong and constant. At best I was ignored, as if not even there.

Worse was when someone bothered to make my presence known.

"Why don't you come with us and forget her?" a woman asked my husband in Arabic right in front of me in a restaurant one day. "We are Arab. She is unclean. She is Christian. You can't eat the food she cooks for you. Why do you want such a cow?"

Everywhere we went at least one covered woman would ask this and make vulgar comments. Most always in Arabic to taunt me further as if I was a goon by not understanding. They were determined to show my flaws and get my Arab husband back from this inferior woman.

"You are the cow!" Max answered back defiantly. "Why would I want such as you? Just to cook my food? I can eat halal by cooking for myself. She is of the book, you are of a pig."

My gratitude for his love and loyalty to me proved endless. I would endure hell for him for the way he took up for me at all times. My knight in shining Arab armor.

The number one sin in many Arab women's eyes is to marry outside of their race. This was true before the latest post-911 nationalism, which only exacerbated it. They can't stand to see interracial, intercultural, or interreligious marriages in many parts of the Arab world.

But coming from the baby boom era of Texas, I had seen something of this type rigidness, bigotry if you will, before in my own culture, so can assume it's a human trait of some sort. But having been told constantly by liberals that America, especially the South, was the only place on earth that seemed to be this way, and then to face this Arab hostility half way around the world, I wanted to drag every liberal over here and shove this in their face. Not that it would do any good. They would find a reason how every other culture is innocent and a victim, while mine is the only one guilty. I obviously deserved all this treatment somehow. Just somehow I caused this and was now stewing in it. My chickens coming home to roost or whatever.

Each day it seemed, openly in front of me, women tried to get Max to go with them. They harassed him night and day about Arab women being better than Western women and how dare he marry a non-Arab. It is more than bigotry, but a competition. Either way, the contempt and disrespect shown me seemed unprecedented.

"Come with me," yet another covered woman would say to Max in Arabic in front of me. "Let's go to my car. I think you call it a quickie in America. My husband is out of town and I know he is cheating on me. I don't care. You are much nicer than he is. Leave your American sow here. She will wait for you. It is her place, my dear. Why did you marry an American Christian anyway? Who wants such tripe?"

While the liberated female in me got a kick out of seeing the male dominance here defied, what was flaunted in front of me at my expense was too personal. Thus celebrating their liberation was a luxury I couldn't afford. These women were abusing me and that took priority to any female dominion rite. Plus Max was a man I admired incredibly. It seemed an insult to him and not just a slander to his wife. It so cheapened him.

Yet this sort of behavior apparently is quite common in the Gulf. These types of Muslim women have their own code. This ruse about their chastity, but Western women being prostitutes, disgusted me. Whether they were nationalists or not, if they seduced my husband, it was not me who was the tramp. It had nothing to do with who I was and everything to do with who they were. But they didn't see anything wrong with it. I was left to brew.

How many Arab women are like this, I often wondered in befuddlement and exasperation? I didn't know them. So many flaunted themselves and abused me, yet many did not. Were those that didn't of the same temperament? I didn't know. Even the non-abusive barely tried to befriend me or even extend a common courtesy. So, was I being unfair? I had no idea. The hate towards me was adamant with so many, while indifference was cold with the rest. It left me angry in return. Blaming. Maybe the vast majority were kind and decent, but minding their own business. But maybe they were just as hateful and judging, just not bothering to display it. I can only relate what happened to me. And I quit trying to be fair. I used that up in the first weeks.

For a woman to be covered is cultural and has nothing to do with the Quran except in the traditional mindset. Women often wear the *hijab*, a head scarf that hangs down past the shoulders and covers all the hair to the forehead. Many forego the *abayat*, which is a one piece robe like dress often seen in pictures. Women might wear instead, the most tight fitting knit tops and pants to show off their bodies. These were tighter than any respectable Western woman would wear back home. Their mothers promote this behavior in the hopes of getting money from a man and not necessarily through marriage. These oil rich, liberated, male dominant figures, play right into the hands of the more cunning pseudo-liberated females. Men bribe them, for lack of a better word, to show off. Much like a macho man might do back home with liquor and gifts for a pick up at a bar or disco.

Many women in the UAE still wear traditional attire, but many of these same women only pretend piety and openly admit it. It is their goal to land a man with money and take him for everything he has. As if it's a game for them. For the bored and restless ones. Which is another reason my husband got tired of Arab women.

The Quran does not specifically ask women to cover their head. Rather, it tells them to draw their garments over their bosoms. In pre-Islamic Arabia, women, as well as men, covered their heads. The current form of hijab is drawn from this inference, as well as the sayings of the Prophet Muhammad. The cultural and personal interpretations vary. The majority of Gulf women wear a hijab that covers their hair and body, but not the face.

Others wear *niqabs*, which are similar, but expose only the eyes. Still others wear the head-to-toe covering called the *burka*.

The hijab, in Islamic culture, is closely related to modesty. Modest dress applies not only to women but also to men, who, in addition, are told to lower their gazes. The idea is that the hijab moves the gaze from the external to the internal, thus making the beauty of the inner self the most important focus.

But where there is a will there is a way. Meaning, this concept might sound good in a pious sense, but in much of the real Arab world, it is pure rhetoric for many women as well as men.

The color of an abayat is always black. I don't know why, since black is so hot and we were in the desert. Black denotes a symbolism, including nihilism. Look at black and strip your ego of desire, I suppose. The only differences in any abayat I saw were embellishments that some had. Underneath them women often wore, I was told, provocative clothes. No one ever saw this because to go outdoors, wearers of abayat would cover up to where only immediate family ever saw what was underneath.

No modern country, except in Iran and Saudi Arabia, requires a woman to wear a hijab or abayat. Sisters walk down the streets of the UAE hand in hand, one covered, the other not. It is personal preference for most places in the Arab world these days. The Western world makes too much of the hijab. It is an intricate part of the culture and women do like wearing them. But those that don't, refuse to. Even Iran is beginning to lighten up on the issue, so I'm told.

Wearing a hijab says a lot of things. It identifies the wearer as one who conforms to the rules of modesty and celibacy as instructed by her faith. Or perhaps, it's a cultural expression of a religious necessity. But it's also something that's open to interpretation in how it's worn, depending on the cultural context. Variations of the hijab have turned into something other than religious necessity. It has now become with some, especially in the Gulf States, as a beauty accessory advertising their wares. Not many admit this openly, but I often saw how celibacy that is instructed by faith, has been thrown to the wayside. There are many covered women, under pretense of chastity, who blatantly flaunt themselves in the open market. I don't know the percent of the pious as opposed to not so pious, but the flaunters are prevalent enough to be noticed.

So, I was not impressed with their airs of superior moral authority to me or anyone else. It was used for the same purpose any hypocrite uses anything. For smugness, ego, competition, or hate. At least the pious weren't hypocrites, but I wasn't impressed with them either. If your religion inspired you to hate me, then to hell with you too.

All I know is, I got sick of being hated. Abayat or no abayat. Pious or free spirited. Every day of my life there, wherever I went, the looks of hatred I received from seemingly every Arab woman was obvious. And it only got worse when I was with my Arab husband. Not one kind word was ever said to me, whether in a business place, or otherwise.

"They are jealous of you, Olivia," Max constantly assured me, as if that was the best he could come up with to make me feel better.

The ones that spoke English to me were no better. In English they could be more blunt.

"America has no culture," I was told smugly yet again at a restaurant Max and I were at. "The Arab culture is so superior to yours. Why are you here? You don't even speak Arabic. You Americans don't deserve to be married to an Arab man."

Many of the Arab women were beautiful and I looked for any opening I could find to befriend them. I admired their beauty. Wasn't that big of me somehow? When I got here I envisioned a home. Even an exotic one. A chance to share my husband's culture and upbringing. To appreciate it. That's what we harped on back in America and this was my chance to broaden my horizons even further than the multi-racial-cultural aspects abundant in Texas. I easily loved much of the music in the Gulf, as well as the architecture. There was so much promise to become a broader, more open person. And to see a modern, youthful Arab woman made me want to be a part of the new spirit with women here. I hoped for some kind of symmetry of cultures.

Not only were many of the women beautiful, but the hair of most Arab women is gorgeous. It reeks, however, from the smell. Many douse their hair in camel urine to give it a soft silky texture. Somehow, no one but me noticed the smell. To be open minded, I tried ignoring it. But as time went on, with all the vindictiveness towards me, I judged them by it. With no regrets.

Finally Max found a job. Was it possible to acclimate now and make a home after all? We sure hoped so. But after only a couple of months Max was dissatisfied.

"It's worse than ever," Max informed me one day after work. "Worse than anything I've expressed to you so far. The Salafists are taking a stronger hold in Qatar. I detest them. All the worse for how they harangue me for having an American wife. The mutual animosity is coming to a head and I don't like the odds. I'm homesick for Kuwait."

I looked at him trying to follow his thoughts, afraid to say anything. Even afraid we were losing the security we finally had.

"I want to show you something of me I am proud of," he continued. "I want you to have a home. A true home here. I am thinking of going back where I grew up in Kuwait. The company I work for cheated me of a bonus. This can be my excuse to file a complaint with the labor board in Qatar. I have contacted a human rights organization to have the company investigated and included how the company's Indian laborers aren't being paid. Slavishly low wages that they often don't even receive at all. They are trapped here and there is nothing they can do about it."

It kept getting worse seemingly each day. I saw the stress on Max's face as we dined at our favorite restaurant. We were grateful for the employment now, but it presented new problems. Severe ones even.

Max was barely talking as we ate. Barely acknowledging my existence, in fact. I considered being a good wife and asking him what was wrong, but the concern he showed made me want to leave him alone. Let him work it out. I sat quietly and purposely minded my own business. So intently, in fact, I hoped it caught his attention. The silence is deafening angle.

"A Syrian employee works for me as a salesman," he finally said, looking up from his food. "He openly supports *al-Nusra* to overthrow Assad in Syria." He studied me for a second to see if I knew what he was talking about. "Do you know who al-Nusra is?" I shook my head no. "They are of the mindset of al-Qaeda. That's the best I know to explain. That shows you who they are politically, but also shows you they are Sunni. I am no great lover of Assad. He is aligned with Iran. Iran is at least Shia, but Iran is not good. They are not Arab. They are foreigners making mischief in the Arab world. I do not like Assad for aligning with them, Shia or not. But these Sunni terrorist groups against him are much worse. But America is backing them. To America somehow, al-Nusra is just the opposition. It's as if Americans do not recognize that al-Nusra is of the same ilk as al-Qaeda. This guy working for me is using the company telephone at least five hours a day trying to recruit for the radical opposition. And like I say, America is supporting and giving arms to al-Nusra so this guy feels justified in his pursuit. Our company is in construction and has contracts with the American base in Qatar. But our company spouts nonstop about the Big Satan America and how they were going to mess them up."

"Can't you do anything?" I asked incredulously.

"I complain to our owner, but he is a Salafist. I was even told to mind my own business because I am Shiite. They hope America crumbles. I have some bitterness about America and I am Arab first, but America in many ways is a great country, and powerful. I feel a pride I didn't know I had in being American. We Arabs need America. But look what is happening. My company works for America yet laughs at how they will help put America in their place as they support the terrorist opposition. I have tried to alert the American base and the embassy about this at my own risk, even feeling like a proud American. But no one responds to me or even agrees to see me. I'm telling you, Olivia, no good is going to come of this. Even Assad is better than what is going to happen."

As it turned out, Max lost the lawsuit against his company. Still, he used their breech as an excuse to break his contract. Just as he had planned. They were glad to get rid of him.

So, with farewell in mind and no looking back, we spent our last days in the UAE dwelling on what we liked. It made us sad actually, in how there were so many things to like that we overlooked. To have been so overwhelmed in all the negative that happened to us. We looked now for good things Max loved before when he lived here and what he was determined to show me before we left for Kuwait. This beauty is what we longed for. To share appreciation for my husband's culture and heritage.

One of our favorite restaurants was an outdoor café on the beach. At this particular locale were many pearl diving boats as we had seen the first night I arrived.

"The pearl industry used to be the mainstay of Gulf countries," Max said sentimentally as we sipped at our tea while watching them. It was just as things had been our first night in the UAE. I let him repeat his stories of the pearl trade, as much from the joy we had our first night together, as for the stories themselves. "The pearls produced were the most famous in the world and more glamourous and romantic than all the oil in the Gulf. To this day, their pearls are extraordinary." He looked at me with longing. "I picture the two of us here hundreds of years ago. As pearl divers or traders."

I held his hand affectionately, in spite of the cultural taboos. It was the best we could do as we shared what we couldn't before.

Not as romantic, but more exciting, were the camel races. Standing room only for camel races was the norm, though Max always got us seats.

"It's the first time I've seen more than one camel anywhere other than a zoo," I chirped like a little girl. Max beamed at my happiness. "This, my darling, is a complete blast. I want to ride one. What a hoot that'd be. Look at them go, Max. They're hilarious. Each has its own personality. They're so grumpy though. And I can't believe it, these camel races have robot jockeys. I prefer the human jockeys. Maybe I'm just old fashioned. But I like personality and these robots today act the machines they look." I looked at Max in confusion. "They're fun to watch, but I don't get it, Max."

"Look!" Max shouted enthusiastically as he pointed. "The Emir and his royal family. There in the special box seats. They truly love their camels. Camels are like children to the Emir. An owner of a camel treats him better than he would a person."

We didn't have time or money to do much around town on most days, however. Everything was so expensive and we had to save for our move. The market places, called *souks*, were nice, but unaffordable. As were their malls, which are among the biggest in the world. Among the most expensive also. For entertainment though, souks were nice to walk around and feel native.

The one thing we could afford to do more now was to dine out. To enjoy the local cuisine. The reality is we mainly ate Indian food since it was by far the best. Indian food had become like local food, much like Mexican food has in Texas. It was much less expensive too.

Even at the end of our stay, the local food in the UAE was not exciting to me. I never got into it. The exception was their seafood. It was marvelous. Our favorite restaurant, the one near the pearl merchants, had Filipina waitresses and made me miss my sister-in-law Connie. They were as charming and delightful as she and treated us very well.

But there is no denying it. What I mostly saw was not wealth in the UAE, but unimaginable poverty. Incredible squalor right next to, as in a parallel world with, the most immense wealth possible. And that's what I remember more than anything. This poverty. The struggle imported laborers dealt with everyday just to survive.

So, we left in a rage for all the injustices we witnessed, and with great contempt for the government and many of the people that abused us. We hoped Kuwait would soften our viewpoint on how corrupt and bigoted the world we lived in had become. For any inkling of being happy in the UAE for us was always dashed by some harsh element. And Max remained disconcerted with the Salafists until the bitter end. They seemed a glimpse of things to come. It constantly reaffirmed his commitment to return to Kuwait where he had connections, including a sister, who had taken him in when he was a boy. I shared his excitement to go home again.

CHAPTER 7

It was hate at first sight between Fatima, Max's sister in Kuwait, and me, as my introduction to my new home where Max spent most of his boyhood days. The Arab culture mandates for the new bride to be welcomed as a sister, once married into the family. But Fatima thrived on competition and proving she was better at anything and everything with whoever she met. Especially a female. The competition.

Max did not tell Fatima we were coming to Kuwait. He knew she would be jealous of his new American wife. She had caused many problems in the past with those he cared for. She wanted to have her brother to herself. As much for possessiveness as affection. She was a nightmare in the best of circumstances, including for her mother or other members of the family. She had her own agenda and that was all that mattered.

"You must stay with me," Fatima insisted, as a greeting upon our arrival. "You must save money. But I have no bed. I have a mattress we can put on the floor for you. We have many rooms, but few furnishings in them."

"I'm game," I said cheerfully. "Beggars can't be choosers."

But soon after moving in, Fatima's motivation to help us for the sake of control came out in full force. Meaning, control of us. Of everything we did, said, thought, wanted, and needed.

The estate where we all lived, the one shared by Max's father and mother when Max and she were growing up, was rather large. The fact that the father later lost much of his wealth before leaving Kuwait, meant it was rather empty. If a piece of furniture got old, it wasn't replaced. Everything Fatima needed to live was in the living room, dining room, and two of the bedrooms. She kept stealing from one of the abandoned rooms to replace the need in the inhabited rooms that she used.

The house was a traditional Arabic style house with two stories, a courtyard, gardens, but also with a few stables, and a corral. The house was built of concrete blocks of stone or of concrete façade, painted white or cream, with bars on all the windows and doors. The floors were tiled throughout every room with the kitchen and bathrooms having tile on the walls as well. There was a salon used as a sitting room, plus a smaller salon with a television as well. The kitchen and bathroom on the lower floor connected in order to share plumbing. Each room had some sort of Persian rug on the floor, though not wall-to-wall, and there was old style furniture. The couches were long and lined the wall from corner to corner with many cushions. Tables were low to the ground because in many homes it is still the custom to sit on the floor to eat around these very low tables. There were a few European types of tables and chairs, in addition.

DNA was not kind to Fatima. The athletic build, good looks, and height that dominated the men in her family, which made them most sought after, did not translate in an attractive way for her. Just as Max had told me back in Texas while we were getting to know one another. She was generally taken for a man most of her life. She had a low masculine voice, a strong muscular body with no waist, while she held herself in a manly way as well. Then, as if to self-inflict more problems concerning her masculine features, she wore her hair short, as well as unisex shirts and jeans. With no cosmetic makeup. If anyone needed makeup, it was her.

There is an oft-repeated story about one of her half-brothers offering to broker her marriage for a huge fee in order for an Iraqi friend to acquire a Kuwaiti passport. It was illegal at the time for a Kuwaiti to marry an Iraqi because of resentment and distrust left over from Saddam Hussein's invasion in 1990. But before they could try to curtail legalities, the man took one look at her and stated, "I'd rather marry a man, or go to bed with another man, than to marry her."

You would think her self-confidence would be so shaken that she would keep a low profile. Not so. Instead, perhaps as a defense mechanism, she became a pathological liar and made up the most extreme scenarios and dramas in order to impress people.

At first I thought mental illness was the root of the problem with Fatima. Max had warned me of such within his family. But I soon determined mental illness only exacerbated her problems. The huge cultural clash that divides the West and the Middle East caused the rest of the problem with myself and her. The rest of her problems with her life and the people in it, I can only guess. Though Kuwait, overall, was a huge step up for Max and I from our days in the other parts of the Gulf region, Fatima in many ways, made it seem worse.

Women such as Fatima are not particularly unique in the Arab world. It is the females' role there to be intrusive, critical, and non-nurturing. Or so it seemed to me. Although the Arab wife takes great pride in cooking, cleaning, child-rearing, and being a housemaid, she also is a dominant force in the household. Westerners hear many stories of the misogynous Arab male who rules the home with an iron fist while abusing the poor woman in all areas of life. Though this often happens, the best kept secret in the world is the behind the scenes domination and general ruthlessness of the female in the typical Arab household. For there is more than one way to skin a cat. While the male deludes himself as being head of the household, the wife often nitpicks him to death, or intimidates by nagging and harping.

Fatima was like this and more.

Some of this may have been defensiveness beyond her looks and demeanor. She may have felt alienation culturally, in that, according to Max, her psychological and cultural mindsets were so fiercely Lebanese you would never know her birthplace was Kuwait. In Kuwait you are not automatically a citizen by birth. You can become a citizen if you apply for it or through marriage. But it is difficult to achieve and Max never did attain citizenship. Though she exuded her Lebanese heritage, she spent most of her life in Kuwait. But as if she didn't belong.

Her argumentative nature however, mixed with a general ignorance on all subjects, was not unusual for her Kuwaiti upbringing. In this she was very much like the Kuwaiti people, who in general, are very argumentative, though in a more elegant manner than Fatima. She seemed to entail the worst of both worlds.

All I can say is, there was never any peace with her.

"Where did you get these horses, Max?" I swooned excitedly one day while my husband showed me around more of their family's estate -- what was left of it.

"My father loved horses," he said with a smile. "Even after we lost our fortune, we kept some of our horses. It's an Arab thing. If you have any money, you buy horses. For show, but mostly it's in an Arab's blood to have horses."

"We had horses sometimes back home," I related from my memories. "I didn't ride much. I don't know why. But I loved to roam the pasture with them. That's where our cattle tank was where I'd fish and go swimming. I just liked being out there and the horses were the biggest reason. I'd always bring some sugar cubes and apples to feed them while I stroked their foreheads. Maybe horses are our common denominator, Max."

He looked at me approvingly at the thought.

"We have some apples," he said. "Just for that. It's good food for them, of course, but we mostly feed them apples for the affection. Just like you said."

"Great. Let's do it, baby. Get me an apple, sweetie."

Max walked to a bin in a room adjacent to us in the stable. I stroked one of the horses on the forehead as I waited for him. This horse had a white patch on his forehead that continued on down to between his eyes. As if a pad for me to please him.

"Here," Max said upon his return as he handed me a ripe juicy, though slightly shriveled, red apple.

I placed the apple on my palm while extending my fingers out so the horse wouldn't nip them accidentally as it took the apple with its teeth. I learned that trick the hard way as a little girl.

"Here boy," I said. "Look what mommy has for you. Look at you. You are one happy camper. Best apple you've had in years, I bet. Remember who gave it to you."

I heard a rustling sound and footsteps so heavy it sounded like a game of basketball. I knew who that had to be.

"There you are, brother," Fatima bellowed. "I need you to lift the television set onto my new bookcase in the bedroom. It is hard to watch TV in bed with it on the table there. It strains my neck from all the pillows I must use to fix my head so upright."

She then watched me feed the horse yet another apple.

"What do you make here, Olivia? Why do you feed this horse this way? It is not a child. I be so clever I make the horse beg me for a favor. I be so clever to know it is me who is in charge. Why you want to spoil this animal? Here let me show you." She shoved me out of the way while at the same time grabbed an apple from Max's hand. "Here, critter, here. Beg me. Beg me. I be the clever one. Not you. I am your master. You are my horse. Beg me, fool."

Every time the horse tried to take the apple from her hand with its mouth, she quickly moved her hand backwards or to the side. A bitter smile broke onto her face with each movement she made to tease the apple away from him.

"I am the master," she said again before dropping the apple to the ground in front of him.

She is the master of whom, I wondered to myself. *Me or the horse*. I was sure I knew.

What was I supposed to think from all of this? I had my experiences in the UAE and now things started off with an encore performance in Kuwait. Was it me? Was I too sensitive? Was I too culturally insensitive? Even if there was a cultural problem here with a white skinned American woman marrying an Arab man, were they really good people and I didn't get it because all I knew was the feeling of being attacked? It's happened to others in other places, including in America. Do I just try harder? I only knew that with this culture clash, including a language I didn't know, and being treated like a parasite, it was hard for me to form a good picture of what I was experiencing. I could try to use perspective, but I also had to be honest about what was happening to me. And what to do about it. I had been warned by Max that his sister was really off the beam and had a mental disorder, which included nonstop talking. She even talked in her sleep. So, maybe it wasn't me. Be patient, in other words. Things will pick up.

As I sat at the table one morning eating hummus, *zaatar*, cheese, and olives, Fatima sat across the room on her couch chain smoking and staring. In the process, according to Max later on, she kept harping in Arabic that I was evil because of my blue eyes. She did so consistently now. At first Max didn't tell me the things she said, but she wouldn't stop talking. So, as Yogi Berra supposedly said, *deja vu all over again*. I was again slandered for my being. But now there was no home place to which I could run as there had been in the UAE. I was more stuck than ever. In her house. Being treated as I had by the Arab women in restaurants in the UAE as they tried to seduce my husband away from me. Except with Fatima, she jabbered away in Arabic trying to belittle me away from him just to control us. All the while looking at me innocently, bestowing what Arabs call *a yellow smile*. A yellow smile means insincere or duplicitous. There was never a moment when she didn't flash that yellow smile my way while slandering me to my husband.

"She's a burden to you, brother. Why do you keep this white monkey? She eats all my food and is so wasteful like a typical American. Be done with her, brother. You made a mistake marrying a white American. Americans are lazy, can't cook, they are so arrogant, wasteful, and don't know anything about anything. Why did you not marry an Arab?"

All this slander seemed hilarious to her. Not just slanderous of me, but of my family back in Texas and America in general. This behavior, from what I gathered, seemed natural for an Arab woman, which my experiences so far backed up.

When I first arrived in the Middle East I thought Max was impatient with Arab women. Perhaps even too sensitive about things overall concerning his culture. Like he had been back in America from being treated like an Arab there in the post-911 world. But it now dawned on me why he seemed to detest some of his own culture. Where the women hide behind bad manners as an excuse to blame everyone else.

With Fatima though, you had to worry about more than bad manners. In spite of Islam, sorcery and the evil eye are still prevalent beliefs in the Arab world. Left over from their pagan days. Fatima, in spite of her brother's devotion and respect for Islam, seemed to prefer these pagan rites over the more enlightened teachings brought by the Prophet Muhammad a millennium and a half before.

"You must leave," Fatima said to us one Friday, which is their holy day. "I need a couple of hours for myself, so that I can concentrate on God. I must pray. I must pray alone. Take your American infidel wife and do some good with her in the mosque. Take her away to the mosque."

By now we expected this behavior since it happened every Friday. Max openly showed his disgust. For he knew what really went on while we were gone.

"She is going against the Quran," he finally explained to me as we walked to a restaurant.

I listened without saying anything. I was sure she was not so pious, but gave her benefit of the doubt anyway, just trying to not be judgmental. But why was he telling me this now, I wondered? Perhaps it was time for me to know, or maybe it was because his disgust with her demanded he finally admit the truth about her.

"She reads the cards and coffee grounds," he sneered. "And predicts the future for a few of her women friends for money. She chooses the holy day of the week to do this. A double blasphemy. For it is written in the Quran that it is man's downfall to deal with such sorcery and witchcraft as does my sister."

Max was so appalled that he pouted the entire time after we left her house to have lunch on the beach. I, however, was just glad to get out of the house. I enjoyed our time away from her during these episodes. For I loved the calming effect of the Persian Gulf. It

84

is so pretty and so peaceful. Though it doesn't have a green Caribbean type beauty in its landscape or any deep crystal blue sea to match, it has majestic clouds with beaches of sand that drew me to its allure.

But as luck would have it.

While we were eating lunch, invariably it seemed, someone had an objection to me being with an Arab. It was as if getting away from Fatima was punishable by the cosmic elements of insanity. And, as in the UAE, it seemed this happened everywhere we went. A young girl would flirt with Max openly and invite him to spend time with her. Or perhaps.

"You American pig," yelled a woman wearing a *chador*, which is an Iranian and Hezbollah style of abayat. A chador has one piece of black cloth which is used like a veil, but does not cover the face except by hand. "Go home," the woman shrieked. "Go home. Go home, you pig."

This rant lasted the entire meal. Not content to be ignored by us, she followed us to our car when we left. Finally, a very disgusted Max turned to her.

"Move away, cow," he screamed at her. "Go fornicate."

She was so out of line Max went to the police to report her.

"And so what do you expect?" The Kuwaiti lieutenant replied as he laughed. "These are disturbing times. The Iranians want to come over the border and take over our country. But you have a problem with an obnoxious woman. Westerners need to understand they can't come to Kuwait and expect things to be as they are in America."

"No," Max scowled back at him. "I will not accept such a cheap answer. I have connections of high rank and you will hear from them soon. Do you know who I am? I know people on the council. Name someone and I promise you I know him. I will personally have him talk to you."

"I am sorry, sir," the lieutenant said squirming. "I did not grasp the significance of your request. We will work on your report of the matter together. Please return to your seat." He then looked at me. "Also you, madam. I am very sorry for the rudeness of some of our citizens. But I must say, except for the report, I am not sure what all can be done. My apologies again."

Then it was time to return to Fatima's.

With each day her dealings with sorcery became more prevalent right in front of us. This included me as she kept her glare and sneer of the evil eye towards me. Max became concerned over it from his fear that I'd truly get sick from this sorcery. He believed so much in Islam I was surprised he put merit in her so called power. It reinforced all the more the pagan links that still exist in this post-Islamic society. I began to appreciate what Islam had accomplished and all that Muhammad had to overcome with his teachings.

To help ward off the arrow of his sister's evil eye and curses, Max one day bought me a necklace with a pendant of a blue eye to wear.

"If you are vulnerable to her arrow, Olivia, havoc could occur. But protection from this amulet could cause the arrow to miss."

I didn't believe in any of this, but I had gotten food poisoning twice while I stayed with his sister. I even felt it was she who poisoned me. But we had our own pagan superstitions in South Texas. Maybe part of me believed in hexes too.

Max was a nervous wreck from fear he brought black magic into my life. But no matter how much he stood up to his sister, nothing would deter her from doing what she was doing.

Ironically, from all of this bad behavior she made a good living. From her challenge of Islam on holy days with her sorcery rituals to her marriages for a living. In fact, she had this aspect of her bad behavior down to an art. How she treated me seemed less offensive when I saw how she treated everyone else.

It humored me how she exploited the system in Kuwait. Women are employed until the age of thirty-five. They are then deemed too old to continue working so are allowed to retire and receive a pension for the rest of their lives. Some women only work two years then retire to receive various benefits from the government. In Fatima's case, she worked for a government agency, but was so unmanageable they retired her after a year. She received this pension, plus disability payments as well. She is not rich, but does all right for herself. She also gets loans from banks for thirty thousand dollars per year. The Emir, usually during the sacred Muslim holiday of Ramadan, then pays off these loans for divorced or single women who don't have a man to take care of them. Medical care is notoriously bad, but they provide it free through the government if you are a citizen. On top of that, on the sly, she often sold her passport to various citizens of different countries through marriage for a hefty sum. Not bad for a woman without a high school education.

Fatima had sixteen marriages under her belt when I met her. Conveniently for her business, with all the nonstop talking, aggression, jealousy, and vindictiveness, no one ever wanted her. Conveniently I say, because it left her open each time to make a nice living out of getting married and then freeing herself through divorce. A real entrepreneurial knack she had. Since all they needed from her was her passport, they didn't consider trying to start a new life with her. Business was business and nothing more. Her behavior guaranteed the divorce. Let's call it a lucrative business resource.

All this with Fatima, her treatment of me, her sorcery antics, her possessiveness and controlling, as well as other traits, made it all the more imperative for us to find a job soon. Damn soon. ASAP soon. Max decided to broaden the search. While he had his applications in locally, he ventured into other possibilities as well.

CHAPTER 8

While in Kuwait, Max and I decided to try the neighboring country of Saudi Arabia in our job search. Max had good experiences there before with various companies. It wouldn't just get us away from his sister, so we hoped, but the pay scale was higher as well. The American compounds are like small pieces of America inside a vast Saudi Arabian province. This oasis of Western style living helped Americans cope within an ultra-conservative environment like Riyadh.

Max had good luck in the past by going to various companies and applying in person with a resumé and references. That actually is the Arab way to look for a job. The norm for Americans in these compounds is to be hired by a huge oil company while still in the States, then sponsored and sent to the Saudi Arabian branch.

Though an invitation letter is needed to get a visa to enter Saudi Arabia, there had never been a problem for Max in the past. With his being a Muslim, all he had to do was tell them he wanted to obtain an *Umrah*, which is the non-mandatory lesser pilgrimage made by Muslims to Mecca. These lesser pilgrimages may be performed any time of the year. With this visa he would go off on his own to the various companies to apply for jobs. To get our Umrah visa we went to the embassy in Kuwait.

"You cannot enter," the security guard at the Saudi embassy told us to our surprise.

I was wearing a Chador that I borrowed from Fatima. Though she never wore any head covering, she occasionally needed one for occasions such as mine now. I felt that as long as I was covered there would be no objection. But my American passport and ultra-white skin proved an obstacle anyway.

"We will not allow a woman onto the grounds," the guard explained further. "She is unclean. Get this infidel from our midst. This Christian donkey. She is a daughter of obscenity. We will never allow a prostitute upon our sacred soil."

"You pig!" Max shrieked at him. "Your mother is a whore. I will get my way with you, Saudi swine."

The scene was so heated that the police came.

As usual, our ace in the hole was how Max knew his environment. He doesn't just lose his temper, he sets up the playing field. Max knew so many of the higher ups in the Kuwaiti police, was so well known and connected, that once he started throwing the names of generals and heads of the secret police at them as being old family friends, the Kuwaiti police backed down. The security guard was severely reprimanded and his job threatened.

"I apologize to you, sir," the security guard said meekly. He then looked at me. "And to you, madam. My apologies also. Please enter our embassy. We are honored to have both of you."

"Please," Max told the officers in charge, "I do not want this man fired. He, obviously, is a good man. I just want him to be polite. To all people including women and Westerners." Max then looked straight at the security guard. "You should change your attitude, you understand."

Amazingly, in true Arab fashion, the insulting security guard and Max became great friends. The guard was so grateful to Max for saving his job. Max has this routine down to an art, I must say.

"I demand to see the consul," Max then said to embassy security.

He was quickly ushered in to see him as a result.

"You may have your Umrah visa," the consul said. "I regret the behavior of our guard. You had every right to be outraged. If not for your graciousness, he would be fired. Enjoy your stay in our country upon your arrival. Good luck to you both."

And we were on our way to Saudi Arabia.

At the airport in Saudi Arabia near Riyadh, we were subjected to their newly instituted fingerprint system. It did not work, so we were kept waiting. The customs people, meanwhile, were agitated we were entering on an Umrah visa. Especially since I was an American woman.

"We cannot process your visas," we were told. "Nor can we allow you entry until we are able to fingerprint you. Since you are not sponsored by a particular company and have no invitation letter, your Umrah visa is questionable." The man holding Max's passport kept inspecting it, occasionally looking up at him curiously before inspecting the passport further. "You have an American passport with a Spanish sounding last name," he said showing concern. "Your wife is an American of European descent. Why is it you want to go on Umrah?"

"I immigrated to America to obtain a college degree and better my skills. I developed those skills further while working in America. Later, I decided to stay and obtained US citizenship. But after the suicide bombings there in 2001, American attitudes towards Arabs and Muslims grew very hostile. To alleviate this hostility I was facing, I changed my name, as you see, hoping I could stay in peace. But the feelings of everyday Americans was so severe I felt I had no future there. Being a proud Arab and Muslim I chose to return to my homeland to live amongst my own."

The man looked at him skeptically.

"You are Shiite," he said coldly.

With that we sensed our doom. After an eight hour delay where we slept on the floor of the airport, the powers that be sealed our fate.

"Upon deliberation we have decided," the agent stated point blank, "that your visa was obtained illegally. Perhaps it is a forgery. Your entry is denied. You must leave. Go back to Kuwait at once."

So we returned by way of Bahrain, where we decided to stay before continuing on. We spent three days eating and shopping in order to erase the bizarre and ridiculous turn of events. And to psyche up with facing Fatima again.

There was nothing to do, but be optimistic upon our arrival back to Kuwait. For we were now acclimated to our fate. Even with the failure of our mission in Saudi Arabia, it felt like a vacation just to get away from her.

Then happily, shortly after our return, came the wondrous day Max found a job. As joyous an occasion as that was on its own account, the biggest joy was knowing we could get the hell out of Fatima's house. I was ready to move at just hearing he was starting work soon. But I could play the game a little longer knowing the end was near.

"Let's celebrate, sweets," I said, all smiles upon the news. "Let's go to that seafood restaurant we like so much. I'm in a good mood."

Before Max could speak, Fatima's mouth began.

"And spend the money before you even make it," she scowled. "I be so clever I save my last penny if I start my new life. You have furniture to buy and you must have money to get a good apartment. You have no business to spend money before you make it." She looked at Max as if she were his disapproving mother. "Are you going to allow this, brother? Why you always giving in to this American wife of yours? She think you must be big shot American. Can just buy whenever you want. You are the man. Stand up to her. This is not America. You are not spoiled brat. Tell her. Is she your master? This is Kuwait. You are the husband. You are the master."

"Let's go, Olivia," Max said looking at me while ignoring her. "I'm in the mood to celebrate myself. Seafood sounds perfect."

"Yes," Fatima sneered. "This is how it is. The big shot American tells the meek little Arab man who is the boss. How you say it in America? Is your wedding ring attached to your nose?"

Still ignoring her, Max got up from the couch, waited on me patiently to follow him, then opened the door courteously for me as we left her house.

"I'm sorry I got you in trouble," I said as we walked. "I knew she would do something like that, but was so excited I lost my head."

"I'm glad you did it," he said supportively. "She's always spoiling things we want. I'm sick of giving in to her. I've wanted to defy her already, but we live under her roof and wanted to have peace. To even show respect. But this is our sign we are free of her. I don't care if she is insulted we disobeyed her nagging or not. We give in too much. Now we are in charge of our lives."

CHAPTER 9

When Max got his job at a logistics factory, it opened new doors for us. We could put Fatima aside, even memories of the UAE aside, and begin again with a new life together in his homeland. That made us happy and that's what we wanted. Happiness. I liked more things in Kuwait overall, and hated the social structure less, than what I experienced in the UAE. It also has more history and better relations with Americans since Desert Storm, the war in the 1990's which liberated them from Saddam Hussein's Iraq. I didn't have what I called friends yet, especially with Fatima monopolizing our social life, but overall I was treated better with most of the people.

Still, of all the injustice, abuse of power, and exploitation of the foreign worker, Kuwait was more savage than the other Gulf States. I first heard stories about such in the early '90s on television during that war called Desert Storm, in fact. I was shocked by what I heard, how Kuwait was so hated by other Arab countries. Then I listened with dread, all the stories Max had about where he grew up. But now that I was full-fledged out among the masses, I was all the more shocked by things I now saw. With all the abundance in Kuwait, these injustices, mixed with the bullying of Fatima, I found it hard to like Kuwait overall. As much as I wanted to like it. To show I wasn't spoiled, or bigoted, or politically incorrect. I even wanted to know I could like things here. I only managed to like things better than in the UAE, however.

On the other hand, there was some good going on in our lives. Max's job paid well and we loved the new apartment we found. It was a roomy two bedroom suite with nice Persian carpeting, brown carved furnishings, lavender walls, and a steel latticed balcony with a gorgeous view of the city overlooking the Gulf. And as an added bonus seemingly, a view of the landmark Kuwaiti towers in the distance.

We also now had a newly acquired cat that we named Mimo. So, things were looking up, but still not happy overall. I was even ashamed of myself for this unhappiness.

For there was no escaping it. There was an imminent problem with Max's immediate boss. This man did his best to steal Max's work and took all the credit for whatever big contract Max brought in.

"I just brought in a million dollar contract," Max mimicked his boss at a board meeting.

Meaning, Max just brought in a million dollar contract for which his boss took credit.

"This happened to me before with him," Max complained to me regarding his situation. "Just last week I got our company a three million dollar contract and my supervisor took credit for that too. This affects us, Olivia. Our bonuses come from these contracts. Him taking credit for all my accomplishments affects my promotions and our yearly income. We need money for security and for our future. Especially with how volatile the Middle East is. We must do well while we can, not knowing an uncertain future."

"Can't you stand up to him then?" I asked incredulously. Naïve little me just assumed there had to be a solution to our plight at hand. "Just tell the board the truth."

Max looked at me as if searching for a way to get me to see the picture.

"It would embarrass my boss," he explained. "He would get caught in a lie and then big arguments and hard feelings would ensue. That would not turn out well for me."

Max does not tolerate abuse very well so I backed off, giving him benefit of the doubt. Surely things would come to a head soon enough with his boss and he would figure something out.

After a few months Max was ready to tell the company to go to hell. The good thing about the job was he was well paid with benefits. Indeed, we needed this security. Plus, he genuinely liked the owner of the company. But the conflict with his immediate boss was driving him crazy.

Then there was Fatima. Still adamantly in our lives. She came over to the apartment every night. Our little refuge from her wasn't a refuge hardly at all. And our pretending not to be home did not deter her in the least.

"Have you seen my brother Khalil?" she bellowed in Arabic to one of our neighbors. "Or his wife the American?"

She had no shame. She would do this door to door with our neighbors or the front security desk until she got her way.

"My brother," she barked. "Have you seen my brother? Surely you know of his American wife? Are they home? Will you answer me please? Are they at home? I must see them. It is urgent for me to see them."

A shrug or negative answer from whomever she tortured with inquiry didn't alleviate the situation at all.

"Do you know where they are?" she demanded further.

Invariably the neighbor or security desk would say, "No, we didn't see them leave. I think they must be there."

Fatima would then come back to the door and pound on it until we answered. It took a strained smile by me to get her to walk past me silently. Her inspection of our lives would begin.

"What is this in your refrigerator here?" she asked pointedly. "American food." A sneer of disgust in my direction was the only interlude before she dug further into the refrigerator shelves for what else was there. "Why imported food, Olivia? You spend too much money. My goodness what a waste of my brother's hard earned money. Americans are so impossible. You must buy in local shops. You must buy cheaper items. You are such a burden on my dear, poor brother. How wasteful you are. Have you no shame whatsoever?" Each room was inspected by this makeshift drill sergeant. "Your cat don't need cat litter, Olivia. I'm sorry to tell you this. You spend too much money on this animal. Save money, Olivia. I tell you this. Save money more better."

This wasn't all, as far as run-ins with Fatima about our cat. There is a psychological disease, it seems, with Arab Muslim countries anyway about pets, but Fatima brought it home personally.

It is traditional among Muslims all over the world to regard the dog as a dirty animal that when touched would void the *wudu*, or ablution, and infect the one who touched it with *nagasah*, which is dirty and impure.

Sadly, this concept comes from fabricated *hadith*, which is scholarly clerical comments on the Quran, claiming that the Prophet ordered the killing of dogs. There are also numerous hadith prohibiting the keeping of dogs except for hunting and guarding. Likewise due to their dirty status.

However, I have not seen anywhere in the Quran, nor been shown by anyone, where dogs are prohibited, nor is there any mention of any contaminating effect of them. Consequently, these hadith may well enamor predisposed tradition. For those Muslim who interpret the Quran from these hadith set forth the cruelest treatment of dogs I ever witnessed, though there are individual Muslims, Sunni and Shiite, who do love their pets.

Cruelty exists back home, of course, but those are exceptions and often condemned with fines or imprisonment as a result of cruel behavior towards animals. The opposite is true in Muslim Arab countries where indifference, even cruelty, is the norm. Even to the extent of sport made out of running over dogs by car for the fun of it.

Even pet stores I visited in Kuwait had many dogs in cages in the open heat with no water where some of the puppies had parvo. The poor animals sat in their cages shaking and dying with no reprieve. There is no humane society, though the British started their own shelters trying to rectify the situation. Some British ladies that lived in Kuwait for several years became personal friends with one of the royal family and convinced the emir to sponsor a shelter and rescue system that was beginning to catch on.

I bought Mimo at a booth in a flea market. Max soon became an animal advocate because of his attachment to Mimo. Growing up Muslim, he never cared one way or the other for pets, with the exception of their horses, but we soon had fifty abandoned outdoor cats that we fed shortly after Mimo came home with us, who we kept inside.

But Fatima so resented how I loved Mimo, and the money we spent for his care, that one day while we weren't there, she deliberately let him out of the house.

"Stay away with your accusations, brother," she yelled as we accused her. "Your wife is crying over this animal, so you take it out on me. I had nothing to do with your cat being gone. He probably hates it here. I am sure he jumped out your window."

"Get out of here!" Max screamed at her. "You intrude on us even when we are not here. You never liked animals and are always telling us what to do about our cat, even our horses. Be gone. You are not welcome here. I prefer our cat to you."

I searched for Mimo for days to no avail.

"I have seen your cat, Olivia," our Iranian neighbor told us one day. "On the stairwell."

Sure enough, we looked and there he was. He had lost half his body weight and had a fever. We took him to a Filipino veterinarian friend of ours. Mimo got flu shots, but was sick for three more days.

We never let Fatima near him again. Later, she told their mother how indeed she had deliberately let Mimo out. Simply because she thought it best to get rid of him since he ran our lives and we wasted too much money on him. Somehow she was doing us a favor.

And if she wasn't at our apartment, she called seemingly every five minutes. If we went to a restaurant she would later say we were wasteful and should eat at home.

"How dare you spend so much money, brother! Because of your spoiled brat American. I buy you fruit and bring it, hoping you eat this instead of gourmet diet for your wife everyday."

"Your fruit is rotten," Max snapped back. "Mind your own business, Fatima."

"My fruit is not rotten. Are you so spoiled now that you marry American? I save you precious money. Listen to me. Do what I tell you to do."

Then she looked at me.

"You leading my brother down bad path of spending and wasting money. You just using him. Go back to your America and get fat there."

"Get out of here, Fatima," Max spewed. "Get out of here. You are not welcome here if you are going to act like this. Who asked you?"

"Is this how you treat your sister?" she bellowed back at him. "You no treating me like this before your American comes here."

We both had to recover with each visit from her.

So, between Fatima, Max's supervisor at work, and me being considered a prostitute in many of our encounters when we went out, I was desperate to find things to like about my new home. Even for my own sanity. It even got me defiant. There were things to love here. There were reasons to have a happy life here. I was going to do exactly that. Come hell or high water.

And indeed, it was exciting for me when I first saw Kuwait's most famous landmark, the Kuwaiti Towers, as I mentioned upon our arrival in our new apartment for the first time together. The way they greeted me everyday from our balcony. How many times had I seen pictures of these towers during the news broadcasts on television during Desert Storm back in Texas? They were a symbol to me of the Kuwait I insisted on loving. There was a rotating observation deck and restaurant on one of them. Max and I immediately ate at that restaurant on our first day alone just so I could say I had done so.

As in Qatar, I loved going to the souk, Kuwait's street market. It was near us and had a complex, bustling, convoluted majesty about it in the city center. It is partly housed in a modern building complete with cubbyholes of lockable wooden shutters. It carries on its antique practices, from the sharp haggling over ribands of offal and ox tails, to the trading of olives and dates in the food stalls of Souk Marbarakia. It's a wonderful place to spend time, plus they encourage the sampling of their food without ever having to set foot in one of the numerous snack shops that line the outer rim of the souk.

The souk also comprises the small covered Souk al-Hareem where Bedouin women sit cross-legged on cushions of velvet selling *kohl*, which is a black eyeliner. There were pumice stones, gold-spangled dresses in the red, white, and green livery of the Kuwaiti flag. Beyond the covered alleyway, the souk opens out into lanes stocked with woolen vests and Korean blankets.

The souk that was closest to us was Souk ad-Dahab al-Markazi. It was the city's major gold market with many shops spangling with wedding gold, as well as local pearls along the perimeter it shared with Souk Marbarakia. I so loved the pearl markets in the UAE and the pearl diving boats. Now here they were again in my life in my new home. Many of these markets were old, but still in use. It was such a charming sight.

I easily got integrated into Kuwaiti life, quite unlike before in Qatar or the UAE. Had it not been for living with Fatima when we first arrived, I may have been happy here immediately, even as we endured Max's boss, as well as the continuing harassment of my American being by many of the locals. At last, I began to think I was open minded, tolerant, and adventurous. For this was Max's home once and we felt comfortable here, as well as safe. I loved sharing it with him. He was so proud to do so. Indeed, those days on our own were happy days overall that gave us promise. I couldn't claim any deep friendships, but many of my everyday acquaintances turned into happy social bonds soon after Max and I settled down in our new apartment.

In addition, the food was marvelous in Kuwait. Their cuisine is an infusion of Arabian, Persian, Indian, and Mediterranean dishes. A prominent dish is *machboos*, which is a rice-based specialty usually prepared with basmati rice and seasoned with spices, mixed with chicken, mutton, fish, eggs, or vegetables. Adorably delicious. Soon, Kuwaiti food became my favorite food even over Mexican, which seemed blasphemous to my South Texas heritage.

Middle Eastern foods are basically the same dishes, though each country does their regional take. You can tell the difference with each region. As much as I found the food bland in the UAE and Qatar, the food in Kuwait was astounding.

A significant part of the Kuwaiti diet is seafood. A local favorite is *hamour*, which is a grouper. It is typically served grilled or fried, often with *biryani* rice, because of its texture and taste. Then there is *safi*, or rabbit fish, and *sobaity*, which is a fish called **bream. This is my absolute favorite.** They have large fish markets where Max and I loved to shop. Arabs love to haggle to get the perfect selection. I felt he loved to go as much for the haggling as he did to get his choice foods.

Our favorite thing of all to do was go to the beach at a kiosk-style stand run by an Egyptian. The beach was nice, but we went just to eat his fish. The owner grilled it on an open fire with whatever herbs and spices he selected until the skin was crisp. This was a meal unto itself and better than any restaurant. Simple. And simply the best.

Kuwait's traditional flatbread is called *khubz*. It is large and baked in a special oven. There are many other available cuisines as well due to the international workforce in Kuwait. We ate at many American and British chain restaurants also and they were all good. An interesting and unexplainable phenomena regarding these chain restaurants is that in Kuwait they were and are the best anywhere. Whatever restaurant America or England has, Kuwait has. Except that Kuwait's version was the best. I wondered why. Freshness may be a factor.

Yet some make fun of Kuwaiti food. I determined it came from feelings they have about Kuwait in general. For whatever reason, neighboring countries consider Kuwaitis as buffoons. I think that must be because they are survivors. It may be ugly at times when one struggles to survive, but survive the Kuwaitis have done through the years. And again recently during the Iraqi occupation.

To be a South Texas girl and raised on barbecue dishes and Mexican food, then replace them as my favorite food by my new home's cuisine may sound blasphemous, but I can tell you, I double dog dare anyone to come to Kuwait, acclimate to it, and see if the same thing doesn't happen. I adore Arab food and recipes. Here is a list of my favorites. Many dishes won't have the point of reference to understand what I'm talking about even then, but here goes anyway. Take note. This is not a travel guide, but the food gods demand this of me.

Balaleet – sweet saffron noodles served with a savory omelet on top.

Bayt elgitta - a fried cookie filled with a mixture of ground nuts and tossed in powdered sugar. It was named after the egg of the crowned sand grouse, common to the area, due to its similar shape.

Biryani – a very common dish, which consists of heavily seasoned rice cooked with chicken or lamb. Originally from the Indian sub-continent.

Gabout – stuffed flour dumplings in a thick meat stew.

Gers ogaily – a traditional cake made with eggs, flour, sugar, cardamom, and saffron. Served traditionally with tea.

Ghuraiba – brittle cookies made from flour, butter, powdered sugar, and cardamom. It's usually served with Arabic coffee.

Harees – wheat cooked with meat then mashed, usually topped with cinnamon sugar.

Jireesh (*Yireesh*) - a mash of cooked spelt with chicken or lamb, tomatoes, and some spices.

Khabees – sweet dish made of flour and oil.

Lugaimat – fried yeast dumplings soaked in saffron syrup, which is sugar, lemon, and saffron.

Machboos – a dish made with mutton, chicken, or fish accompanied over fragrant rice that has been cooked in chicken or mutton. It is a well spiced broth.

Mahyawa – a tangy fish sauce.

Margoog – vegetable stew, usually containing squash and eggplant, cooked with thin pieces of rolled out dough.

Mumawwash – rice cooked with black lentils and topped with dry shrimp.

Mutabbaq samak – fish served over rice. Rice is cooked in well-spiced fish stock.

Qouzi – Kuwaiti dish consisting of roasted lamb stuffed with rice, meat, eggs and other ingredients.

Zalabia – fried dough soaked in syrup, sugar, lemon, and saffron. It has a distinctive swirly shape.

Hummus – a dip consisting of mashed chickpeas, also known as garbanzo beans, tahini, garlic, and lemon.

Rice – numerous types of rice exist and it tends to be either a side or a base for many dishes.

Tabbouleh--a "salad" generally made of parsley, bulgur, tomatoes, garlic, and lemon.

Falafel – fried chickpeas rolled into balls and served with vegetables inside pita bread.

Kebab – numerous styles exist, usually with a base of roasted lamb or chicken and vegetables inside pita bread.

While on the subject of food. When eating in Kuwait there are some etiquette rules one must know and follow since Kuwait is a Muslim country. First, dress on the conservative side. Second, in conservative homes and even in some restaurants, it is not acceptable to eat with a person of the opposite sex unless it is your child, sibling, or spouse. While this is not as common in Kuwait today, to some conservative Muslims, and in some restaurants, this is still important. So, it is best to observe the local restaurant's situation and follow a local's lead. Since men dine only with men and women only with women traditionally, it is best to not bring a guest of the opposite sex to any meal unless you are specifically invited to do so.

It is best to arrive on time for a meal. If eating in a local's home, remove your shoes at the door if others have done so. Greet the elders first, then everyone else, by shaking each person's hand individually. Prior to sitting down one should ask to wash their hands. If others wash their hands, follow their lead. Let the host seat the guests, then while sitting, be sure to keep your feet flat on the floor, or pointed behind. Pointing the soles of your feet at another can be offensive.

The guest will be served first, followed by the elders. Once the food is served, follow the host's lead. It is good to try a bit of everything offered as turning down food or drinks can be offensive. Eat as the locals eat. In many houses this means eating with your right hand. To touch any food with the left hand is offensive. As you finish your food, leave a bit on your plate to show there was more than enough. Then place the fork and knife together in the five o'clock position. The meal isn't truly over, however, until the host indicates it is by standing up.

This is true for most Middle Eastern Muslim countries. They are meticulous about these rules. A violator will be scowled at. Many people these days, however, are beginning to follow European standards more for eating. But many still don't feel comfortable doing so.

Since no one should hold hands in any of the Muslim countries, or show any type of affection in public, married or not, we often had to show a copy of our marriage license so we could stay in the same room. Even if everyone else on the floor was partying with prostitutes. This was common actually. They want to prove that a Western woman is a prostitute so they can feel superior, I decided. While it is okay if one of their own really is a prostitute.

Texas is known for hot, dry summers. But even Texas did not prepare me for weather and climate like in the Middle East.

Nor did Fatima, though this time she tried. I dreaded the pounding on my door knowing who it had to be.

"Quick, Olivia," she howled as I opened the door, only to be shoved aside as she bowled past me. "You must do what I say. There is no time."

I had heard such alarm before, but instead of skepticism, I wore a blank, neutral look as I learned to do when she barked out orders to me.

"Don't just stare at me," she bellowed. "There is no time. I must get back to my house before the storm hits. Did my brother not tell you?"

"What storm?" I asked, still wearing the blank look. "No one told me anything about a storm. Max is in Iraq for a couple of days."

"Do as I say," she ordered as she opened each of my closet doors. "Seal all the windows."

She saw my still skeptical stare her way and sneered.

"I tell you this, Olivia. Help me here. I be so clever I must save you from the sand storm that is almost here. I have finished my house, but I must go home soon or be caught in it. Help me. I tell you this. Help me."

"What do I need to do?" I asked.

"We must use everything you have. All your blankets and sheets. Even your clothing. Every crack in the house is a leak in a sinking ship. The sand will blow in and you will have a huge, horrible mess. It will be hard to breathe. Trust me. Give me all your cloth material. We must begin sealing every single crack and hole in the doors and windows and vents."

We barely had any blankets, but did have several sheets. Even old ones. As I learned growing up, they make good rags to clean things up.

"March through July are the worst months," Fatima explained as we stuffed bedding and rags into the cracks of the window sills. When Fatima said every crevice, she meant it. I wondered how an insect could possibly breathe with all the patching we were doing. I felt gratitude for her efforts on my behalf. For the first time it was like she cared about me. "These months are horrific. Many times, I tell you, terrible red dust storms, Olivia. Horrible."

We had finished the main bedroom and living room when Fatima left to go back home ahead of the supposed onslaught of dust storm on the way. It was up to me to get the guest bathroom and the dining room. I had just finished when I heard the first howling winds outside.

It seemed the end of the world. The windblown sand completely blocked out the sun outside and it grew dark at midday. Like out of the Bible. From the region of the Bible. Even with all the sealing I had done, I still missed edges in some of the vents in the house. Even covered windows weren't totally sealed somehow once the wind pierced its way. The smallest of cracks let in streams of sand. Even with the air conditioning units closed, some portions of them had a crack still open somewhere. In each oversight of even a molecule left uncovered, a coat of thick red dust bullied its way into my apartment.

When the wind finally subsided, there was sand everywhere. Inches of it on the floor as if a flood of sand instead of water. It all smelled like petroleum. Even though I had been warned, I could not fathom the consequences I was now stuck with living. Every blessed couch, chair, rug, floor, and kitchen appliance was coated with an inch thick of red dust.

"This will take weeks to clean up, Olivia," Fatima scolded me the next day. "I tried to tell you. I tried to tell the spoiled brat American about the sand storm. But you insist on staying lazy."

My next encounter with this plague was at least somewhere else. Max was having a conference in Basra, Iraq, and brought me with him since it was a drivable distance.

"I have to pull over," Max said as the wind rushed by us on the streets of the city. "It will soon be unbearable to drive."

And sure enough. Within minutes the ominous cloud of sand reached us.

"My God," I gasped. "I can't see anything in front of my face from this wall of dust."

"The red dust blows in from northern and central Iraq," Max explained. "Even the storm you encountered in Kuwait City originates from other parts of Iraq. It is notoriously bothersome. Sometimes the storms last an entire day. Sometimes three or more. I'm glad we have bottles of water in the back seat. I don't know how long we will be stuck. I'll drive towards the hotel with each let up at all in the clouds of sand blowing on us."

Lucky for us, this storm lasted only until night fall. Our room at the hotel was a mess from the sand, but it was an inner room, away from outside windows, and didn't get the brunt of the storm.

Even then, after a change of our sheets, residue of sand still tormented us in our bed, disturbing our sleep that night.

So, between my social turmoil and then this supposed Biblical plague type weather, I often felt overwhelmed. I endured hardship growing up so, overwhelmed or not, there was a confidence in me. In fact, I was challenged by it all. Texans experienced many hardships in their pioneering history. Then, in church, we lived stories about such in the Bible. History and religion both, in fact, were for this very moment. To prepare me to endure. To overcome. To grow. Part of me even wanted to defy and taunt my circumstances. *Do it, Life*, I challenged. *Give it your best shot. Hit me again.* Every crevice of my psyche and nervous system strained to cope and to grasp these new elements. This was somehow a test. And I was going to win it. *God didn't put me on the planet for a white picket fence and soap operas on television*, I decided. *I'm going to come out of this on top of this. And pass it on to whoever I can help later on.*

That said, I was amazed how every part of me came to the fore as I faced these elements. Every weakness in me I had to deal with. But every strength was there too. Every superstition I had and every false conception haunted me. Every single facet of me came to a head. But that's what bad times, even crisis, are for. My Texan heritage and my Christian faith, my upbringing that my parents passed on to me, all were there for me. To use if it had any substance, or to overcome and discard where weak or fallacious. Life was school. Which included the school of hard knocks as my big brother would harp.

115

This brought out in me more than homesickness. I missed my culture's mammary glands to nourish me. And my faith's. I was a Christian in an Islamic setting. I wanted to go to church again, desperately at times. For renewal. For reinforcement. For nurture. I knew I could win this. I didn't want a crutch, I wanted a hand. I must learn to sing the Lord's song in a strange land.

As a Christian, on a personal level, I was not welcomed in Kuwait. The Muslim men often treated me suspiciously and disrespectfully. Not because I was American, but because I was uncovered. This assumption I was a foreign prostitute.

To add to my personal problems about this, I also had to worry about Max. A simple outing easily turned into a fight for him because he felt compelled to defend my honor from the insults. The blessing about this was. I saw firsthand the quality of man I married. And indeed it was a blessing. This man was so honorable and he was my husband. I can tell you, it was worth marrying him just to experience him.

I remember going to the hospital for an antibiotic. In the waiting room, as I'm sitting next to Max for my turn, an elderly covered lady started asking me in Arabic why I was there.

"You don't belong here," she chastised me. "You take space for a Kuwaiti woman."

I thought Max was going to burn the hospital down from his anger. Then the culture kicked in because in Arab countries respect for the elderly is the primary thing. He had to deal with his anger and show her respect, regardless. Sort of.

"Kuwait was my home," he replied. "Your behavior makes me ashamed of being Arab."

That got everyone in the waiting room involved. Yelling ensued between Max and many of the patients. Just as in the UAE, such as this seemed an everyday occurrence for us. Whether we were at a restaurant, a grocery store, a recruitment office, or his sister's home.

Nor was it just with his sister that he had to deal with aspects of the evil eye or sorcery. I developed an appreciation for Islam so much more from how the Prophet tried to uplift his people out of these pagan notions. Max held himself above such pagan aspects because of Islam. I think Islam, overall, was one of his strengths. But he too believed in the evil eye. And this 'eye' thing was the bane of my existence while there.

Similarly, one had to counteract the 'arrow' of the eye by giving the word, *Inshallah*, which stands for, 'if it wills Allah'. Being American, I was taught at an early age to be agreeable, positive, and polite. So, my positive, bubbly, Pollyanna attitude to promote or encourage something was totally disagreeable to the Arab culture. I had devoted my earlier life in Texas encouraging colleagues when something good happens. Showering greetings such as, 'I love your shirt', or 'My word, you're just beautiful'. But if you say these things to another Arab, even Max, you better say, 'I love your shirt, Inshallah', or you'll be accused of jinxing things. If something happens to stain or tear an object, then it is all your fault because you gave it an 'eye' with your praise.

In fact, I could not even say, 'It's a beautiful day'. This would cause any problem incurred afterwards to be my fault. Much like in the scene in the movie *Young Frankenstein,* where the aid to the young scientist said, 'At least it isn't raining'. And then immediately a monsoon exploded. That captures, metaphorically, the need for Inshallah to counter each cultural evil eye. To see such negative attitudes blew me away.

"Your eye is very strong, Olivia," Max often told me. "I know you don't mean these compliments of flattery you give in an envious way, but things are jinxed anyway."

I nodded my head in agreement from all my experiences.

"I'm constantly getting into trouble for my compliments," I acknowledged. "So, now I'm going to start using this word Inshallah. I just can't stop being me and not compliment things and people so I'll acculturate it. Does that sound like an idea, Max? Then I can live with the hidden me of it. A cross cultural compromise. What ya' think?"

So, I adapted. Instead of saying, 'Hopefully I'll see you in Lebanon', just adding the word Inshallah means it will never happen because of little old me and my eye thing, but only if God wills it. I loved this loophole. By saying Inshallah then, everyone knows I have no intention of really meaning it, but pass it off as God's will. I began to say this and loved how it got me off the hook. Don't blame me for any jinx then, or any 'eye' you think I have. Just blame God. So there.

Then one day, in some Arabian twist of fate, we got word that Max's mother needed an operation and wanted us to come home to Lebanon. She wanted us to live near her in the home that Max built for her and his family there. How we would be one happy family.

"But we finally found happiness here, Max," I whined.

He looked at me sympathetically, but then went back to his own thoughts.

"I appreciate how hard you've tried for happiness here, in spite of all the things that happen to you, but we could build an addition on the top floor of the house I built for my mother there," Max said wistfully, as if talking out loud to himself. He then looked back at me. "We could have a family compound and come and go as we please."

This would get us away from Fatima, I lusted inside. *We could help his mother too. If I can be happy in Kuwait, I certainly can be happy away from Fatima.*

So, the idea began to appeal.

"We don't need to stay long," Max explained. "We don't have to stay for life, Olivia. We won't retire there. But we have a home as a base until we figure out where we will end up. Lebanon is my home even though I was born in Kuwait. My family was strong there and the mountains of Bekaa are so incredibly beautiful. In my lifetime it was once called the Switzerland of the Middle East. But mostly I must go to take care of my mother. She is aging and my half-brother does not care for her well. Mahmoud is not very intelligent."

So off to Lebanon we go.

CHAPTER 10

Never have I seen a people express such pride over even the most minimal things as do the Lebanese. I had no preordained thoughts about Lebanon going into my new life there. I knew little about them. They were in the news sometimes, a tad of history about the Phoenicians in early history, some things in the Bible, and a few current events. I didn't know much about Hezbollah, even though they were in the news a lot, beginning with the suicide bombing of over two hundred Marines that were used in a peace keeping force as part of NATO during the time of President Reagan. That got my attention because my brother used to be in the Marines.

Lebanon was not in my consciousness. I imagine if you asked any of my friends who I count as intelligent and well-educated, none of them could have told you much about Lebanon either. Or Hezbollah, or the Middle East, other than we got much of our oil from Saudi Arabia, that we went to war in Iraq, and that the Desert Storm Gulf war was in Kuwait. My scope of friends were lawyers, judges, and various professional people. We all worked twenty-four hours a day, it seemed, plus enjoyed all the American past times. None of our lives included worrying about the politics of Arab countries other than we lost good young men in Iraq.

The major exception in my immediate life to all this lack of knowledge was my brother. A Marine and a history buff. But unless you were in the military, or Congress, or a history buff, no one much cared about the troubles of Lebanon, or the terrorism of Hezbollah, because we did not understand it. It was something somewhere out there. Lebanon would only be briefly mentioned in some news story. I did not watch the news much because I felt the media portrayed things to sell stories and jack up ratings. I didn't find actual truth in much of it. My friends and I were more concerned with domestic problems like the economy, unemployment, the various natural disasters that came our way, and the day to day survival mode in our own little part of the world.

Such narrow outlooks is what drove my husband, and my brother for that matter, crazy. Both considered Americans to be shallow and naïve. I respected my brother, but he seemed not just an exception, but a bit odd for it. He's the guy that joined the Marines to go to Vietnam. Who the hell did that? And my husband was Arab so that answered that. Except that it didn't. My husband knew the world. I could shake off my brother as being an outlier, but with my husband in my life too, I did feel naïve. And now, here I was, smack dab in the middle of my innocence and naïveté with my new life in the middle of all this turmoil.

I was vaguely aware of the civil war in Lebanon a few years back, because it was long, brutal, and in the news frequently in the States for awhile. I remember how booming Lebanon was before that civil war. So, it was with excitement that my husband and I traveled to Lebanon now because Beirut had once again become the hub of Middle Eastern Mediterranean life. The Lebanese had high hopes of rebuilding the area to its former glory.

Beirut potentially becoming the Paris of the Middle East as in the old days, renewed its reputation for being cosmopolitan. So, I looked forward to Lebanon as being a relief from all the severity I encountered in the Gulf countries. Both in religion and culture.

Lebanon was well known for its various cultures and beliefs. It still, however, was struggling with sectarianism from its past. America played no small part in the tumult of the recent civil war. There were still many Lebanese Americans in Lebanon, either through marriage or birth, that kept the embassy quite busy meeting their needs and demands. Americanism seemed to be quite established in Beirut. All of this looked promising to me.

My flight into Beirut was innervating. There is no other place like this glorious city, which is the tenth oldest still existing settlement in recorded history. I was mesmerized just looking down from the window of the airplane. How it is situated on cliffs and hills overlooking the Mediterranean. With this scenery I felt as if stepping back in time. A pristine, beautiful time.

To intrigue me further, my husband related much of Lebanon's history on the flight. Not just about Lebanon itself, but as part of the Levant region of Northwestern Asia. This cross roads of three continents, Asia, Africa, and Europe. It was a bonding moment between us. One adorable to share. The near erotic experience of something I never considered as important before and to share it with the man I loved the most. To see his pride as he related things added to it all the more.

"It would take volumes, Olivia, to give justice to the Levant's importance and place in history," he beamed as he sat next to me on the plane explaining things. "Recently, it was part of the Ottoman Empire. Lebanon, as part of the Levant, has various phases throughout history. Its place in history means different things to different factions living there, both current and past. All of this history put together gives a strong spiritualistic pull to both expats living there now and we native Lebanese."

I listened starry eyed and felt girlish for doing so. Max's style of explaining things reminded me of a college professor. On opposite ends of the universe from the brawler he could be while protecting his wife or defending his heritage. He had a heart for knowledge like no one I ever came across. I loved him seeing me in awe and in love with him.

"And you'll love this," he continued. "Beirut has some of the finest dining I ever experienced in all my travels. They are rich in seafood delicacies as well as many Middle Eastern ones. You will love them even more than what we had in Kuwait. There's nothing you cannot get in Lebanon, as far as material goods are concerned. We were once colonized by the French. This occurred after World War I when the French and British divided what was left of the Ottoman Empire in the Middle East. How they betrayed the Arab states that helped them defeat the Turks. Colonial treachery. This is another reason the Arab countries are so embittered. But the French influence has its good points and is in every aspect of modern Lebanon, especially the food. The European feel is everywhere, mixed in with Arabian. The best of both worlds as they say."

"Better food than in Kuwait?" I drooled. "Am I going to get fat, sweetheart? How am I not going to eat myself into oblivion?"

"That is probably why most Lebanese women are fat," he said. "Unashamedly so. It is a badge of prestige among them."

"Max, I can't get fat. Not. But what a way to go if I do."

"But back to the history, Olivia. It is the history that is nourishing. It is the Phoenicians, these ancient Sea Peoples, that made the largest impact on Lebanon. They are revered to this day, and esteemed as the highest imprint on Lebanese national identity. The Phoenicians were one of the major forces to ever occupy this planet, in fact. You hear of Mesopotamia, of Egypt, or India, or of China. But among them were the Phoenicians. In fact, it was the Phoenicians that developed and spread the world's first alphabet. That changed the course of history."

What did my Arab husband really think of all this, I wondered? As much as he was shamed by much of his culture, he was the proudest man alive about it. So how did he really feel about all those in Lebanon that preferred the Phoenician to the Arab?

"Wasn't Carthage Phoenician?" I asked timidly while searching desperately in my mind to retrieve the tidbits of history I ruthlessly ignored in school. "I know the Philistines were," I added boldly, then held my breath, hoping I was correct in my memory.

"Yes, Olivia, you are right. Both were Phoenician. It is this strand in the Lebanese race and culture that is the most significant. Being Phoenician and not Arab is a very important distinction to the Lebanese. Separating themselves from the lowly Arab Gulf countries with this trait makes them feel more refined and elegant. All this makes Lebanon one of the most unique places on earth. Here, along with its Phoenician past, are Sunni and Shia Muslims, Maronite Christians, Catholics, Greek Orthodox Christians, as well as generations of Druze. All co-existing."

As encouraged as I was by all my husband said, to my American eyes, from the Lebanese I observed in other Arab countries, their culture seemed the same as any other Arab nation. I say this because of the mindset. The one I had been plagued with since my arrival in the Middle East. The arrogance. From my aspect, that's what I saw the most pronounced. Arrogance based on a need of self-worth.

Even the Lebanese I met in Kuwait would drone endlessly about how terrible America is and how Americans have no culture. How we are lazy, fat, stupid, uneducated, greedy, wasteful, warlike, racist, and so on. Every cliché of need an inferiority complex demands of things it feels left out of.

Still he made me hopeful I would find better in Lebanon's own environment. I was game. I don't need to name call anyone just to get back at them. I had to live with them. I was so ready to feel Lebanon was glorious.

But I immediately learned they were indeed more of the same. What I had already experienced in the Middle East was waiting for me here in my new home. Again. Even the longing I felt to be a part of my husband's heritage got swallowed up by harsh reality as soon as I got off the plane. Calling names to their arrogance just seemed a waste of time. I can only relate the life I led while there.

It became apparent they were sidetracked with internal bickering over who is superior among themselves. Businesses seemed to base their focus on stealing resources and money laundering. There was religious sectarianism beyond what I lived growing up in Texas. There were remnants of civil war in some form endlessly. Perhaps their smugness was an escape from their problems, but I determined it was more the cause of those problems.

During the civil war it is well known that America backed the Christian factor, mainly the Maronite Phalange Party. America basically kept these Maronite from being tossed into the sea. The thanks America got from the Phalange for it was condescension, ridicule, and hatred.

Among the first things anyone asked me upon my arrival was, "Can you help me get to America?" Then was quickly followed by rhetoric regarding how horrible America and Americans are.

Max's family lived in a small village in the Bekaa Valley called Al-Habib. This was home to Max's mother's second husband. This second husband divorced Max's mother, but not before they had a child together. His name was Mahmoud.

Mahmoud was seven years old when Kuwait expelled a large number of Shiite malcontents. Including Mahmoud's father. Mahmoud was sent back to Lebanon without his mother, who chose to stay in Kuwait with its large Sunni population. So, Mahmoud lived with his half-brothers, half-sister, father, and stepmother in Lebanon until his father was shot down by a stray bullet from someone trying to kill the person next to him. After Mahmoud's father died, his uncles and the rest of the family kicked Mahmoud out on the street.

Mahmoud had a low IQ as well as being stunted physically. Emotionally he seemed no older than nine. So, Mahmoud's mother left Kuwait to take care of him. They lived on charity until arrangements could be made to find a place for them to live. Max was abroad working when this happened. He began sending money to them to purchase land to build a home. Twenty years later, after sending hundreds of thousands of dollars home over the years, a three story house with two outer buildings for rentals and storage was built and furnished.

This is what we called home upon our arrival.

The Bekaa Valley is famous and coveted for its fertility. From Beirut it is a drive into the mountains. A gloriously beautiful drive. All of Lebanon is, in fact. The hour and a half drive from Beirut to Al-Habib looks like scenes out of Monaco. The cedar tree with its Biblical significance, and which is on the Lebanese flag, is evident everywhere. Everyone's property seemed to have them. There were also citrus trees, bananas trees, olive groves, orchards of almonds, as well as other fruit trees in abundance. Vegetables grown in Lebanon were prevalent and of high quality. Radishes grow as big as oranges while colorful vegetable stands populate every street corner. Flowers and plants are also lush. All in this beautiful mountainous terrain I now called home.

But Al-Habib had become a Hezbollah village by the time I got there. Hezbollah are not only terrorists, but also foreign trained. Puppets. They are easily hated for both reasons, including by my husband.

My first introduction to the Hezbollah village of Al-Habib was a most unusual start. It is a cultural custom to be welcomed to the area or home by visitation. Arabs are very sociable people and any excuse they can find for sitting down with tea or coffee and good old fashioned gossip is greatly appreciated by them.

Max, over the years, became well known to the town and neighborhood because he visited everyone he knew constantly when he came home from abroad. Plus, he was responsible for creating this large compound for his family. So, upon our arrival, we began going house to house so everyone could meet the new wife. Me.

By the few pictures I saw of Hezbollah through the years, I expected to see men in their turbans wearing Afghan type shirts with long growths of beards. But as Max kept mentioning to me who was Hezbollah and who wasn't as we visited, it was obvious they dressed like everyone else, and many were without a beard.

For Hezbollah men it is a t-shirt, often with American logos, and blue jeans. But it depends on what they are doing. The clerics wear traditional Arab dress with headgear and robes. But the everyday person wears, since most of them work at some family owned establishment in the village, buttoned down sport shirts and jeans. Casual dress is usually European, mainly Italian. If they are out in the field or in town doing official Hezbollah business of some sort, they usually wear camouflage attire. Much like the Lebanese Army does. They would be indistinguishable except the Hezbollah have their own arm patches and dispense with bars defining rank.

As Max had explained to me earlier, the women were quite hefty in physique for the most part. Many wear the traditional hijab and abayat. But the really hardcore Hezbollah members who are married to clerks or fighters, wear the Iranian chador.

The first house we visited was that of Mahmoud's half-brothers, which was right next door to our compound.

No one said a word when one of the brothers opened the door to let us in. They just stared, first at Max, then at me. Then at Max again, then at me again. They were obviously surprised, but somehow it was the same old same old I had seen everywhere I went.

"You were always the playboy," Mahmoud's half-brother said in disgust to Max.

That was the cue to unravel the rest of local society. This man was shoved aside by the pack of wolves known as the women in the house, all of them Hezbollah.

"How could you marry an American?" each howled in Arabic. "Why not someone from the village? Have you no pride? Have you no decency?"

Welcome to my new home indeed. Perhaps with all my aspirations about coming here I should have chirped, *Inshallah* before I left Kuwait. But this would have happened anyway and I knew it. It couldn't get worse except that it did.

For the moment, only the half-sister, her stepmother, and a few other women were there. They pounced on Max before glaring at me, then yelled at him some more. These were his people, the Shia of Lebanon. Culture demands politeness to a guest if you are in their home, even if you hate them. My presence defied that polite custom. Did that make me special?

This custom of greeting the new bride, in fact, is an important tribal custom. If bread is broken or a meal shared with someone in a home, even if a sworn enemy, protection must be offered from that point on. This custom dates back to the beginning of time, even before Muhammad's day. Yet, these women were verbally assaulting Max and insulting me, his new wife.

As if to set your watch to it, Max lost his temper.

"Leave this house!" he yelled. "You soil my floors. You are a cyst on the neck. Leave this house immediately!"

"But this is my home!" one of them yelled in return.

"I allowed you to stay," he reminded them. "This is my house. I lent it to swine. To pigs. Get out! All you sows get out!"

I loved it. *Go Max go. Inshallah.*

Things calmed down and he allowed them to remain. Then, as we sat drinking tea.

"America is corrupt," one of the women began her new rant to Max. "You bring this woman to be among us. What a betrayal to your family. You run to marry an American. Such an honor. You are too good for a Shia woman it seems. She is a Christian also. You are disgusting."

Max stood up, then turned over the table for dramatic affect.

"Get out of this house!" he bellowed. "Leave! Now!"

"But it is my home," she defied. "We pay good rent for this. You can't kick us out of our own homes. Did you learn this in America?"

"I hate Arab women. You are typical. Who would want such as you?"

She stormed out. When quiet returned her stepmother approached Max.

"I am sorry for my daughter's action," she said before breaking into a laugh. "You had the audacity to kick my daughter out of her own home." She laughed further and shook her head. "You are the same man we knew. Nothing has changed at all. This is what you did before, such behavior. I don't blame you, my dear friend. She deserved it. It is good to have you home."

The daughter, however, huffed straight to a Hezbollah secret police officer.

"A man, a criminal," she spewed out angrily, "came into my own house just now and forced me to leave. He is trespassing in my house as I speak to you. Come, arrest him. He wants my house to give to an American prostitute for his pleasure."

The police officer rushed over with a gun just to see what was going on. But when he spotted Max they both laughed.

"It has been a long time, old friend," the police officer said. "You just return and already such a commotion. Nothing has changed, Khalil. I was told you forced out a poor Hezbollah woman. I know you do not like us, that we are puppets to what you consider invaders of your homeland, but where will this woman live now?" He then looked at me. "Is this the American woman you intend for this house?"

In spite of ill feelings politically between many native Lebanese, such as Max, and the Iranian-Syrian backed Hezbollah, Max befriended many of them and had a reputation bigger than life among them. He smiled as he greeted his old friend.

"This is my wife. She is American. We only just arrived and I came to visit, but my presence with my American wife upset this woman."

Max paused for a second, as if wanting to say more, then continued.

"I don't really consider the Iranians that trained you as invaders. I know you meant well by asking them in to train you. They are Shia, you are Shia, we all are Shia here in much of Lebanon. But knowing you want to take up for yourselves is one thing. The Iranians are mischievous. They don't just train and pat you on the back. There are consequences. They are mischievous and ambitious. They are not Arab and they do more than protect Shia Arabs. The devil takes his due someday, my friend. And Hezbollah invited them in. We will pay the cost for this someday."

"We need the Iranians, Khalil," the police officer said in English for me to understand. "We were weak until they came. But back to your wife and the problems here. I can see the woman behaved outrageously." He turned to me again. "Welcome," he said to me. "I apologize for the way you were treated upon your arrival. There is passion in my people. Sometimes misplaced. I do hope you feel welcomed here in your stay with us." His grin broadened when he spoke again to Max. "But did you have to marry a blonde also? American wasn't bad enough?"

Everyone laughed. The women seemed put in their place. I was satisfied. For now.

Every house we visited the women erupted with similar scenes. The rhetoric never varied and Max always got upset and told everyone to go to hell.

The men, however, were absolutely wonderful. While the wives were screaming shrews with their attitudes and jealousy, the Hezbollah fighters showed us every respect, clapped Max on the back, gave us welcome, and insisted on tea or coffee as they sat talking to get acquainted.

As a further introduction of his American blonde haired wife, Max took me by the hand to march me down main street to the Hezbollah headquarter office.

"This is my wife," he said boldly to the Hezbollah leaders of the village. "She is American. She has blue eyes. She has blonde hair. And she is the greatest wife of any man in this village. Who wants an Arab for a wife, or an Iranian for that matter, with such a prize of a wife as I have?"

As he dared anyone to speak, spontaneously the village leaders rushed to meet their old friend, then hugged him in fraternal greeting.

"You are under our protection," they said loudly to me, showing proper respect to make their point as if to all in the village.

Everyone now knew they would have to deal with the full force of Hezbollah, as well as Max, if they gave me further problems.

Max's brazenness worked again. The village women continued to glare at me on a daily basis and still gossiped, but they realized I was here to stay.

Such was my first day in Lebanon.

CHAPTER 11

Max did not ask a penny rent from his family for the house he provided them. In addition, he donated a substantial part of his income to their living expenses and in sustaining the compound. I was excited that we would have a house that we owned ourselves.

I was in awe when I saw it. It contained an Old World traditional setting where an entire Arab family could live in one family compound. This layout is the norm for most Middle Eastern cultures. Each child or family member takes a room on a floor of the main house. The center courtyard provides a summer retreat from the heat. Everyone has their own veranda where drinking tea or coffee is seen at all times of the day and night since the Arab culture is a social one. They have figured out how to make the most of limited space. It is all very pleasing to the eye as well as functional.

If there is air conditioning at all, individual air conditioning window units, as well as radiant wall heaters, are the norm in the Bekaa Valley. So it was in our house. Any room not used was left uncooled or unheated. In the mountain villages and towns, since most homes date back hundreds of years, not many people have air conditioning in their homes due to the naturally cooler air. But another reason is electricity. It is sporadic and very undependable. Also the wiring is precarious.

I must have a fan and I ran it constantly. That seemed so absurd to Max's family that it became a topic of conversation at every opportunity. The wasteful American. The same logic applied to heating as I was afraid of literally freezing to death in winter without it. I never saw a centrally heated home in any country in the Middle East. The winters are incredibly harsh in the mountains. I often was buried in snow and not able to leave out the front door of my home.

Diesel is the crown jewel of the Middle East for heating. It is smelly, smoky, and thoroughly unpleasant. But my life blood in the winter. There is the equivalent of a potbelly stove in each common room and bedroom, while the hallways, kitchen, and bathrooms are left unheated. I spent as little time in these unheated areas as possible. I wore three layers of clothes in winter plus socks and whatever else I could get my hands on. I buried myself in my bedroom with a TV and books for the whole of winter.

The cold was even harder to bear because all the rooms in our house, as well as most Lebanese houses, have tile floors. This makes it easier to clean, which I appreciated, though would have traded that problem for a good old fashioned, warm, cozy rug. *Whatever happened to a Persian rug when you needed one*, I often wondered?

Water heaters are on a boiler system. In order to have hot water, the water heater must be lit a half hour beforehand so the water can heat up through the boiler. This mattered to me since there were no hot water capabilities in my kitchen. To wash dishes, I had to heat the water on the stove first.

Since the price of diesel was so expensive, I could only run the heater twice a day. A little in the morning and a little in the evening. Even that was unaffordable to many people.

Housing there is very primitive by American and European standards. I must say, however, as a little girl when we visited my maternal grandmother in Pueblo, Colorado, it was even more primitive. My grandfather plowed by mule and there was no electricity at all on the entire farm. My grandparents used a hand pump for water, a metal tub for a bath, a potbelly stove to cook with, and an outhouse for unpleasantries. So, I was grateful for my not as stark exposure in the Bekaa.

Residential *sahns*, which are part of a courtyard house, are the most private areas. The scale and design details differ. No matter the locale or climate, and no matter the era or culture, the basic function of security and privacy remains the same for them in their design. The sahn can be a private garden, a service yard, or a summer season outdoor living room for the family, or for their entertainment. In our case, instead of one veranda of three walls overlooking the sahn, we had two verandas facing out into the garden of fruit trees. We also had climbing roses with every color in the rainbow, as well as tall pine trees and Chinese fig trees, all wildly growing among each other in a very colorful display of foliage. On either side of the courtyard, enclosing it on each side, were three-story apartment buildings rented out to tenants. This was also the case for the ground floor of the main house.

As gorgeous as our house estate was, and as beautiful as the Bekaa Valley was to live in, we needed employment. Luckily, soon after we arrived, Max found a job in Beirut, an hour and a half drive away.

"I have to get an apartment in Beirut," he informed me after a week of driving back and forth. "In the village here I have to plow through the snow and ice almost everyday in winter. That makes the driving hazardous. Our house is just too far away if I am to have a life worth living. So, I must live in the city if I am to work there. People have summer and winter homes in Lebanon, so this will be our getaway home. It is even a Lebanese tradition to have a summer place in the mountains and a winter place in Beirut. As if we are rich. Everyone in Al-Habib lives and dies in their same house generation after generation. But we will have two different homes because of circumstances."

The good part about residing in Beirut was seeing two parts of demography in Lebanon. Beirut was on the ocean and there were beaches. Since I had grown up on the coast of the Gulf of Mexico, this suited me fine. The Mediterranean Sea became my favorite body of water. From the moment I first flew over it to land at the airport in Beirut under a full moon, I called it my Mediterranean. There is nothing to compare. The ocean made the temperatures in Beirut more manageable also. And there was the added benefit of being away from Hezbollah.

For me, the focus was on the food. I had to eat and I sure as hell wanted to enjoy what I ate. Max promised me I would adore the food in Beirut. I was ready to find out.

"You'll love *kibbeh nayyeh*," Max promised.

Kibbeh nayehh, meaning raw kibbeh, is a common Levantine mezze. This consists of minced raw lamb or beef, mixed with fine bulgur and spices, often served with mint leaves, olive oil, and green onions. Flat bread is used to scoop it. There is sometimes a sauce of garlic or olive oil served with it.

I held my nose, closed my eyes, and indulged. I nearly gagged.

"Sweetheart," I bluntly said, "I hate this. I hate lamb. I was sure you knew that. Even though I love beef you can forget about raw beef. This isn't a good way to start me off in Beirut. I'm sure I'll like the seafood and Indian restaurants, but don't ever do this to me again."

I was so disgusted, but the dish is the Lebanese pride and joy. That's why Max gambled and had me try it, even though he knew better. Just what if. Well, it was official. I hated it. Huge.

Arab women eat this for breakfast if they are lucky enough to afford meat. They serve it with great abandon. When offered, no matter how much I wanted to be polite and not offend, I could not abide the thought of eating it again.

I constantly heard, "I told you Americans are weak," as I gagged while they shoved it in front of me. But go ahead and humiliate me. I still hate it. What part of 'hate' and 'no' do you not understand?

The pride of eating kibbeh nayehh comes from having the strength to eat raw meat, no matter what the doctors say regarding the health of doing so. Even the babies are weaned on raw meat. I admired this. It made me want to be up to eating it. But I never did manage.

After all these years, Beirut still suffered the affects of their civil war. It never fully recovered. Even so, it was a glorious cosmopolitan city. There were Phoenician descendants here, Europeans, Americans, Muslim. And Christians. At last. I wanted to wallow in the Christian elements and structures.

Most Lebanese, until recently, were Christian. The Christian population has dwindled to one-fourth of the population now, half of what it used to be just a few decades ago. But Christians are still a large sector. That part was a relief to me. I could retreat, perhaps, to Christian enclaves, and relax a little.

"Excuse me," I said to a street vendor at a kiosk I came across. "Do you speak English?"

"Of course," the lady selling newspapers and cigarettes replied. "So many speak English in Beirut. You are a tourist?"

"Oh no," I answered. "But my husband and I just moved here. He's Lebanese actually, but I just moved here with him. We were living in Kuwait."

"Oh, then your husband is Arab," she surmised.

"Yes."

"And you? You are not Arab. Are you American?"

"Yes, I am. And I'm looking for a Christian church. Is there one nearby?"

"What do you mean by Christian? There are many different Christian types here."

"I'm Episcopal."

"What is this Episcopal that you speak?"

"It is Protestant."

"Oh, you are Evangelical. You must say so then. Yes, there are some Pentecostal churches in the area. I don't know if you can walk to one, however."

"No, no," I answered. "I'm Episcopalian. It is like Catholic."

"What you mean Catholic? There are so many Catholic. Which kind Catholic are you? You sound a bit confused."

"I'm a Catholic. Is there a Catholic church nearby?"

"So, again. What kind of Catholic are you? I can't tell you the church unless you can tell me what kind Catholic are you. Are you Roman or Orthodox? What kind of Catholic please?"

"Roman Catholic."

Her look turned sour. It was if someone threw water on her.

"You mean you are a papist. You follow this anti-Christ then. Yes, I can tell you where is a papist church. I am Maronite. There are many Maronite in Lebanon. While you are here you must find out more about us. It is good education for you. But your papist church. There is one in two block walk from here. You will see a large bell tower on the left. There is your papist church. This pope of yours, you know, says the Savior was born in Bethlehem. Not so. You must find out the truth while you are here in Beirut." She studied me further. "And your Arab husband that is Lebanese from Kuwait? He is also papist? There are so few papist in Kuwait."

"No, he is Muslim. A Shia."

Somehow the look turned even more sour.

"Why would a Christian marry a Muslim? It is because the papist are not really Christian, that is why."

"You have been very kind and helpful," I said to her before walking off.

She looked contemptuously the other direction from me in disrespect as I did so.

I almost appreciated the encounter in my own subdued way. It put my feet even further on the ground. It is so easy to judge others when being confronted by bigotry. People are people. Flawed. Some more than others. The tormentors I faced in Gulf countries deserved to be judged by me, but the encounter now with the Maronite gave it the perspective I was forgetting. Everyone has their own problems. This isn't a religious thing, a political thing, or a cultural thing. It is an all the above thing, and more. If all a person knows is what they think they know, this happens.

Suddenly, right in front of me there it was. A church belfry. My heart leapt. The peace of even lighting a candle melted me at the thought.

Once inside, the solitude of the church moved me. At first I sat quietly at a pew. Just for the serenity of it. Slowly I studied all the fixtures. The stained glass windows, the stations-of-the-cross, the crucifixes. It was as if my past life flashed before me. Everything that I held precious. My family. My upbringing. My faith.

Peace and love comforted me. How fulfilling Christianity was to me and the messages I learned in church. It surged within me. I wasn't proud to be Christian as much as comforted for the things Christianity gave me in my life.

I knelt and prayed. Me praying in a Christian church again. How sacred it felt.

I stood up to leave. Candles were near the door entrance. I lit one and prayed again. I prayed especially in gratitude of my husband. In spite of everything that had happened since I married him, I had gained so much in my life because of him. No one loved anyone the way he loved me.

"Max, darling," I whispered as I lit the candle, "you and I are of the book. Amen."

CHAPTER 12

I had insisted to Max to find us a more traditionally Arab apartment this time. I was acclimated now and wanted Persian rugs, Arab furniture, arched entry ways, and tiled floors. The whole works. He chose well and threw in a view of the Mediterranean, my Mediterranean, as well.

The more I experienced Beirut the more I grew to love it. There were educated, sophisticated people in my midst. Enough to mingle with and feel sane with. But as much as I loved Beirut and its cosmopolitan lifestyle, I decided to do the unbearable. Move back to Al-Habib in order to take care of Max's mother. Back into the center of turmoil itself. Where division within the country was now more divided through outside forces, namely the takeover by Hezbollah. Since Mahmoud was letting his mother rot, I had to help. Duty called. As hard as life was in Al-Habib, I was needed there. Max would make the trek from Beirut as much as possible. Even knowing he was available comforted me.

After my first rocky start upon my arrival from Kuwait, going back became a smooth transition, to my surprise and joy. I soon acclimated to the locals and as I lived among the Shia in Al-Habib, I grew to love and admire them. It is my husband's ethnic group. My loving husband that I greatly admired.

But overall, I had problems with the Shia women because culturally, and as human beings, we are too different. In my eyes it was their fault we couldn't get along. I could forgive them and move on easily, except I never got the chance. The clash kept hitting me in the face on a daily basis and I never learned how to deal with it. These women never compromised in any way, shape, or form. All of that aside, Shia women are truly some of the toughest, no nonsense women I ever met. However, most of the uneducated ones think in a linear way that won't allow for anything outside of what they are taught to believe.

I understood, on the one hand, that it is their cultural heritage they are fighting for. To them it is a survival stance. All of this turmoil they've faced and their ancestors before them. I see their need to protect it. Yet I could not just stand around and take it passively. I had my own surviving to do. I had problems with them that were personal. Even damn personal. I could never appreciate the way they treated me because of any perceived threat I was to them. But I could at least understand their perspective in my spare time. I even felt a duty to do this. It seemed hopeless to work things out, but I could start by trying to understand. On the other hand, I was not going to wimp out of my own causes. I had to learn how to handle all of it. I was even grateful for that.

I soon learned, however, that some of the Shia women from rich families, who were educated abroad, are some of the most brilliant people I ever met. Their hunger for knowledge and thirst for adventure outweighs any criticism I might have of Shia or Arab women in general.

Thus the problem. Thus the challenge. Endure what I must from the adversarial Shia women, and find friends among the more open minded. I was game. I had no answers, but was determined to work on it. It's why I was there. Or so I had the feeling.

In my search for meaning, I thought of Westerners back home, as well as new ones I met in the Middle East, that had much of the same closed mindedness my adversaries displayed. I had encountered some of this growing up, in fact. To be single minded and bigoted seemed a human trait. A very complicated one. But finally, in my stay in the Middle East, I now began to meet wonderful Shia women who treated me protectively and honorably. I began to see things in better perspective. And I came to admire my husband's people. I felt better off for doing so.

"We have lived in Texas, Olivia," my new friend in Al-Habib told me soon after I moved back. "We lived in Corpus Christi. My husband was a doctor there."

"Corpus Christi?" I chirped. "I grew up on a farm just south of there. Near the King Ranch."

"Yes? Oh my goodness. The King Ranch. This wide open ranch that goes on forever. It is as big or more as some of the emirates near the Persian Gulf, I think."

"We're neighbors then," I said. "Or were. We just didn't know it. But now we do. Somebody from home. I can hardly wait to tell my mother. And now here we are again. Really neighbors now. So, why did you move here? Or back here. What's your story, babe?"

"The same as you, I'm afraid, Olivia. How you said things were for your husband. After 911 it became so impossible for an Arab to live anywhere. We were lucky enough to live in a community with many Hispanics so that we could mingle and hide among them so to speak. Pass as one of them. At least some of the time. But even then, there was so much distrust and anger with Arabs and Muslims that my Shia husband, and I must admit, me also, got fed up."

I nodded sympathetically.

"And then we come home and so many Hezbollah look at us like traitors," she sighed. "It must be hard on an American like you."

Should I be honest, I wondered?

"It can be trying," I replied as straight faced as possible. "But then I meet people such as you. And from my neck of the woods even. But even some of the Hezbollah are so good to me actually."

Dealing with Max's family again, however, was a different story. *Did Max take all the good genes for himself*, I often wondered? I thought, or at least hoped, Fatima was the exception for bad results in his family. Instead, she was just a chip off the old family block. I couldn't blame Max's father or uncle for how the family turned out. They had passed on. All the marvels I heard about them seemed believable, if for no other reason than seeing such attributes in my husband. So, I had to assume, the relatives of his I met that were lacking came as a result of those ancestral heroes being gone. Long gone. And the matriarch mother being the reason for the insanity I encountered with his living siblings. I don't know how Max came out so good, but he did. His ancestors be proud.

All through the years Max sent money to his family in the village where they lived. Those were good times for them. They had tons of money to do what they wished with no one to tell them what to do or how to do it. They built the three story house we now shared and rented out the bottom portion. Then proceeded to tell Max how they needed to build more so they could rent that out also and not be dependent on him anymore.

Max's half-brother, Mahmoud, never worked a day in his life. He spent the entire time, day in and day out, sleeping until noon, then leaving the house in the late afternoon to pursue his mischief. He was divorced by the time I arrived, having made his wife miserable with arguments and beatings. She threatened to kill herself if her family did not take her back.

The two of them had twins, a girl and a boy. In Islamic culture, the man gets the children if he deems it, while the woman is left with nothing. They agreed the daughter could go with the mother back to the nearby village of Kom Hasa. The son stayed with Mahmoud and his mother.

I determined early on that the majority of blame for my brother-in-law's disastrous marriage was the mother. She was mean, cruel, and nasty to Mahmoud's wife, so I heard. She would not let her daughter-in-law have any say over her own children. She also starved her, locked her in a room much of the time, and constantly insulted her. She would then instigate Mahmoud to beat her for the reason that the daughter-in-law hated how she was being treated, which was worse than they treated their housemaid. After four years of this, Mahmoud's wife staged a protest on the roof of the house.

"My mother-in-law is a whore!" she screamed to the village. "I want to kill myself! I demand a divorce! Right now! This minute! I hate my husband! I hate my pig of a mother-in-law! I want to go home!"

In Arab culture the wife is not usually granted a divorce. The man can divorce at a moment's notice and it is legal. All he has to say in front of witnesses is, "I divorce you, I divorce you, I divorce you." And it's done.

Mahmoud's father-in-law, his wife's uncle, and her brother all lived nearby. During visits to the family, sporadically, they noticed bruises as well as heard stories from her of her treatment from her husband and mother-in-law.

"We will not accept this treatment!" they shouted. "You cannot treat her this way!"

So an exception was made and she was allowed to come back home to her family with her daughter in tow. Part of the marriage contract was that if there was a divorce, then Mahmoud's wife would get ten thousand dollars. This is very common. Max sent the money for the divorce, just as he paid for everything.

As I entered this scenario, I became a threat to both Mahmoud and his mother's dependency on my husband for their financial livelihood. Mahmoud, all these years later, still would not get a job, even with pressure from his relatives, including Fatima in Kuwait. He claimed his job was the maintenance of the compound and what amounted to playing housemaid, with the exception of the cooking. He took out trash, washed floors and did errands.

My new life with them also meant I inherited Mahmoud's son in the mix, who was now twenty-three. The son, like his father, would sleep until noon, then leave in the late afternoon to drink with his friends. He was known as the town drunk. To a Muslim, this is even more humiliating than to other religions because such behavior is strictly forbidden. In the Hezbollah headquarters in town where the young men are true believers, they not only do not drink, but they fight any wars that occur, often losing their lives in the worst way. They had no respect for Mahmoud as a result. Though Max never liked Hezbollah, he befriended many of them and admired many of their dutiful ways. The behavior and lifestyle of his brother and nephew embarrassed him. His entire family did, in fact, for their attitude, laziness, and greed.

So, I could see it coming. Here I was, new to the environment, and an American. Same song, different verse. Sure enough.

"Why did you bring this American back to us?" Mahmoud and the mother said to Max when he returned to visit one day. This, in spite of the fact that my sole purpose for being there was to help them. "She is lazy and only causes us trouble. Take her back with you to Beirut. She has been a problem for us the whole time of her return to us."

Max, more shell shocked from this type reaction to his marriage than even I, read his family the riot act instantly.

"I will not accept your belligerence," he sneered. "After all the support I have given you through the years. She is my wife. You will not judge her. You will not judge me. You will treat her as you treat everyone else. If you insult her or treat her badly, I will no longer support you."

His mother did not take this well, and even though in the beginning she kept away from me, behind the scenes she instigated trouble at every opportunity.

"Your wife wastes money," his mother said to Max as yet another complaint. "She is an infidel. I will not allow her to touch my food. She will take all your money. Americans are greedy. They take and never give."

"You are my mother," Max said for assurance. "I still support you. Do not be afraid."

"Why did you marry an infidel, Khalil?"

"She is my wife. But I will continue to support you," Max reiterated. "I allow her to control much of the money now. But do not fear, Mother."

Max's loyalty to his family was such that even though he saw their behavior and attitudes, he would not allow me to comment because he was embarrassed.

"I don't listen to them, Olivia," he assured me. "Please be patient. I know it is a hardship on you, but I will take care of you. They are family. I must be there for them."

I stared at him showing some of my contempt.

"I'm tired of putting up with it, Max," I said. "I mean fed the hell up. I was happy in Beirut. I had friends. Even American friends. Yet I'm beginning to like it here in our village. For the first time I've been in the Middle East I'm treated well by most. I even have my friend from Corpus Christi now. Some of the uneducated little bitches here are still mean to me. But many with some education like my new friend that have been abroad are very good to me. Even your friends in Hezbollah are good to me. They make me feel like they like me. I feel safe and secure because of them. I can't fathom they are terrorists actually. I know they are by Western standards, but they aren't starting any wars. I know they get involved with Israel. I'm not naïve. But they don't blow people up. Maybe someone does somewhere, but not our friends here. I even admire them. As long as they don't blow up Marines or something. But your mother and your brother are another story. I want to show respect, but I have had it, Max. Had it. They lie about me all the time to you too. I'm glad you don't listen to them, but I didn't come here to be their competitor nor to antagonize them. I'm the one that helps them. I finally have a home. I'm finally on the verge of happiness. But right here in my own home, the one you bought and paid for, I get treated like dirt."

Max let out a sigh.

"They are my family. You are my wife. I have to honor both of you. No, I don't listen to them. They are petty and they are liars. I can only ask you to be patient. They receive the rent for the house, I make sure they have food and medicine. But we will live our lives without them except for this."

"I guess you know Mahmoud wants a Mercedes Benz," I said with a smirk of contempt. "You know that, right? This whole village laughs at him like he's the village idiot. Well, Maxie baby, are you gonna buy your brother a Mercedes Benz?"

"Food and medicine," he repeated. "Clothing if they need. I must provide that. I will not support every whim of my worthless brother or his worthless son. When I supported him from abroad, even after I got here, I gave him two hundred dollars a day. No more. Since last year even. No more money. He is on his own. I am also fed up with his greed and his laziness. This is not because of you. He thinks so. He hates you even more now. But he knows I am fed up with him. He hates you and blames you anyway, but he knows the real reason. I have told him so. One pathetic excuse after another to get my money. There is little money left for us and it means nothing to him. How can he blame you? But that is what parasites do. In his mind it is the world's fault he doesn't have everything he wants."

CHAPTER 13

"I hate to leave you stranded here, Olivia," Max told me one afternoon, "but I found a better job in Iraq. I will be leaving soon. If the job wasn't better than what I have now, and if we didn't need the money so badly, I wouldn't be doing this."

I stared at him at a cross between scared of being left alone and fear at the name of 'Iraq', with him going there.

"You'll be killed," I said fretfully.

"Iraq is stable now," he replied. "There are still dangers, but it is mostly pacified. I have the bigger fear for you being here in the same house with Mahmoud and my mother. But our friends in Hezbollah have vowed to protect you. I feel safe with them to do so, but they cannot deliver you from the insanity of my family. I'll send for you in Iraq when I get the chance. This company is headquartered in Baghdad. It is owned and operated by Iraqi Shia. It's a small construction company looking for a General Manager. They think a Shiite with an American passport is just the ticket for creating new business opportunities with American companies, as well as other Western companies. They promised me a lot of money with the chance for bonuses. Money is so tight here because of my family. I must take this job even though I face a risky environment."

But it was obvious from the beginning this was *not* an up and coming company after all. The owner was making promises he couldn't keep. He didn't complete many projects, either for individual entrepreneurs, or for government contracts.

Max had many meetings with various unhappy customers upon his arrival. He immediately set about trying to rectify the problems.

"I must speak frankly," Max told me one day over the phone several months after he arrived in Iraq. "I should not have come here. I didn't want to worry you, but it's evident now, the company is bankrupt. I can't save it. There is no money to honor any debts or start new projects. That's the key. It has no money to even start new projects. No way to make money then. The company has not paid employee salaries for six months. They paid me for my first months. They needed me to see what I could do. But you can't bleed a turnip. So now, I also have not been paid in three months. It is time for me to leave. They can't even fly me home, however. But it's more than that. I'm not leaving until I get what is owed me."

My heart sank. How were we going to make it? But we had been through worse.

"So how did you come up with the thousand dollars your mother asked you for?" I asked him. "The money for the lawyer for the will?"

"I had to borrow it," he said meekly. "I didn't want to tell you yet of the trouble I was having. I have a rich friend here. I'm not in Baghdad anymore, but in An Najaf. That's where I am staying now. It's in another province. My friend is an Imam and really likes me. We really hit it off. I am staying mostly with him and his family now. It is a great honor, actually. Somehow good happens to us, not just the bad."

"Is he helping you get your money or something?" I asked. "What are you up to?"

"The owner of this company I work for," Max replied, "has a family in Najaf and business connections with a well-known cleric there. Najaf clerics are very strong and beloved by the people of both Sunni and Shia. They carry a lot of weight in both politics and tribal disputes. This particular Imam is very high in the hierarchy and is both wealthy and well respected. We did much business in Najaf. Through the company I became an instant part of this cleric's family. I not only am staying in their home, but I'm being served food by his wife. This is an honor in the Arab culture. I have formed a strong friendship and bond with this Imam and his family."

"Why am I not surprised?" I stated while beaming. "That's my Max. I'm glad you told me that. It will help me get some sleep tonight. While I'm worrying if I'll ever eat again."

"I wish I could bring you here," Max said. "Najaf is the pinnacle of Shia. If I had any money at all, I could let you see what true Shia is. In all its glory."

"Yeah well, I'm on the phone with you, baby. Go ahead. Knock me down with this glory you're living. While we're struggling to pay the bills, ha."

"Najaf is a city of half a million people approximately one hundred sixty kilometers, that's one hundred miles, south of Baghdad. It is the capital of Najaf Governorate and is considered to be the third holiest city of Shia Islam and the center of Shia political power in Iraq. The city is home to the Imam Ali Shrine and hosts millions of pilgrims yearly."

"You're there?" I gasped. "I know about this Imam Ali. Sort of. Wow. I'd love to be there with you. Even for the experience."

"Najaf is considered sacred by both Shia and Sunni Muslims. It is renowned as the site of the tomb of Ali ibn Abi Talib also known as Imam Ali, the First Imam of the Shiites, the cousin and son-in-law of the Islamic prophet Muhammad, whom the Shia consider to be the righteous caliph. Sunnis consider Ali the fourth Rashidun, or rightly guided Caliphs. The city is now a center of pilgrimage throughout the Shia world. Only Mecca and Medina receive more Muslim pilgrims. As the burial site of Shia Islam's second most important figure, the Imam Ali Mosque is considered by Shiites as the third holiest Islamic site."

"Oh, Max," I swooned. "You're killing me here. How can I not share this with you? Just sharing it on the phone is exciting me. We're going there someday. I'm telling you this."

"I want you here, Olivia. I even need you to be here. But I live on rice and beans when I'm not staying with the cleric. Someday I can bring you here to visit. But in the meantime the Imam told my employer that he needs to help me. How he brought me here then cheated me. The Imam told him that I feel no ill will, how I just want my back salary, a ticket home as promised, and I'll be on my way. They had a tribal council meeting and the owner had his say and then I had mine and the tribal leaders and the Imam all agreed that the owner should pay what was owed me and to honor the contract. The owner explained that he was broke and could not pay all of it. The Imam said that he would pay some out of his own pocket, but the owner should pay what he could so I could go home."

"So, when will all this happen?" I asked hopefully.

"It is complicated," was Max's response. "I was happy after the meeting and went back to Baghdad to my apartment. I stayed for awhile waiting for the owner to honor his promises. Days go by and nothing happens. Then the owner disappears for a week. His employees are starving, I'm on beans and rice and getting angrier everyday. When the owner gets back from no one knows where, I had it out with him. The owner says he will not pay because he doesn't have the money, he doesn't care what the Imam or the tribal council said. 'I should find my own way home', he said. In the Shia culture to openly defy and ignore the Imam, especially the Najaf Imam, is total sacrilege. No one does that. I couldn't believe it. It is the same as if a Christian tells the pope to go to hell. Everyone was horrified. The Green Zone by America is still in Baghdad. It covers twenty miles. What that means is, there is still a large CIA and US embassy presence here even though the troops are now gone. The courts in Iraq have many Western style laws. The Iraqi law that governs employment is very similar to current US and British law. So, I filed a lawsuit with the Iraqi government for payment of my salary and for the company to enforce the contract. The lawyer said it was a solid case and I will probably get my payment in ninety days even if the owner had to declare bankruptcy and sell his assets. So, I came back to Najaf to stay longer with the Imam at his invitation."

"Well, I'm glad you're in a better mood," I said, "because I found out what is in the will your mother took your thousand dollars for. I've also been holding out on you, not wanting to hurt you. I'm glad I did with all you've been going through. They cheated you, Max. I found out. They can't keep their stupid mouths shut and I heard from your mother and from Mahmoud that the will gives everything to Mahmoud upon her death. She didn't protect you at all. She suckered you."

There was dead silence on the other end. I then heard a moan.

"I did threaten to cut them off before," he said solemnly. "They apparently got scared. That's what all that was about. In getting the will, I mean. They wanted to protect themselves from me if I ever got mad and disowned them."

"You would never do that," I comforted.

"I understand why they did it. I suppose I do. But it hurts me. I do everything for them and it's never enough. I have not disowned them up until now, but continue to support them. Even borrowed a thousand dollars I don't have just to be jilted by them. Adding insult to injury."

"I know, sweetheart. I'm so sorry to tell you this. That's why I waited until better times. If that's what these are. Better times. More like less than as sucking times."

It was two weeks before I heard from Max again. I tried believing no news was good news.

"I'm calling from jail," he said just after the greeting.

"Jail?"

I went blank after that response. I could not think of even one thing more to say.

"Yes. This is the Middle East for you," he sighed.

"You're sounding so philosophical about it, Max. Are you gonna let me do all the panicking here? What do you mean you're in jail? What the hell is going to happen next? Did you kill somebody? Did you knock their lights out or something? What happened, sweetheart?"

"I didn't get the chance," he answered. "They got the best of me on this one and I need your help."

"I'll do whatever, Max. So, what happened?"

"This owner of the company I work for has connections with certain judges and police officials. So, he waited until Friday evening, this was two weeks ago, then had an employee of his, his assistant actually, call me at my apartment to invite me for supper to talk. We were friends by now, so I didn't think anything about it. I waited outside the compound of my apartment, saw him and waved at him on the sidewalk. He was pacing nervously for some reason. As I approached him, suddenly police surround me and arrested me on the spot. I still don't know what the supposed charges are. This is the Middle East. That's how things are done here. I guess it's none of my business why I'm in jail. But the setup is that even though the charges are misdemeanors, according to my lawyer, because it was Friday, I have to stay in jail until Monday. They did this on purpose. The owner said he would drop charges if I dropped his lawsuit for back pay. But I refused."

"So, you're just gonna rot there?"

"No, I need you to call the American embassy. I've already done so, but I also need you to do it."

"How will that help?" I asked.

"I talked to them already. They are the ones that got me my lawyer. America still has some pull here, but it is out of their hands for the most part. They can only help me because I'm an American citizen. They send someone everyday to make sure I'm not being abused. That is helpful for now. I can't follow through on things like I need since I'm in jail. That's where I need your help. Get in touch with them to help me coordinate legal matters."

I couldn't refuse him, but didn't know what to do. I started by calling the embassy, then played it by ear from there.

"A hearing was arranged and bail was set at three thousand dollars," a representative of the legal attaché in Baghdad told me when I called. "Our hands were tied on behalf of your husband. America has handed political power over to the Iraqis now. We're not occupiers, in spite of anything you may have heard. But this means it is not in our jurisdiction anymore for local disputes. We cannot interfere with foreign law. We only have jurisdiction to assist one of our citizens. I'm sorry."

"So what next?" I asked.

"We told your husband he must leave Iraq for his own good because we cannot ensure his safety from this owner. There are many corrupt Iraqi companies. Many Americans get caught in these situations. The best we can do is get them out of the country once they're released from jail. In fact, our embassy can't get him out of jail. We can only make sure he isn't abused in any way."

But with Max it was the principle of the thing. He spent his entire life fighting and the fight was still there, strong as ever, in him. He knew that if it came down to it, he could contact his Hezbollah friends in Lebanon, knowing they would help him through their Hezbollah friends in Iraq. It is something like the Sicilian faction in New York or Chicago. Even if you are not in the mafia, if you are Sicilian, in need, and you haven't made them angry, they might come to your aid. Though you might regret you asked that help one day if they came knocking on your door expecting a favor back.

"I need you to call Fatima to see if she can help," Max told me with his latest situation update one day. "See if she will make my bail. I will pay her back someday. But let her know the situation and it is important she put up the bail money now. She could even come to Iraq to assist in all of this, but for sure I need her to put up my bail."

So, that's exactly what I did. But first, I brought it up to Max's mother and to Mahmoud.

"We have no money, Olivia," they both said in unison.

They looked at me skeptically, as if wondering why I even brought it up.

"He'll pay you back as soon as he gets home," I appealed one last time in spite of knowing the futility of it.

They didn't even bother to answer me. Now to face Fatima.

"I don't believe you, Olivia," she said to me in a rough, harsh tone of voice over the phone. "I don't believe Khalil is in jail. You are a lying American. A scammer. He is in Iraq working to spoil you, but still you do not have enough money for all your American food and luxury. I will not give you one penny. Go back to America where you belong."

"Get my mother on the phone," Max instructed me when I told him the news of the failures.

Max's mother called Fatima in Kuwait after a heated conversation with Max. After several minutes with her, she hung up and explained things to me through Mahmoud.

"Fatima will give five hundred dollars for Khalil's bail," Mahmoud explained hatefully. "She will give it as a stipend, but she knows we will use it for Khalil in Iraq. Or for whatever you really intend to do with it. We will play your silly games. But only five hundred dollars."

Max wasn't here so I took the liberty to hate them. I walked away as civilly as I could to make sure I received the five hundred dollars from them, but I knew I would never forgive them.

"Maybe they think I'm just trying to get my thousand dollars back for the lawyer I paid for them to cheat me," he said when I told him. I could hear the hurt in his voice.

After a couple of days I approached Mahmoud about the five hundred dollars from Fatima. He looked at me with disdain.

"No, Olivia," he said spitefully. "Of course not. What do you think of us? That we are stupid Arabs? You can't have our money to cheat us with."

Max absorbed everything stoically when I told him the news.

"I got in touch with the Imam who promptly paid the bail," Max explained to me shortly afterwards on the telephone from Najaf. "He is putting me up at his own expense and treating me like family. The Imam quickly called a tribal meeting in order to discuss what to do about this owner who betrayed everyone for his own gain. All of this takes time, however. Meanwhile, the embassy consuls are very conscientious on my behalf, Olivia. I can tell you, I am proud to be an American. My life and circumstances are so complicated. I have so many friends and benefactors. It's a complicated world and somehow I am a melting pot of it all. The embassy is so concerned, but can only make sure I'm being treated fairly during this distress."

"America is made up of all sorts of people, Max," I said as philosophically as I could manage. "As is the Middle East. I'm sure the whole world. Anyway, I'm glad you have friends here and with the embassy. We need all the help we can get, for sure."

"The Imam and tribal council are having another meeting with the owner soon," Max explained further. "The council will recommend for the owner to provide all my back pay. The owner is still insisting, for now, for me to withdraw my lawsuit as it will damage his business. In the meantime I have found another job. Can you believe?"

"How is that possible?" I gasped.

"I can't trust this owner so I kept my eye open for opportunity while I waited. I don't want to just sit and impose upon this gracious Imam. We need the money anyway. So, I found a large dairy firm in Baghdad. I start working for them next week. I'll let you know how it is."

A week turned into a month, however, and I never heard from Max again. I was frantic from worry. He would never leave me intentionally hanging. I did not know how to get a hold of the Imam in Najaf, so I talked to the embassy who told me they also had not heard from Max since he had been bailed out of jail by the Imam. According to them, the Imam also didn't know of his whereabouts. I wanted to fly to Iraq myself, but knew it would do no good.

Then one day, there he was at our doorstep in Al-Habib. His clothes were a mess, he hadn't shaved in days, and all his possessions were in one handbag.

"Max," I yelped as I rushed to him. "I was so worried about you. I was beside myself. I didn't know what to do. What on earth is your story? Just looking at you, it's like you escaped as a prisoner of war or something."

Max just held on to me for a moment without saying a word. Just hugging me and rubbing my back affectionately. Then his story began.

"The company I found to work for," he began, "the dairy firm, turned out to be a total disaster. In just a matter of days I began to turn sales around. They couldn't praise me enough. Until they found out I was Shiite. Why didn't it matter before, I wondered? If it was so important, and Iraq is mostly Shia anyway, they should have checked. But the owner was living in Dubai because apparently he has over thirty lawsuits against him filed by employees, distributors, and the government of Iraq. He is Sunni and supports this al-Nusra faction I told you about before. Same as the company we left in the UAE. They hate Shia. He has five factories and four of them are shut down because he tampered with expiration dates on products and sold them anyway. Then, on top of that, he was not paying incentives and bonuses to employees. He is as crooked as they come, but I did not know this until I got to Baghdad from Najaf. I was just so happy to get a job under the circumstances, I did not check this company out. Then word reached him about this Arab-American that is Shiite. Nothing mattered to him except for that. His company is rotting, I'm immediate help, but it didn't matter. All that mattered is that I'm American and a Shiite. The devil."

I pushed myself away from Max for a moment to kiss him sympathetically on the lips. I started to say something, but decided to continue our embrace while he finished his story.

"I was told I must live in a suburb of Baghdad named Monsour. Monsour is notorious for a radicalization going on. A Sunni one. Not al-Qaeda. Another faction is being formed. In Monsour there are stories of kidnappings of expats. So, why would they insist that I live there? No one will live in Monsour. But there were orders from this owner himself from Dubai that I must do so. He is known for being mentally disturbed and has trouble everywhere he goes. It turns out he cannot travel to Iraq because he is wanted. He especially hates Shia and calls us names, I'm told. And the managers in Baghdad are very sympathetic to this hatred of Shia. Saddam Hussein was Sunni, and though secular, he created a divide among the two groups that grew worse than before he took power. What I was hearing about the owner and this company made me suspicious and I refused to live in Monsour and said I would resign immediately if they forced this on me. That's why I didn't call you. I was ready to come home with my first paycheck."

"Max, Max, just call me when something happens. I know you worry about putting me through things like this, but telling me at least lets me know what's happening. And that you're alive. The not knowing is the real problem."

"I know, Olivia. I do know this. But it was all happening so quickly. I thought I might go back to the Imam in Najaf soon and call you from there. But I wanted to get paid first."

"We need the money, but that's not what's important now. Somehow you Shiites think you are indestructible. You've been through so much in your history, survived so much, that you think you can handle everything."

"There's more," he sighed.

"I'm sure of that," I said with a chuckle.

"Baghdad is mostly Shia, so I stayed in a hotel there while I fought the company about moving to Monsour. I was mostly stalling until I got paid. The leadership and owner of this company hate the Shia, but fear them. Not just Hezbollah, but Shia are so hot headed and passionate. Just days after I moved into my hotel it got blown up. I happened to not be there, but in a nearby restaurant. I heard the blast. There were casualties, of course, and I lost all my belongings. Except for what's in this bag. I still had not been paid. I went to the manager of the company and demanded my salary, but his contempt for all Shia was so extreme he threatened me instead. It was time to come home. So, yesterday, I went to Najaf and asked if he would pay for me to go home. The owner of the construction company still refused to pay and now my new company refused to pay. We're broke, Olivia. The Imam paid for my ticket and enough to get me home. So here I am. Strange things are happening in Iraq since America began its withdrawal. Strange things in the UAE, too, with all the Salafists."

"All that matters is that you're home and safe," I said as bravely as possible.

"Yes, for now that's all that matters. We have yet another experience in our lives, Olivia. Is this why you married me? You were so bored with peace and prosperity in America that you came for all this adventure?"

"I wonder that myself sometimes, sweetheart," I said with a mischievous giggle. "One thing I definitely am not anymore is bored."

"I talked with the Imam about the owner of the construction company before I left," Max added. "The construction company went bankrupt. That part makes me happy, but the employees were never paid. The Imam asked if I would drop my lawsuit. I agreed to do so out of respect to the Imam, since he was paying for my trip home anyway. It was like beating a dead horse just to keep stubborn if I did not."

"I want this owner to get his just reward," I said. "Sick justice or what. I'm glad he's bankrupt. I hope he rots."

"No one knows where this Iraqi owner is anymore," Max explained further. "He is supposedly on the run because he crossed other people as well. But the Imam said that the owner did go to the Green Zone to talk to the CIA and the embassy people. But I already told them everything I knew about this Iraqi owner previously. The CIA knew about him then by the time he ran to them. I was told that the owner applied to the US for a visa. The CIA promised me they would stymie any chance of this happening and would investigate him more thoroughly. The Imam said that the owner was very upset the last time he saw him because his application for a visa to the States had been denied."

"Good," I smirked in celebration. "Good. But I guess you know now to stay away from these small, unknown companies. All of them."

"Yes, I do," he replied. "It's a learning experience. But little consolation for all the trouble and financial setback I went through. But that's all I have. More experience. But there is good news too."

I waited in anticipation. Good news seemed hard to come by anymore.

"In my stay with the Imam I met some Lebanese Shia that do business in Baghdad. They are opening a branch in Ghana in Africa. They want me to help them open it."

"Africa?" I swooned. "You're telling me we're getting to go to Africa?"

His smile answered 'yes'.

But first, there were accounts to settle with his family.

"You would have let me rot in jail?" Max asked his brother, hate spewing from his eyes.

"We should believe your American wife?" Mahmoud answered in defiance.

"Yes, you should have. Absolutely, you should have. I trust her. I don't trust anyone else in my family but her and this is why. You talked to me on the telephone yourself. I explained it all to you personally."

"You would do anything to give your American luxury. What do you care of our problems? Only your American wife matters to you now."

"And then you cheated me out of my own estate," Max said pointedly. "I spent hundreds of thousands of dollars to build this house and estate. I borrowed another thousand for the lawyer for the will that you used to cheat and humiliate me more."

"I built these buildings," Mahmoud confronted. "These are mine. Why should you inherit them? Did you learn theft from America? Are you American now? Have you no shame?"

"My wife and I are leaving," Max said angrily. "I disown you. I'll have nothing to do with you. I have a better job in Ghana and refuse to live with you. I bought and paid for this house you live in and gave it to my mother as a devoted son. I allowed you to stay, worthless that you are, and gave you your first responsibility in your pathetic life. A chance also for the son you raise who follows your disgusting ways. I borrowed a thousand dollars for my mother's lawyer to make a will to disinherit me from my own merit. You are the result of the takers who envy and steal from the makers. Only this greedy fantasy of yours lets you believe you could make a fortune on your own. You will never understand those that can. Like a typical loser, you only know to envy the winners. There's a knack to making money, but losers can't fathom competence on that scale. Therefore I must be cheating you somehow. In your pathetic eyes it is me that is greedy. You will fail in life. Not because I curse you or will it, but because parasites eventually lose their hosts. The host that kept them alive. All for greed. The greed you project on me. Good riddance."

CHAPTER 14

The job Max found while in Iraq was as a Business Development Director. They needed someone to open an office for them in Accra, Ghana. This he was glad to do, especially in his rebellious mood against his family in Al-Habib. Family housing was included so I, and Mimo our cat, were on our way with him to Ghana for an unknown length of time. To see Africa was beyond my wildest, adventurous dreams.

Since Lebanon is Max's homeland, in spite of how he disowned his family, I knew he was too devoted a son and brother to really mean the disavowal. I knew we would see his family again. We would visit there and perhaps one day even live there again. So, leaving Lebanon was fine with me though I liked the thought of someday returning. Of not closing any doors behind us.

Ghana is in the western part of Africa, almost due south of Spain, at the bottom of the big bulge section of the continent. It is in the tropics and very pretty terrain wise. Accra, its capital, looked much like Mexico near where I grew up. I felt right at home.

Ghana was colonized by the British until their independence in 1957. The roads were made up of wide tree-lined lanes with beautiful, decorative foliage.

Where there was wealth in Accra, we saw lovely homes and yards. The majority of the population, however, lived in squalid housing with little electricity or running water.

The people were very laid back, warm, and friendly. I was touched by their kindness and sweetness to me. After all the antagonism for greetings I had received in every stop of my Middle Eastern life, it was good to experience the Ghanaians. It reinforced to me that it wasn't necessarily anything I had done to my Arab tormentors.

The compound where we lived was populated by diplomats from many nations around the world. It was by far the nicest place we lived anywhere to date. Surprisingly, however, the cost of living was extremely high.

But alas, it was a third world country. Not an oil rich one with a near starving immigrant population to do the bidding, but a pathetically dirt poor, desperate third world country. It was not unusual to drive along where swarms of beggars at every stop light were hoping to get lucky.

One particular time near our home we drove to a restaurant. We passed a ten year old boy on the side of the road in school uniform crying. Max looked at me and sighed.

"I have to stop to see about him," he apologized. I nodded that I both understood and approved, for I adored my husband's heartfelt devotion. "What's the matter?" Max asked him.

"I am hungry. I am so hungry. My parents can't give me food for lunch. I only get one meal every day. That's with my family in the evening. There are six of us in our family. I barely get to eat."

We were eating ice cream as we listened and now felt like gluttonous pigs. Guilty conscience sirens screamed inside of us.

"Here, Son," Max said. "Take our ice cream." After he handed both to the boy, he said as well, "Here is some money. Be careful with it. Let no one know you have it. Get it to your parents. God loves you. He sent us to you. Have hope. Make something of yourself when you grow up. Help your family. Help your country."

This was a normal story for day to day living in Ghana. Expats sent there by companies lived in compounds who could enjoy Accra. Not so for the average Ghanaian. For them, electricity may cost as much as three months' rent. Food is expensive as well. Unemployment is high, so there is much crime. We found little trouble ourselves, but the newspapers were full of tragic stories of burglary and home invasion. We felt safe walking on the sidewalks or driving along in Accra, even throughout Ghana itself. But theft was a common occurrence so we had to be vigilant. Even with the desperation and poverty, however, I had nothing but kindness bestowed upon me by the locals.

The vendors and sales people were a different story. Social life was such that one layer of life created a living for another. A vendor automatically assumed an expat was rich, which we were by their standards. They bargained for every item beginning with as high a price as possible for any wares they were trying to sell. I had to bargain hard. But being a South Texan from near the border with Mexico, I had encountered some of this before. My upbringing prepared me for a lot of my new life so far, in fact. I got more grateful for my upbringing.

Accra stretches along the Atlantic coast. I found the tides very charming, but the undertows are strong. Because of that, the Ghanaians don't care much for swimming in the ocean, but at resorts will swim some. They fish a lot.

It was nice to see after the religious bigotry where I grew up, then even more in the Middle East, how the many religions in Ghana co-existed peacefully. Religious tolerance was very high, which I relished. This was my kind of place.

I was amazed at the amount of evangelical influence in Ghana. The three most prominent religions are Christianity, Islam, and Traditional, or what some call animism, which may best be described as nature worship.

Ghana has the highest percentage of Christians in West Africa. Sixty percent of the citizens of Ghana are Christian with the majority living in the southern part of the country. Being Christian, in particular Episcopalian, I loved the beautiful Catholic churches in the larger cities. My soul could almost breathe again. I walked among these church grounds to experience them as much as to marvel at them. Structures such as the Our Lady of Lourdes Catholic grotto at Kpando with its eight meter statue of Mary. And the grotto with life-size statues at the stations-of-the-cross. The feast of Assumption in August, and the Immaculate Conception in December, were well attended by pilgrims to this location.

To see Christianity so abundantly available made me realize how I was starving for religion before in the Middle East. Just to light a candle gave me so much inner peace as it had in Beirut. I believed very strongly in God. I could feel His breath as I walked among the Christian relics. Belief is so important. Seeing the fanaticism in so much of the world where I had been did not take away from the need for the inner peace of a loving God. A tolerant, caring God. And to be honest, it helped me appreciate the depravity I sometimes lived also. The obvious contrast made dwelling in this spiritual abundance now seem even more blessed.

Twenty percent of Ghanaians are Muslim, which was nice for Max. I didn't want him homesick for his religion as I had been in his homeland for mine. The northern part of the country is heavily Muslim, but mosques are located throughout the country. I could hear the calls to prayer throughout Ghana. I had grown to love them in my stay in the Middle East. There were even Shia in Ghana, also happily for my husband. There were Sunni as well. Ghana also had a unique brand of Islam called Zetahil, This sect includes certain Christian customs.

Traditional, animistic beliefs still play a strong role in Ghana because of their intimate relation to family and local mores. I heard of nativist religions and cults all my life. Now here I was in a country with a relatively strong version of one still in existence. The fact that twenty percent of Ghanaians practice traditional religions, usually in the southeast of Ghana, I was glad with the news Max brought home to me one day.

"We've been invited by the King of Ghana," Max told me. "He's the tribal leader of the Ashanti tribe. He wants us to be his guest for one of their traditional feasts."

My mouth flew open.

"How in the hell did you get an invite from the King of Ghana?" I asked incredulously.

"Pure luck," he replied. "I met a prince on one of my plane trips right after we first got here. It was fascinating, but I didn't think much of it. I just now met him again at a business seminar here in Accra. He introduced me to the king after we chatted again to get reacquainted. The king has fifty wives. They will all be there at this feast."

Nothing so exotic ever happened to me back home or in the Middle East. To see this king we had to fly to the provincial capital of Kumasi in a twin engine commuter plane, but that excited me also. The terrain with its rivers and jungles was just below us. What an overview. I cherished the chance to see a different part of the country even from the air as I experienced a modern version of tribal life upon arrival. I wondered if Tarzan and Jane might be there in my fantasy.

"What is this food?" I asked Max, marveling. I didn't care if he knew or not. This was my way of celebrating the feast. "Grilled meat, fruit of every kind. My God, I want to live here. I know it's a festival and not everyday mundane life, but I love it."

"The sauce on the meat is made out of grass," Max explained.

"Grass?" I asked with a giggle. "How do you make a sauce out of grass? Is it good?" I tried some. "Oh, yes. Yes. I've got to learn how they make this."

The prince that befriended Max soon got up to speak.

"Now we have the honor," he bellowed without the use of a microphone, "of enjoying the pleasure of our beloved king as he dances one of our illustrious tribal dances. Enjoy please."

Oh, the rhythms we swoon over when we picture African dances. The king was magnificent as he bobbed his head, fluttered his shoulders, and strutted his feet to the drums. This seemed the greatest day of my life. The joy, the festivity, the friendliness of this magnificent African tribe. I wanted all my friends back home to see me here somehow.

Kumasi itself, as a city, was superior to Accra, which had turned in many ways to the stiffness of a national government settlement, immersed in one giant ghetto. Kumasi was not only more pristine and beautiful, but quieter and quainter as well in its more manageable size. I realized I was seeing it in ultra-magnificence, but I wallowed in that magnificence while I could.

"Look at those gold bracelets on the king jiggle while he wiggles," I laughed to Max. "So many rings. But look at his fifty wives. I can't call him a chauvinist can I? They are plain Jane in their attire. Great being king, I guess. And he's not going to let them forget it."

After the dance, the prince presented Max and I to him. Thus, I met my first king. None of my hick friends, I was certain, ever met a king. King of the prom maybe.

"Welcome to the Ashanti," the king said with an exuberant smile. "It is a joy for us to have you among us. Please stay as long as you like. Enjoy us. It is our pleasure."

"Thank you, Your Majesty," I said girlishly.

I had no idea what to say to an African king, but I felt like he was majestic, so that's what I said. 'Your Majesty' it is. Proudly so.

But sadly, our first stay in Africa soon came to an end. I thought I found happiness, but it was just a reprieve instead. An Africa with giraffe, lions, hippos, and cheetahs. Just driving among the villages was an experience, but the jungle areas with exotic wildlife put the rush back into my spirit every time.

"We have to leave Ghana, Olivia," Max told me a few months after our arrival. "The Ghana economy is in a free fall and their dollar gets devalued on a daily basis. We never know exactly where we stand because of the volatility. Our company headquarters back in Beirut is too unsure of the future here. It is not worth the risk, they are thinking. There is no sound financial basis to stay. Many Lebanese companies here, in fact, are going bankrupt. We may be next if we stay. For you and I even, if we accumulated much money here, we could not get much of it out of the country. It is to our benefit as well to leave. While our money is trapped here, we lose value on the daily devaluations. So, I met with Ghana's president. I had to get special permission to do so. I got that permission from the king we met. It allowed me the privilege. Luckily, I was able to cut a deal because of it that gets us our money back. The company back home is very pleased with me for doing so. We are one of the few companies that did not lose our shirt."

Max saw the deflated look on my face from our having to leave.

"When do we go, sweets?" I finally asked. "Somehow it was just too good to be true."

"I have one other assignment first, so we can stay a bit longer. Or at least you can. Tomorrow I must fly to Benin. It is a country in this region. The company trusts my judgment, so they want me to do a feasibility study if it is worth starting a branch there."

"How long will you be gone?"

"I'm not sure. I have to scout around and form an opinion. Then make my judgment."

He was not gone long. A week later, from out of the blue, on my doorstep you might say, appeared my husband.

"I was warned," he began after greeting me, "not to go to Benin. I didn't want to tell you, so you wouldn't worry about me while I was gone. I wanted you to enjoy your last days in Ghana in peace. Foreigners are in danger in Benin. I was at risk. It has many Muslims there from many different Islamic groups. Some are very militant. The country itself is very primitive. Not just poor, but primitive. More than here even. I thought that since I was also Muslim I would not have anything to worry about. I wanted to please my company. I am grateful to them for hiring me and giving me so much responsibility."

I sat beside him stoically. He wasn't just relating things to me, he had a very deep, disconcerting look on his face. Something had happened, I could tell.

"I thought being a Muslim would give me an advantage to do business there," he continued. "When I arrived at the hotel, I had to give my passport. The entire front desk saw my American passport. So, word got out that an American was in their midst. After two days scouting out areas and talking to locals, I was approached by a man and we began talking. I love social contact, plus it opens avenues for business. Like meeting that prince on the airplane. One thing led to another and this man in Benin and I decided to meet again for dinner that evening at my hotel. During our conversation it came out how this man made contact with me on purpose." Max then looked at me directly. For emphasis. "The intent had been to kidnap me since I'm an American," he said. "They would hold me for ransom."

Max increased the intensity of his stare.

"This man was from a faction of al-Qaeda. They wanted an American who was foolish enough to be there on his own. But during lunch earlier that day it came out I was Shia, therefore a fellow Muslim, even though al-Qaeda is Sunni. He ended up liking me. Actually, I liked him. Just as I have many friends in Hezbollah back home, even though I detest them as bullies. It is easy for me to like people. With my business experience I developed instincts of how to work with diverse factions. Business is not just about war on competitors. Competition is just one aspect of business. Cooperation and mutual benefits are much bigger aspects of business. Anyway, to make a long story short, we liked each other, so they decided not to kidnap me. Besides they didn't want any trouble with the Shia because we are notoriously hot blooded. They might retaliate if one of our own got hurt or in trouble."

"My God, Max," I gasped. "Just like that I'm almost a widow. Stranded in darkest Africa as a widow. I'm glad I'm hearing this after the fact and didn't have to witness any of this."

"So this al-Qaeda guy and I had a great time after all," he continued. "Again, that's the world of business. People think of business as so cutthroat and it is. Politics is cutthroat. Sports are cutthroat. Religion is cutthroat."

"Al-Qaeda is cutthroat," I said, not as a pun.

"Businesses must get along as much as anything there is about competition," he continued explaining. "There is often an interdependency in the economic world. So, one Muslim to another, one business man to another, business to customer, this al-Qaeda man and I are now best of friends. Not only that, I met many other al-Qaeda while there. They came to see me later and we had tea together. I was even offered a job in one of their businesses. They think I'm competent. Of course, I don't want to work for a terrorist organization even in a business way. Even for my own safety I want none of them. When would I cross them somehow and be taught a lesson? Or be marked by one of their many enemies? Plus I hate terrorists. I hate the Shia one too we live amongst. Terrorism is not the way to do things. I will live the life of peace my religion and my conscience demand of me. I hate the terrorist mindset. It is a pollutant. But many of the people in terrorist organizations are very good people in their way. There are things to work with. I must do that as a man of faith. As a business man too. I will deal with terrorists the best I can. I am trapped in their world."

CHAPTER 15

The most touching thing I ever experienced was when we came home from Ghana. As we drove to see Max's mother, the Hezbollah fighters were on the street all throughout the village. Everyone, to the man, when they saw us drive by, tipped their hat to salute us. This is the greatest sign of respect they could give. It brought tears to Max's eyes.

"We know you despise us," they told him. "But you treat us as your friends. We know you were treated badly by your family even as you cared for them. You are a special man. The way you deal with your family is the way of the book. To be loyal to them even as they betray you. This is the way of the Prophet. We also heard of your time in Benin. You are very brave. You are a man among men."

I had no problem, terrorists though they were, to acknowledge and appreciate the human side of Hezbollah. To find ways to live and work together in a manner that did not contradict my own values. On top of that, they were protecting us. But any appreciation and affection I might attain for them for such, I had to find ways to keep my feet on the ground about them. They did take over much of Lebanon. They were aiding Iran in taking over what they could of the Middle East. They did have much mischief about them. But I appreciated many things about them too.

The glow of our return was soon tempered by other realities. Not just closer to home, but home itself.

Now that we were back, the scars of Max's treatment by his mother and brother from before, hit us as if it was yesterday. We had not gotten over it, in fact. I saw how it hurt Max deeply as he had to face them again. He needs family, love, and respect. He gets it from me, his American wife, and from terrorists he admires as friends, but hates as an entity. But not from his own family.

In spite of the hurt he felt, there remained an overwhelming sense of responsibility to see that his mother died well. For she was ailing. He knew he must put animosity and bitterness aside. He couldn't let his mother die on the street. He knew that even though his mother and Mahmoud owned the buildings legally, they would never keep them maintained, or make an adequate living from them. Plus, his mother required much medication. Neither Mahmoud nor his son took care of her. While we were away they neglected feeding her. No one cleaned the house.

Which means we came back to take care of her during her last days. As long as she lasted. With Alzheimer's everyday saw rapid deterioration.

After our return, I was there for her while Max worked, which sometimes took him out of the country. Her hated infidel, me, was the only one to care for her. There was karma in that somehow. Still, there were limitations to my helping her. Since I am an infidel, I was not allowed to touch her food. This would make it dirty. My Hezbollah friends helped with this.

Still, I did things in caring for her needs which she loved me for in her own crazy way. There were things to work with in our relationship. I worked with them. If I had not been there for her, she might possibly have fallen and not be able to get up. Mahmoud and his son would not find her until the next morning when they came in. Max cooked and cleaned for her when he could, in order to comfort her about halal.

"How long will she last?" Max asked me one night before we went to bed for the evening. "There is no humanity in Mahmoud. He has passed this onto his worthless son. It all sprang from her actually. My mother knows this, she even hates him for it, even knowing he is of her making. But we can't stay here forever. She has left him everything, even what we gave her. Perhaps it is for the best I did leave them everything after all. Even though it hurts me to be so badly treated. Then we can bid him to be on his own while we live our lives somewhere else. But we must be here for her in the meantime."

"You know," I broke in. "Both Mahmoud and your mother are so sure everyone thinks like them. They are still convinced we are trying to take back the buildings. It's as if they think I am caring for her in order to get the buildings back actually."

Max nodded his head acknowledging the truth.

"Treachery is the only world they know," he said. "They do not understand anything else. To them we are just hypocrites. That we are here only to live cheaply so we can steal the buildings away from them." He looked at me sadly. "When I have no money, they don't want me here. I am of no use to them. I do not understand that way of thinking. Such a shallow life. Like that of a terrorist. I have broken free from them emotionally enough to live with this reality. I am able to leave them to themselves. But she is my mother. I have responsibility to her because of her circumstances. I cannot in good conscience leave my mother to die in filth. So, here I am."

I reached over to hold his hand with all the affection and love for him I felt.

"Here we are," I vowed.

There were other problems in our village though. Similar to what we experienced before in the Gulf area.

"Why do you want this American?" said a woman with bad teeth.

"She just wants your money," the woman's Shiite sister said.

"You are home now," the first sister said. "Abandon her. No one is impressed with your American."

"You are still so good looking," said the second. "We would care for you. My sister is right. Americans are greedy. She just wants your money."

Max looked at them with disgust.

"I hate obnoxious, disgusting Arab women," he sneered.

But it was like a rotating door with all the visitors we received on the pretense of welcoming us back from Ghana. Mothers kept coming relentlessly, dragging their daughters in tow to show him what he could have.

Except for Max's temper, which still failed him at times, we did our duty to show as much respect as possible. Still the flirtations came, some beckoning him to marry. Max's mother sometimes intervened and declined generous offers of affection toward her son. I wondered if that meant she was accepting me.

"In America," Max tried to explain as patiently as possible to his suitors, "divorce is expensive. My wife would get half of everything. I don't want to lose so much."

To explain this way became a joke to him. It showed his disgust as much as shouting at them. In fact, this excuse worked better than shouting. For anything monetary is taken seriously.

Other times he stated bluntly, "I love my wife. I would never consider anyone else but her."

They would never believe him. They couldn't get past how a Westerner mattered over an Arab. It was months before anyone realized Max wasn't traditional. It never registered to any of these women how much he grew to hate Arab women.

Finally, they left him alone.

"You have been brainwashed in America," they said in their mindset of denial.

CHAPTER 16

I think back to the life I lived in America and how naïve I was. How naïve so many I knew were. But ignorance is not at all bliss like you hear. It's empty. I almost pity my naïve friends. I guess that means I'm grateful for the life I've lived since I left home and for the things I've experienced. I must say I am. I wouldn't change a thing except to do it better.

So, yes, I had to deal with these hot blooded Shia. They are indeed an emotional and crazy lot when it comes to fighting for what they believe. Just saying the word 'Shia' instills fear in the hearts of many people for a reason. The political minds of our nations must deal with the extremism of Islam, but what I did while living in their world was personal. For my own growth. Not for political resolution. I can't make excuses for them or for my naïve friends back home, who know so little about them. I must only grow with the opportunities presented me.

Historically, in Afghanistan, the Persian Gulf states, and Saudi Arabia, it was the Wahhabi and other Sunni radicals that dealt the most misery. But the Shia are no slouch either. Most of their rage, hostility, and violence comes from oppression throughout their long Islamic history. Hezbollah, which is Shia, or Hamas, which is Sunni, as well as those of their ilk, are brainwashed into believing what they are doing is right. How does a moderate Arab Muslim like my husband, or a Westerner like myself, deal with this while living among them?

In the case of Hezbollah, this Shiite group that I lived among in Al-Habib, I feel if shown a different path, these highly spiritually motivated individuals could do better. But like all fanatic, brainwashed, dogmatic groups, getting past the brainwashed state is the hardest part. Fanaticism is solid, but immobile. The ability to adapt is the key to survival. Therefore, they are very vulnerable, in other words. Fanaticism may be hard to penetrate, but once broken, chaos easily occurs. They feel invaded and fall apart. It is human nature to resist change. It is nature's way, in fact, since we need stability to survive and grow. But since the key to survival and growth is also the ability to adapt to changes, fanatics are left vulnerable by design. Fanatics of any ilk then, are stuck with a long, evolving procedure of change they resist fanatically.

Hezbollah, being Shia, seems preordained to the lowest esteem of world opinion. Being Shia himself, Max likes much about them, but sees them as fanatics and puppets. Their allegiance is to non-Arab Iran. So, tribal and religious loyalty is what dominates his beloved country instead of Arab nationalism. At least in Lebanon we saw opportunity to see them more for all they are. But we weren't just at odds with them. We felt comfortable, even affectionate, for much about them as well. I cherished this chance to understand. Was there some purpose for my being there then? It makes me fatalistically think so.

What I loved about Hezbollah is how they put their entire life on the line fighting for what they believed. I questioned whether it was right or wrong, but I won't simply judge them. In their minds they fight for a way of life and their right to believe the way they choose. They want to take care of their families because tribe and family are everything to them.

I suppose every military man in the world worth his salt, feels much of this. Including our own military men in America such as my brother. He is so different from them culturally, but there are points of reference where they can identify and appreciate each other. How many brave young men have I known that fought for their country and died trying to provide a better way of life for so many? My brother and his friends that I met absolutely felt that way. I am swayed theirs was for a better cause. Even a more sane and moral cause. But my objective now in Al-Habib became to search for more details about my own country and also with the people I opened up to in my husband's homeland. To not let preconceived ideas remain so black and white, yet without getting swept up in any Hezbollah terrorist cause. For they are terrorists in my opinion. I did not take their side against my own. I might have if I saw them as right. But Iran is trying to take over the entire Middle East, and already has taken over much of Lebanon through Hezbollah proxy, as well as made a puppet out of Syria. So, this is their cause not mine. This is also why my Shiite husband sees them as terrorists. Yet I didn't mind trying to see more about them than this terrorist side.

And that's the key to me. I wanted to see more of what I was learning about them now. The human side of them. It all required keeping my feet on the ground and maintaining perspective.

Beyond the religious and cultural differences, I saw this.

Western countries, especially America, have all the money in the world to provide weapons, military intelligence, and a massive war machine. I am glad of this because it makes me feel safe, and I overall believe in our causes. What astonishes me about Shia fighters, however, is how they fight to preserve their cause, both religious and for self-preservation, *without* the massive backup that bigger and stronger countries provide for their warriors. Hezbollah is the boots on the ground. In America, the debate goes on about bombing people into the Stone Ages, but how you cannot win without boots on the ground. Shock troops like the Marines have to be the foundation. But with Hezbollah, boots on the ground gets little other military support.

In the American Civil War, the South often faced obstacles like the Hezbollah that I saw in Lebanon. We are very proud down South for our fervor and fighting prowess in history. So, in Lebanon, I could identify with that aspect of Hezbollah. In their case, they receive support from Iran with arms, money, and moral rhetoric, but little if any from Naval or air support. They do well enough to bully the already divided Lebanese, which my husband rightly despises about them. But they are just as courageous and fervent against stronger odds they face.

Many became my protectors and my friends. That matters to me. My husband has many of the same ideals I grew up with through both religion and in the foundations of America itself. So, we must determine how to deal with diverse peoples and situations. Failure means division and war, which happens too often.

Hezbollah fighters, if killed, know their families are given a monthly stipend for the rest of their lives. These families have the pride their son or sibling was martyred while fighting for what they see as a just cause. Poverty and unemployment are so high in Lebanon that the stipend Hezbollah gives to every member or family on a monthly basis is the only means of survival many have. Winters are harsh, diesel is expensive, as is food. So even this stipend is not enough. To the dependent and destitute, Hezbollah equates with survival and strength. They have a job.

Also, everyone loves a winner. The fighters that join Hezbollah know that part of that financial package may require them to be a suicide bomber someday. They may well agree to this due to belief in the cause and a sense of choosing the winning side. The family often is torn with worry and fear, but are made to feel disloyal if they don't show a brave face. That shows passion for life that not many people experience. Knowing how death can come at any moment. Indeed, Shia are the most passionate of people.

The antithesis to all of this is very sickening, however. These brainwashed, fanatic people easily give up their lives for a cause they see so out of context. It leaves them incredibly susceptible to being used as pawns. Our soldiers back home are also used as pawns by our politicians at times. It's nothing new or unique in history. But the world of the Hezbollah is not a democracy. The individual American soldier has more access to information and alternative options. He is more able to make choices. Hezbollah soldiers, however, live in a narrow world and are easily duped into obeying without questioning. A dangerous environment. Not just physically, but spiritually.

So it was a sick world I found in Lebanon in many ways. Local politicians are often corrupt and drain much of Lebanon's resources on frivolity. They have bankrupted the country. They are much to blame for any local Lebanese who now join organizations like Hezbollah. The spirit and passion of the fanatic Shiite shows the world the darker reason for its existence.

But overall, Max received such respect in Al-Habib, that in spite of the pettiness of some of the locals, many warmed up to me because of him. Especially those with education and some travel behind them. On a daily basis I adapted to my new home. As much as I found to despise, I found much to love.

And one must understand the Lebanon that nurtured a Hezbollah. A civil war, and the aftermath of one, does unimaginable things. The extreme bigotry and hatred that is so pronounced between the different factions is unfathomable to someone that has never experienced it. Some attribute it to the cultural momentum of tribalism in Arab societies. Even if you are on the sidelines as an outsider you pick sides in your head with the faction of which you most relate.

With my background, I assumed the Christian viewpoint and lifestyle in Lebanon was the most accurate. I held a certain fear about Islam and the Middle Eastern world because I perceived it to be hostile and unfair to anyone outside Islam. To a great extent I was right, but what I never delved into or questioned was, why the hostility and brutality on either side. I had pre-conceived ideas and lived with them. Now I was deep in the middle of this East-West conflict. The result of being a Westerner living in the Middle East. These misunderstandings amongst the varying factions in Lebanon have created so much anger and oppression that I fear it will never balance out. Much of this is based on Lebanon's East-West divide throughout history. The result of their geographic setting in the Levant. These experiences created the hell of mental illness caused from the war. This causes its own chain reaction.

The Lebanese, in fact, seem to my outside eyes as a nation consumed with mental illness. Perhaps a type of post-traumatic stress. What these people, all factions of them, endured is incomprehensible. Not a single person or family is untouched by what happened in their past. Even Max, whose family was scattered at the time, got bit by the battles. He had an older sister living in Beirut where she was engaged to a very wealthy Kuwaiti man. She planned a new and happy life with him. Instead, she was killed in her apartment when a bomb detonated. It destroyed the entire apartment building and everyone in it. I don't know her name because the family would not speak about it or allow me to ask questions. I was told the story about her once by Fatima while I was in Kuwait, and thereafter was told it was a forbidden topic.

Everyone in Lebanon has a story and it's easy to see how feelings linger on such an emotional level. It seems unfair to me for an outsider to condemn or preach about them when national emotions are still in such disarray. As of yet, they do not know how to move on with their lives. No emotional security blankets exist for them. What stresses me the most about their holding onto all this bitterness, is that everyone plays the blame game about who started the civil war. This remains the number one topic of any social gathering. This is what enflames people constantly and will ultimately create another war between Christian and Muslim. I understand the cause of the war, but until the Lebanese move past these issues, the causes will never be resolved. They will have to reach the ability to grow more than to blame.

CHAPTER 17

"I don't feel like going back to Al-Habib," Max said to me on the plane from a trip we took to Bahrain.

I stared, not sure what to make of his statement.

"It felt good to see you happy while we were in Bahrain together," he said. "I like bringing you with me on my business trips when I can. You deserve to be happy. You've put up with so much since you've been with me in the Middle East. I kept waiting to provide a home for you. One without all the baggage. That hasn't happened yet. But I still want it for you." I smiled in gratitude, but still wondered what he was driving at. "I'm tired of all the fighting and turmoil with Mahmoud," he said further. "More for you than for me, but even for me. He is worthless and destructive. I want to get away, to minimize all my family drama. So, I've been thinking. There is a Christian community just a few miles from Al-Habib. I have a good job now. We don't need free rent anymore. Let's go to Zahlé when we arrive home and find us a flat there. Just you and me. It is close enough to my mother's house that we can still keep an eye on her. We can still be there for her in emergencies. Zahlé is closer to Beirut also than Al-Habib. That's good for me. You could finally be among your own faith there. Other Lebanese-Americans live in Zahlé also. Shia live there, though in small numbers. I'm fine with that. And Hezbollah doesn't control it. At least not directly."

The apartment Max got us in Zahlé was luxurious and situated on top of the tallest mountain in the area. A big, beautiful apartment with spectacular views in every window. There were three balconies which looked down onto the valley as well as the town itself. It was springtime and we were surrounded on every side by almond groves that were gorgeously in full bloom. The sight took my breath away. The apartment itself had hot water in both bathrooms as well as in the kitchen where it warmed with the flip of a switch. Every room had a heater.

Our landlords and neighbors lived in a spectacular house right behind the apartment complex. From the moment we moved in they treated both Max and me like family. Before long all of Zahlé treated us as one of their own. Everyone was thrilled I was Christian and became protective of me. My landlords offered to take me to Church with them. Zahlé even had a wonderful veterinarian for my cat. I finally found bliss.

In a perfect world I would live and die in Zahlé, Lebanon. The fact it is a Christian community was appealing, but beyond that, there is something movingly spiritual about the place. It is paradise, wrapped in majestic beauty, to go with Old World charm.

Zahlé could easily be an Italian village with its red tile roofs strewn throughout the narrow mountaintops. I felt nothing but joy there. The winters are rough, but bearable if dressed appropriately and living in a heated house. Travelling to Beirut every day for a job can be hard to bear without snow tires and a heated car. Otherwise, stay home. The town is self-contained and as quaint as they come.

Zahlé is the largest predominantly Christian town in both Lebanon and the Middle East. Christians form approximately ninety percent of the total population. It is the town with the largest number of Catholics.

As I learned when I first arrived in Beirut, there are multiple types of Catholic Churches. The majority of the Christian population in Lebanon, sixty-five percent albeit fifty percent in Zahlé, is Greek Catholic. Greek Catholic is made up of the Byzantine liturgical rite in the Koine Greek and modern Greek languages. This is not the same as the Greek Orthodox church.

Fifteen percent of Zahlé is of Maronite Christian. The Maronite lady at the kiosk in Beirut misinformed me about this church. It is considered by many to be fully Catholic and in compliance with the pope. This lady, however, is indicative of the divisions in much of Lebanese society. Somehow there isn't enough to fight about, so a Maronite Christian Catholic needs to fault Roman Catholicism. The members of the Maronite Church are part of the Lebanese people who are the present day descendants of the Phoenicians, a Canaanite people. This difference may be pronounced enough to spur the dissension I encountered with the lady at the kiosk.

The Greek Orthodox make up ten percent of the Zahlé population. This group is of the Eastern Orthodoxy, related to such as Russian Orthodox. They make the sign of the cross in a more pronounced way while using icons rather than the crucifix. Their calendar places Christmas and Easter a few days after the Western church.

Then there are Syriac Christians comprising ten percent of the population. These handle their liturgies in ancient Syriac, akin to ancient Aramaic, which was the language spoken by Jesus. Tradition has this branch started by the apostle Thomas, who spread it as far away as India.

Zahlé's Muslim minority is also ten percent of the population. It is concentrated in the districts of Karak Nuh, where Noah's tomb is allegedly located, and Haoush el Oumara, on the Northeastern and Southwestern edge of town, respectively. Seventy percent of these Muslim belong to the Shia, while the remaining thirty percent are Sunnis. In the past, the town also had a Druze minority, even a small Jewish population, most of which emigrated during the Lebanese Civil War.

Zahlé is built upon a series of foothills in the Lebanon Mountains at the Western edge of the Bekaa plateau. Mount Sannine towers above it at eight thousand feet. The hills form a narrow valley. Because of this, most of Zahlé's neighborhoods spread vertically on steep hill slopes. The municipality also extends onto the Bekaa plateau all the way to the Litani River. Zahlé was Lebanon's capital until the occupation of Syria over a hundred years ago. The capital was then moved to Beirut, but its place in Levant history is fascinating. It was the hub of education for seminaries and universities for centuries.

Now suddenly this historical and scenic town was my town.

Being a Christian in a Christian area did not entitle me to acceptance. Somehow, of course. The Maronites abhor, for the most part, any religion except their own version. The majority Greek Catholic population is more open to other factions, however.

These days, the majority of Christians align themselves politically with Hezbollah for purposes of self-preservation. Since Zahlé is so near to Al-Habib, cohabitation with the Islamic community was deemed important to attain.

Even with this more open forum, I soon encountered typical Arab response to a non-Arab.

"This is my wife," Max said proudly to four Christian women agents as he introduced me to his favorite travel agency, one he had used exclusively for years. They were old friends and very welcoming until he reiterated to them that I was his wife.

"Why did you marry an American?" they shrieked in unison. "Arab women are so much better. Isn't being Arab better than having an American?"

Max got up to leave immediately, as he took me by the hand to rush us out of the office in a huff. Hate was exchanged between them in Arabic seemingly forever before we got to the door.

"I will take my business elsewhere," he said angrily as we walked out. He then stopped, turned, and glared. "I hate Arab women. Do you understand? I would never marry an Arab woman."

At least my life was consistent. I couldn't be oversensitive or dreaming this up. It verified to me how this attitude was based on culture more than religion. God couldn't be blamed after all, even if He was so often referenced.

I had so many friends by now, between my landlords and those in their church, that the rude Arabs in Zahlé were the exception rather than the norm.

"An American," the people at my adopted Roman Catholic church exuded upon my arrival. "We love America. We are so happy you chose to live among us."

I let my smile answer for me. At last. A further reminder that I had a real home. This warm response became the happy norm in my happy life.

The cost of living is very high in Zahlé. On a par with the cost of living in Paris. There is also the constant worry of impending war as a deterrent to tranquility there. So, as far as a place to retire, we would really be stretched on a daily basis to make ends meet, while the potential of civil war at a moment's notice meant we might have to leave everything behind. If these two matters were not an issue I would live my life happily ever after in Zahlé, Lebanon.

Since the dominant religion in many of the Christian areas outside of Zahlé is Maronite, I ran across many as I travelled Lebanon. I began to see them as more bigoted than the Muslims. To them, if you are not Maronite you are a pagan. They even have their own pope. Thus *my* pope was the anti-Christ, at least to some of them. That I was Christian meant nothing to them since I was American. Meaning, I was someone uncultured who only worshiped money. And to the Maronite, I had downgraded myself by marrying a Shia, which was even worse than Catholic to them.

There are reasons the Maronite are so bigoted. They have a story to tell just like everyone else. The civil war can never be forgotten. For future generations, it will be as if it just happened. Much like happened in my beloved South back home. Every Maronite had something brutal and terrible happen to them. There was bigotry before, but the civil war made it worse. But no matter the justification, I was not welcomed by this faction in Lebanon.

Zahlé was totally different from every place in the Middle East I had been. I got to be Christian and non-pagan as part of the deal. Zahlé not only welcomed me, but embraced me for who I was. As if I had Lebanese family. Every store owner in Zahlé took care of me. My landlords became my family. It was a truly wonderful experience. The Catholics were genuinely warm to me. And to my surprise, they did not care at all I was married to a Shiite. They welcomed the Shia, in fact, because they had an alliance with them. This made it official to me. As much as in Texas, finally in my Middle East experience, I had a true home sweet home.

CHAPTER 18

Being an expat, I was required to leave the country every two months in order to maintain my visa. I then had to be gone for a week at a time. If Max was out of the country on business, this made it impossible to take care of his ailing mother. A nightmare for us because of the irresponsibility of Mahmoud. Knowing our plight, many of the Hezbollah women offered to intervene and care for her while I was away. What a load off my mind. All the more of a bond with my new friends.

As much as I love to travel, to have to do so can be inconvenient, even knowing my mother-in-law was going to be in good hands. Still, I had all these countries near me I got to experience. My favorite was Turkey.

The Turkish people are very European in their manner and also very friendly. Shopping was wonderful there and the food became my favorite even over Kuwait. The history of Turkey is magnificent. I drew a keen interest in it, especially the Ottoman Empire era with their vibrant past. I decided I could stay in Turkey forever. Especially Istanbul. The Bosporus Strait, the Sophia Mosque, the architecture, the shops.

"Don't you Muslims have guilt complexes?" I teased my two Lebanese-Australian friends, sisters that were visiting Istanbul and staying at the same hostel as me.

"Listen to our cheeky American," the one wearing a hijab and abayat shot back jokingly. "Why should we Muslims have guilt complexes, my imperialist friend from America?"

"Look at this beautiful mosque," I swooned as we entered the compound known as Hagia Sophia. "Once it was a gorgeous Christian church in mighty Constantinople. The grandeur of the world. Then here comes the Ottoman. And just like in Jerusalem, what was once a sacred Jewish or Christian temple, is now a gawky mosque. I couldn't live with myself doing such things."

I let out a chuckle to make sure they understood I was joking. They were indicative of so many Muslim I had encountered once I moved out of the Gulf area. Travelled, educated, modern, smart, and fun. So typically, one of the sisters dressed traditionally, while the other wore chic.

"Can you believe this bitch?" the chic clad sister laughed out. "We Muslims brought Christians out of the slums and this is the thanks. Comes from eating too much pork all your life, I'm sure."

"Actually," I replied, "I love Muslim architecture. It's breathtaking. All the domes and minarets and marble. The arches. My God, all the gorgeous colors. I can imagine what the church before it looked like, but it's so gorgeous as a mosque. And the Blue Mosque too next door."

"Istanbul didn't miss a beat from once being the Byzantium capital," the chic girl praised.

"I'm happy in Oz, but I would love to live here," the hijab wearing sister commented. "It's a secular city anymore, since the Ataturk, but I've felt renewed as a Muslim since we arrived last week. Even considering how we mixed our time with our new infidel here, Olivia."

"But sister dear," the chic sister added, "something is stirring since last we visited in the nineties with our parents. It's not so secular anymore. Ataturk's ghost must be squirming."

As if on cue. Suddenly, I was accosted by two women dressed in the chador.

"Olivia," my friend wearing hijab said nervously to me while pulling at my shoulder. "I think you're getting some notice."

If looks could kill I would have died a thousand deaths. Iranians were everywhere inside with us. We felt threatened and exited out of the door we had just entered. But the two women followed us ominously.

Normally, my presence in Istanbul, even at mosque sites, created no problem since the majority of Turks and visitors alike were Westernized and wonderful to me. But there are some Iranians abroad that take the hardcore stance of their mullahs. With the mindset that anything not of Islam is bad.

"They are speaking Farsi," my chic dressed friend said. "I don't know what they are saying, but it is menacing. All this means they are Shia. That's not good for us."

"Except that Turkey is Sunni," her sister said. "Like us."

"They don't know the difference right now," I interrupted. "It has nothing to do with you and everything to do with me."

Both sisters turned around at five chador clad women babbling angrily at me.

"Go away!" my hijab wearing friend said to them.

"Go," said my chic friend. "I mean it. Shoo. Buzz off. Fornicate in the sewer, you bitches."

"You heard my sister. Be gone. Flee, whores."

My Muslim friends continued to protect me as we walked until we finally came to a market place in which to be absorbed into the crowd.

This incident, however, was indicative of things changing in the region, as was noted by my Australian friends. I had been accosted in the Persian Gulf countries because of all the white skinned Western prostitutes around and the stereotype I fit there. But in Turkey I had few encounters. Until now. Turkey, in fact, was becoming increasingly more militant. Though it is a Sunni country, its recent history thrived as a secular, modern state, and as a key member of NATO. But I became more leery with each visit. Not just because of the militant Shiite Iranian factions within, but with Turkish Sunni themselves.

Things were changing more in Lebanon also. Not so much in Zahlé, but it was getting more dangerous to set out for other parts of the country. All the more reason I was nervous for Max to leave me on assignment. For Max's company now decided it wanted offices in oil rich Angola in southwestern Africa.

"You have a knack, Khalil," Max related to me as to what his supervisor told him while I was gone to Istanbul. "You know how to turn a bad situation into good. We had a meeting and decided you are the perfect man to open our new offices in Angola. We need you to leave as soon as you can. But it is dangerous there. Even more so than here. We must warn you of that. You cannot take your wife. She would be safer in Lebanon living among fellow Christians with Hezbollah protecting the region. You will be generously compensated for both the dangers you may find in Angola and for the hardship of leaving your wife. I am aware that you are taking care of your mother, but your wife can manage that for you."

As soon as I managed happiness in his world, he was taken away from me. But I understood the situation. It was a feather in his cap that his company placed so much faith in him. We could always use the extra money too. So, in spite of disappointment in not getting to live in Africa again, I did love Zahlé. And knowing Mahmoud would never care for his mother, I was amenable to stay.

"Don't worry about me, sweetheart," I assured Max as I bid him adieu. "Our landlady just may be my best friend now. I'm there at her house everyday for tea or coffee. Or she's here at our place. She, more than anyone, has helped me integrate into society here. Christmas is soon. She and her husband, our dear landlord, have already invited me to their flat to share it. So, there will be a sense of family, even without you. And our friends in Al-Habib take good care of your mother. I can easily check on things now and then each week."

In fact, that Christmas with my landlords in Zahlé was the best Christmas I ever spent. They welcomed me at the table and fussed over me as if I was a long lost cousin. I was never so taken care of. It was just as glorious at New Years. Only Max being gone dampened any of it.

"Olivia," the landlady said as we sipped tea the next week late in the New Year evening. "What a wonderful way to start off 2012. Don't you think? I know Khalil misses you, but I hope you don't have an empty heart. Or at least too diminished. You are such a joy for us."

"I love it here," I answered chirpily. "I loved the midnight mass at the church, the fireworks, the food and wine. Just the best time. I love being in Lebanon."

"That makes us happy," my landlord said with a smile.

"You must stay the night with us," the landlady suggested. "In fact, we talked it over today. We want you to live with us. You can keep your flat. That is fine. A place for your things and for your privacy. But we are worried about you."

"Why that's so sweet of you," I said with a laugh. "I love the thought of it, but you don't need to bother. I'm fine by myself."

"I don't think you understand," the landlord said. "Our friends in Hezbollah have been warning us for weeks now. It seems to be more than warnings anymore. There is a group in Iraq, you may have heard, that is very violent. Much more so than al-Qaeda. They are in this area now. In Syria, right next door. In our part of Syria, I mean. Not just near Iraq, but here."

He saw my skeptical look. Who could be worse than al-Qaeda, I thought to myself.

"Olivia, get this innocent mind of yours tuned to reality. Remnants of Sunni from Iraq left over from Saddam Hussein are their leaders. This is what we are told. With the Arab Spring uprising to overthrow Assad in Syria, 'the Islamic State of Iraq' I heard them called, have taken advantage of the chaos there and infiltrated with significance in Syria this past summer. Our Hezbollah friends now say they are beginning to infiltrate Bekaa. Right here in our midst. We are worried about you. A blonde haired American living alone."

I stared blankly, trying to filter what I just heard. All the turmoil and strife in this region, especially after the uprising against Assad's regime in Syria, seemed under control to me. I was worried about sudden civil war like anyone else. But the Arab Spring uprisings recently in Tunisia, Libya, and Egypt were worrisome too. An infiltration by a terrorist group worse than al-Qaeda? I never considered such a thing.

"I would love to spend tonight," I replied. "It's so cozy and I feel so welcomed. But I'm okay. Hezbollah won't let anything happen to us."

They looked at me as if I was naïve, but said no more.

As the days passed inside our new year, however, the rumors became more serious. More threatening. Even my Hezbollah friends were concerned. This caught my attention.

There was no Max to advise me. The group I was told about that called themselves ISI, the Islamic State of Iraq, was taking advantage of the Arab Spring revolts going on in much of the Arab world. Groups of Arab rebels were getting rid of the yoke of their tyrants. Except that groups like al-Qaeda, and now ISI, were taking advantage of the chaos to take on their own agenda. One based on terror. Nazi style terror.

I wanted to live in Zahlé forever, but it was not to be. Danger came knocking at our door in a very real way. A department chief of the Lebanese CIA happened to be a cousin of Max named Abdul. From loyalty and concern he ventured to my house in Zahlé often to check on me.

"There are sleeper cells in Lebanon, Olivia," he explained to me on one of his visits. "You are in danger. We are increasingly concerned at the agency. Our agents and our Hezbollah fighter allies relate more individual stories about all they have heard. Some have experiences. Never has there been such as these. While Khalil is in Angola he also hears stories about them being now more prevalent in Syria and their infiltration on the border of Syria and Lebanon. It seems, in fact, this is the very group that blew up his hotel that time in Baghdad. They are very violent. He is worried about you. I can only assure him that we are here for you. But you are now at great risk. It is time for me to be blunt. This new development of sleeper cells here and his predicament in Angola with the dangers there have aged him, he says."

"But I've never been happier in my life than here," I answered. "I believe all that you say and I don't want any of you worrying needlessly about me. But please, let me stay longer. I will leave and go wherever you instruct me if it gets out of hand, but please let me stay longer."

Abdul studied me, then eased into a smile.

"Then stay," he said. "I am flattered you love my country so much. But when I say you must go, then you must go."

"Agreed," I said, grateful for any reprieve of my departure from paradise.

As it turned out there had been an encounter already with this group in a nearby town. A Christian lieutenant in the Lebanese Army with his men, which consisted of Sunni, were ambushed in a town called Arsal. Arsal had been a blemish on the ass of Lebanon for years. It was a Sunni village on the border of Syria and Lebanon and had been repeatedly warned by the government to cease and desist with their acts of terrorism against the Shia in other villages. The mayor of Arsal was very pro-opposition to the Assad regime in Syria. He used this village on the border to smuggle arms and drugs with damaging results. They constantly raided and murdered individuals that either got in the way of their endeavors, or who didn't agree with their way of thinking. Now, through intelligence, they could be traced to be among the earliest ISI, now called ISIS to include Syria in the pseudonym, infiltration groups. This town grew to be the number one hot bed in Lebanon.

The ambush of the lieutenant and his men was the most brutal act of violence I heard of at the time. The lieutenant was axed in the head and slaughtered out in the open, while the mayor and his son, as well as other leaders of Arsal, laughed and jeered while the Sunni soldiers of the lieutenant were made to watch.

They begged for their lives saying, "I am Sunni. I am one of you."

But the terrorists responded, "You are not one of us just because you are Sunni like us. Look at your army uniforms. You are our enemies."

The Army soldiers were then tortured, drug behind cars, then executed. After that ambush things got worse. We hoped at the time it was just an isolated incident and that justice would be served against this town. After much publicity and promises made to bring action against all that participated, which actually would have been the whole town, nothing was ever done. Arsal became a safe haven for terrorists. Finally, it was one of the first towns hit by Hezbollah in their push to drive out this new terrorist group. No one, however, understood what was actually happening or how it would escalate. This early terrorist group had the first inklings of what became known to the world as the Arab pseudonym for them, Daesh.

I sensed how the next visit by Abdul was not a courtesy call, as I invited him into my apartment.

"Hezbollah caught three individuals in the Christian village next to Al-Habib," he told me. "I'm sure you must know of this village."

"Of course, I know it well," I replied. "I sometimes go to church there."

I waited nervously for the rest of the story.

"These men turned out to be with the group based previously at Arsal. They were working as a silent cell, targeting people in the area to kidnap. They desperately want to gain a foothold in this area. I'm sorry to inform you, they heard there are Americans living here in Zahlé. To tell you directly, Olivia, you will be targeted by them. You cannot live here any longer. Your husband called me yesterday from Angola. In unrelated circumstances, his life seems to be in jeopardy there too, according to him. Upon hearing about this infiltration here, he has decided to quit his job and come home to be with you. Two different threats, but overlapping dangers to you and your husband. I am sorry."

I didn't know what to say. I was afraid for both me and my husband. I also wondered how easily he could find a job if he was going to quit. He had problems there, but I didn't know the extent. He told Abdul more than he told me. I was heartbroken, not sure which hurt the most, paradise lost, imminent danger, or lost income.

"Even our police didn't know about the arrests and interrogations by Hezbollah intelligence when we were told this by them," Abdul informed further. "This group is brutal. Beyond imagination. They behead their captives. They burn people alive. Everyone is their enemy to them. Their purpose is to terrorize in the name of Allah. I know your husband, my own flesh and blood, and how he hates Hezbollah. But he needs them now. We all need them. We must do what is best to survive."

I nodded that I understood.

"Actually, we're very good friends with many in Hezbollah," I explained. "We just hate them as an organization."

"We have to be more than friends with individuals. I am not asking him or you to change your allegiance or politics, but you must understand that it is only Hezbollah right now that stands between living and the worst death imaginable. If you do not want to ally with Hezbollah, it is understandable, but you must be respectful and cooperative. If Hezbollah attacks Christian communities or tries to kill Americans living here, that is another matter. But whatever friends you have in Hezbollah, show them appreciation and respect for being your protectors. I hate to say it, but we need them now. I work with the Lebanese government and I must admit we are very disorganized, divided, and weak. I too have hated Hezbollah and considered them puppets of Iranians. But that is in the past. This is our new reality."

"I have grown to respect those that I know," I answered. "I can't speak for the entire organization or for any Iranian mischief, but the ones in Al-Habib that I know, I have grown an affection for. They have been more than my protectors. They have shown me immeasurable kindness and affection. I will show them the respect they deserve for befriending me and for protecting me. While I was rejected everywhere that I went in the Middle East, including by Max's family and friends, I suddenly found that his enemies, and supposedly mine, showed me respect and protection. Me, the Christian from America. It shocked me from all I've heard of them, but it did not go unnoticed."

"That is good, Olivia. I am glad we have this understanding. Khalil will surely call you any day now. Any moment now perhaps. He cannot leave you alone anymore. You must move back to Al-Habib. Al-Habib may be the safest place in Lebanon now, considering it is a major Hezbollah center. Every villager there is a fighter. You will have a personal army for protection, if need be. As I am sure you know, Khalil has five cousins there, neighbors, along with his brother. All are armed with two handguns apiece. There are even machine guns thrown in for good measure. An armed van will be here upon the arrival of your husband. They will provide you safe transport."

Max arrived within a week of my conversation with Abdul.

"I quit my job," he told me after our affectionate embraces and endearments upon his return. He looked older now. In less than a year he looked five years older to me now. "I won't work for that company anymore. I liked them and appreciated how they liked me and gave me such responsibility. But they would not listen to me of the obstacles in Angola. There is so much chaos and danger there. On top of that it is so expensive to live and do business."

"So, what will we do then?" I asked showing my concern.

"I have connections in Bahrain. We will go there. You can come with me. You like it there too from our visit."

"What about your mother?"

"Yes, first we must take care of our life and responsibility here. But our Hezbollah friends still look after her well. I hate to impose further, but we must."

I let Max unpack, shower, and get settled. We had a lot to talk about. I brought out pita bread and hummus for him to prepare a snack for us, then set it on the coffee table in front of our couch in the living room. He spent several silent, restless minutes sitting next to me on the couch after his shower. He hadn't even bothered to dress, but came in his bathrobe. He didn't bother to look at me while he ate, but stared off into his own thoughts before finally turning to me as if ready to speak.

"Angola was the worst experience I ever had. The Shia I worked with turned against me once I resigned to come home. They even tried to kill me. I'm sure of it. They tried to get me arrested to be brutalized in jail. Thugs pulled a gun on me and robbed me. I escaped because of a most wonderful American ambassador at the US embassy in Angola. I will be eternally grateful to him. I am sure I would have been killed if it hadn't been for him. On the other hand, our embassy here in Lebanon is worthless and cannot provide any sort of protection at all for us. But we are well connected here through tribe and family. I am probably safer here than anywhere for the moment. What concerns me right now is the infiltrations occurring all around. What if this Islamic State group decides to fire long range missiles on us here? We are so close to the Syrian border. Missiles could come from even there. The Syrian border is just minutes away. We are doomed if that happens."

"I don't want you to rehash old, painful memories, sweetheart, but you never told me much about your experiences in Angola while they were happening to you. I had no idea what you were going through there. I asked a few times when you called, but you shook me off. I wasn't sure why and I didn't want to pry it out of you. I assumed you were just caught up in getting things set up. But now I find out that it was a nightmare for you while you were there. So, we can let this go and leave it behind, but tell me now, then we'll drop it. Is that okay?"

He looked at me to give a small jerk of a nod for 'yes', then turned to stare off through the distance in front of him again, painfully in thought.

"My company in Beirut, I found out, was owned by a higher up in Hezbollah. His family lives here in south Lebanon. As it turns out, Angola is famous for Hezbollah money laundering. The United States is working hard to close it off. The President of Angola is complying with the American requests to block off Hezbollah, so most known Hezbollah companies are being shut down. Over three thousand Lebanese were deported in the short time I was there. I'm still not sure why I was sent. It wasn't for setting up a new business, not in the way I thought anyway. This company used connections there as a front of some sort and that's probably why they didn't care if doing business successfully there had merit or not."

Max returned to his own thoughts for a moment. Then looked at me with his serious demeanor to emphasize his concerns.

"I was assured our company was not doing money laundering for Hezbollah and that it was all legitimate. At first I didn't care much, I just wanted to do my job and be successful. To me, any money laundering I heard about was done with someone else. They paid my salary and bonuses and honored my contract. I wanted to set up successful financial links for them. I was suspicious about money laundering, but at first I decided that was not my concern. Then reality became more apparent."

He took a deep breath before taking a bite of the pita and hummus on the table in front of us, seemingly using it as a pause for contemplation.

"I began to get nervous," he finally said. "At the same time, the US embassy was pressuring the Angolan government to shut us down. I detest Hezbollah anyway. The Hezbollah there became more and more hostile to me as a result. Especially since I am American. It became open warfare between me and them by the time I heard of the infiltrations going on here. So I got worried about you. It was time to get out since they wanted me dead. I don't think our Hezbollah friends in Al-Habib will turn on us. But it is yet another concern if they do."

"My God, Max, you had a horrible time. I so wanted to be there with you, but I understand all the more why I couldn't. I was hoping it would be a Ghana for us again."

He nodded and then leaned back into the couch, breathing a sigh as he did so.

"But there was one marvelous incident there," he continued. "Actually, I'm so appreciative of the American embassy there, I must include that as a marvelous incident also. But there was another. Very endearing. Once I went to a local Lebanese restaurant for lunch. I was sitting there eating and struck up a conversation with the owner of the restaurant. It really is a small world. This restaurant owner knew who I was when I gave my name. He knew my family and how so much of my family was in government. The owner of the restaurant said to me after finding out my last name, how he remembered my uncle well. Even fondly. The uncle I told you about that got murdered by the angry tribe. He told me how my uncle was thinking to arrest him once. How he, the restaurant owner, was a smart ass around my uncle and how my uncle slapped him. A hard slap. My uncle was a powerfully built man. But then my uncle let him go. The owner let me know how much he admired my uncle and related how sorry he was about what happened to him. He told me what a great man my uncle was. My family is so well remembered, even in Angola. It gave me courage, all the more, to stand up to my company there and to Hezbollah. I have a heritage I must live up to."

Before we had time to talk more about his problems in Angola, a van with a luggage rack on top and machine guns mounted on the roof, came barreling up our driveway. Within thirty minutes Hezbollah soldiers emptied our flat, loaded our things into a truck, then swooped us back to Al-Habib and home.

We surely looked like a gypsy caravan blazing down the highway with three of Max's cousins, as well as two Hezbollah soldiers, sitting on the roof, machine guns in hand. More Hezbollah hung out the windows of the truck and van, all brandishing their handguns so that no one would even think about stopping us. We made it home in less than half an hour.

I had private body guards assigned to me everywhere I went. By then Hezbollah had Daesh shoved back from our borders. This protection bestowed on us now was a statement of respect and assurance as much as any physical protection itself. My head swirled from all the attention and devotion. It renewed my feelings of affection for my Hezbollah friends, even as stories Max told me about the organization itself, disgusted me.

CHAPTER 19

It is not unusual for there to be violent disagreement between factions in the Middle East, especially among the Shia. They are quick tempered, hot blooded, and passionate about everything, and very willing to announce it to the world. This does not make them wrong, but certainly very volatile. To the point of wronging their cause. There was always some injustice on a daily basis in my Shia oriented world of then. I got used to stories of conflict and violence. That is why I was completely surprised by the Syrian Arab Spring in 2012.

Suddenly, there were innumerable stories of riots and misadventures. Where it seemed that every single country in the region had lost its mind. Even then, I was not prepared for the Arab Spring. When the first stories filtered back to us in 2012 about the opposition forces to Syria's Assad regime, I did not get it. Neither Max nor I thought of it as a civil war. Assad constantly brutalized some faction in his country, so I considered it as another typical uprising against him that would be extinguished as usual. In fact, many of the opposition were normal Syrians fed up with tyranny. Never in a million years did anyone dream of an entity like Daesh, which as mentioned, is the Arab pseudonym for what ISI became when it infiltrated massively into Syria in the spring of 2014 becoming ISIS, Islamic State of Iraq and Syria.

Muslim was killing Muslim, not just everyone else. For the sake of killing. Tortures, beheadings, burning victims alive, sex slaves, the wiping out of entire villages to the man, woman, and child, began to occur readily. To this day, this is the hardest thing for Muslims to take. Not just warfare or dispute amongst Muslim factions, but Muslim killing Muslim in the most systematic, horrific, evil filled way. To my Shia friends, this became the end of days. It was not the way of the Prophet. The Quran did not promote this.

The most shocking thing was how much of world opinion, through the years, seemed to think the Sunni were the voice of reason, if they thought anything at all. Much of Sunni history, actually, promoted such opinion. The Sunni did much right, even much brilliance. But this favorable opinion modified somewhat with the onset of al-Qaeda after 911. Until recently, it was those crazy Shia that blew themselves up when they didn't get their way that was the problem. In history, the Sunni were known as balanced, peaceful, and the cream of the golden era of much of Islam's past.

The Shia were not shocked in the least by modern day extremists in the Sunni world such as Bin Laden, the Wahhabis, and the Taliban. Now it is the Sunni world that has produced ISIS, or Daesh. These extremists are not just trying to bring down the Western world, or create a caliphate, they are vilely and sadistically killing other Muslims, as well as infidels. Upon constantly facing turmoil, invasions, and the threat of civil war in my husband's home in Lebanon, I found myself now witnessing even worse sectarian fighting in all of the Middle East.

And there seemed to be no refuge from it.

In our need for employment, Max and I looked in Beirut, but also in other Middle Eastern countries. Similar to our predicament when I first arrived in the Middle East from America in 2006. But now things were different. Vastly different.

We used our stay in Bahrain as a much needed vacation. But a working one in that we searched for a job. I even hoped I could find work somewhere on the US military complex there. Max and I both fell flat on all of our searches. So, it was off to Egypt. We would be tourists too, but the job search took on a much higher priority. We used everything as a refuge to try to live in denial of the ever worsening situation in the Middle East. While the Middle East was falling apart in turmoil, we were unemployed. Very frightening circumstances.

While in Egypt, we did not claim Lebanese residency. Since Lebanon has such a bad name it would be held against us. We simply passed as US citizens with US passports. Because we were concerned of a civil war erupting in Lebanon, I needed a place to live or escape in case of emergency. Egypt would fit that criteria, if we could get a residency visa. It is only an hour and a half flight from Beirut and easy to get our beloved pet into the country. I loved Cairo and to live there had appeal. It was historical and had an intriguing countryside as well.

Getting residency is a tedious process, though we managed to get a six month residency permit. But not before relentless paperwork and endless lines. There were expats from every nation that we came across, including from Egypt with American passports.

Cairo was hot, dirty, crowded, and loud. In one of our countless lines, we came across four Americans standing in front of us. I never would have guessed they were Americans, however. They were hardline Salafists with beards, dishdasha, and head cover. Thinking back, it was obvious they were ISIS, but we called them Salafists because we still knew so little about ISIS then. They had American passports, but were talking openly in Arabic about American women being prostitutes. I assumed my appearance prompted this. Arabic is so difficult and I am so bad in languages that I never got it down very well. I remained calm as Max translated their Arabic to me. I was acclimated to such slander about me and my country by now.

"America is corrupt and materialistic," one of them said.

"America should be destroyed," another added.

Max figured out, as he listened, that they were part of a movement existing in Cairo. With the overthrow of Hosni Mubarak and the setting up of the radical new government in Egypt led by the Muslim Brotherhood, such movements and open conspiracy were prevalent.

With Max's light olive skin, these Salafists had no clue that he could speak Arabic or that he was Arab, so they spoke freely with one another.

"Is this why you want to go to America?" Max finally asked them. Max is so astute in language skill that he spoke his Arabic with an Egyptian accent. Stunned by this, they stared at him in disbelief. "Is America so corrupt you bring it upon yourselves to destroy it? Are you here to bring enlightenment upon us? Were you raptured by the glory of Allah to do this? Pieces of dung such as you were anointed by Allah to redeem America? Who are you? You are swine bringing darkness. Mind your own corruption first. I am also a Muslim, but fanatics such as you bring shame to Islam."

"You have sold out the Prophet," one of them said angrily. "Has American greed soiled your soul? You fool."

"Why did you shave your beard?" another Salafist asked Max. "You do not like facial hair? If you were a true believer and Muslim like you say, then custom should dictate you must have facial hair. Is it because you choose to look like a woman? Do you enjoy the American way of all men looking like women and being feminine?"

"Facial hair does not make someone a man and you are living, pathetic proof of this," Max taunted them. "The hair on my ass looks more masculine than your rat's nest of a beard. Would you care to check it out yourself? I'm sure you would be pleasured to see for yourselves. You would probably get aroused, in fact."

Everyone in line began laughing at the Salafists' expense. They, like Max, hated them and began clapping Max on the back.

This boldness by Max set the Salafists off and they grabbed at him to wrestle him to the ground. But one sidestep by Max easily freed their awkward grips on him. He followed through by punching one hard in the face knocking him down. He sneered in disgust at the other three who froze in panic.

Feeling triumphant Max looked to me for approval, which I gladly obliged. Even in middle age, his athleticism remained graceful as a deer. I hadn't a clue of the verbal exchange between him and the Salafists, but I didn't need to know the details. I had seen the show before. Dexterity seemed to fill every part of Max's being.

"But this is alarming me," he said soon afterwards, a grave look upon his face. "How did such as they get American passports?"

In fact, our stay in Cairo, though charming as before in many ways, was quite disturbing. The Arab Spring had not been kind to Egypt. The rule of the Muslim Brotherhood was proving to be brutal. Their mishandling of the economy proved just as unbearable.

After a month of futile job searching, though in many ways still adoring our stay in Cairo, it was time to return to Lebanon. We were running short of money and one could never be sure one day to the next what political event might affect our safety. We would have to look for work in Beirut now while staying in our, i.e. Mahmoud's, house in Al-Habib.

CHAPTER 20

"Oh, it is so good to see you again," my Hezbollah friend Khadija said to Max and me upon our return to Al-Habib. Though she was ten years younger than me, she was now my dearest friend in the village, while her husband our number one protector. Maybe it was her endearing spirit that prejudiced me toward her, but I also thought her the prettiest in Al-Habib, even in her plain, sometimes dreary chadors. "I am sorry that you did not find work in Egypt, but I must tell you, you are not just welcomed here, but so needed."

She paused to look us each in the eyes, one at a time, for dramatic effect.

"I went to your home many times daily to check on your mother. Mahmoud is such a problem. I knew this already, but I had to live personally with this problem about him. There are times your mother is very alert, very talkative, and friendly. And many times very demanding and angry. But this is not the problem. I check on her to visit, then leave. But once when I came she was trapped on the toilet. I came one morning and she was asleep there all night long. Mahmoud never checked, nor did his son. She was limp, leaning backwards, her mouth open. Oh my. What if I did not check? She was filthy. And almost everyday I have to bathe her. But that is not the worst of it. Here you are needing to find a job, your income unstable, and now I must tell you some very bad news."

Again she looked at us for dramatic affect. We had a dramatic look of our own now as we waited for this news from her.

"Just after you left for Bahrain, Mahmoud sold the diesel for your house. Your tank is empty. All to spend on a girl. In America I think you call her a bimbo. He sold this diesel not for money for the hospital, or to fix the house, but to make a bimbo think he is big shot. It pains me to tell you this. If you had not come home your mother may have frozen to death this coming winter. Your worthless, disgusting brother would not have cared. The tenants would have moved out perhaps. No money income then, only a bimbo. Of course no bimbo either if no income from no tenants."

My friend and I both looked at Max to see his reaction. His face turned red and his neck veins began to bulge.

"Have you no shame?" Max screamed at Mahmoud late that morning in Arabic before he could make it off to town.

"Why do you talk to me in this manner?" Mahmoud asked with a sneer. "Do you want to remain in my house? Do you think I can't rent out your room? I give you consideration for your room and you treat me this way."

"You sold all the diesel," Max said point blank.

"What do you speak?"

"All the diesel is gone in the tank. I spent thousands to buy diesel for the winter for you and you sold it."

"Who told you this lie? There is diesel in the tank. Don't listen to gossip."

"The tank is empty and you know it."

"Then someone stole it," Mahmoud yelled. "Probably Hezbollah. They are terrorists. You know this. Why do you blame me? They want to fight another war. They always need money."

"They are our protectors," Max countered. "You are the terrorist. You would kill our mother. She gave you this house that I bought for her. I bought the diesel that you sold. Everyone knows you sold it. I talked to the man who sold it to us. He said you came to him for him to buy it back. He is not Hezbollah. Stop your lies."

"You stop believing gossip. Hezbollah obviously threatened him to lie to you. Be gone or I will rent your room. Are you suddenly aligned with Hezbollah? I thought you hated them."

Autumn was upon us. The air was cool and crisp. We had no money to live and buy diesel again, but had good credit and were able to charge it.

Now to find work before winter set in. But there was more to face than the cold. The opposition against Assad, including Daesh, was taking over more of Syria while America aided all as a coalition.

In America's eyes, anything against Assad was good, even though so much of the opposition was of the jihadist genre. I didn't know if America was aiding these radicals unwittingly. Wouldn't America know there was a difference in the factions? Having dealt with al-Qaeda, I couldn't imagine America not knowing the difference between freedom rebels and terrorists. But our friends in Hezbollah told us that even the terrorist factions were benefitting directly or indirectly from American aid. Even my brother in Texas was for this aid to overthrow Assad. In emails he clearly did not understand what was happening here, only that America was fighting Assad. This horrified me. If my brother didn't know yet the difference, it didn't say much for the rest of the masses there. But surely the CIA knew. Wouldn't they? Anyway, I was horrified.

The Arabs have a saying I hear constantly. If given a choice between sickness or death, choose sickness. In the Arab world those are often the only choices you have. When I first heard it, I thought it the most negative outlook imaginable. It annoyed me and I decided they deserved what they get. But after all these years and all my experiences, I must say that now I get it. With the likes of a Saddam Hussein, Bashir Assad, or Muammar Ghaddafi, no matter how bad it is, somehow when these tyrants are overthrown, the aftermath is worse. With the country worse off because of it. Things go from bad to worse. So it seems a punishment to even think of democracy. As if they should say 'Inshallah' while overthrowing a tyrant.

Islam is revered as a way of life with the Quran a guide how to live. That's all that matters to a believer. It is not a religion where State and Church are divided like in Western democracies. Islam is inseparable from every aspect of life because Muhammad supposedly directed how to solve all problems. Followers feel led how to carry on with daily life. Islam, in fact, means submit. Do not question. Question only enough to understand better how to submit.

True believers cannot separate waking up in the morning, eating breakfast, going to work, then praying five times a day. All are Islamic tasks to them, not just mundane actions. They often work themselves into a religious frenzy with each supposedly sacred task. A Shia's life is basically a choice between sickness or death then. In fact, Shia feel they must make death a glorious thing. Fighting for God a glorious thing. If not, they could not get out of bed in the morning. They do not wake up optimistic like an American easily does.

Hezbollah has turned glorious submission, even to the point of death, into a fine art. Shia have been oppressed for so long, and bullied by so many factions, that Hezbollah was created to get them out of bed in the morning, so to speak, for the purpose of fighting this real or perceived oppression.

Just as Hitler instilled patriotism and pride into being German again in order to revive the country, Hezbollah gives the Shia hope. The rest of the story with the Nazis, however, wasn't so redeeming and that happens at times with Hezbollah. Without making excuses for them, I can see more now why these people grasp onto this way of life. They feel validated for once. Now they don't wait to be bullied. But like the Nazis, they often turn into bullies themselves.

Hezbollah, in turn, takes care of their own. Their version of the master race. As I have previously stated, when a Hezbollah fighter becomes a martyr in death, the family is given a monthly stipend for the rest of their lives. If the fighter led a hopeless life, at least his family will be taken care of. Which is more than they had before.

So they allow themselves to be brainwashed. It is sickness rather than death. Or perhaps a death of jihad to enhance sickness.

I felt Max roll over onto his side toward me as we lay in bed in the darkness. I needed to talk, so took advantage of his reverie state.

"Are you awake?" I whispered. His hand touched my shoulder as a sign that he was. "I can't sleep, sweetheart," I said.

"Again?" he asked sympathetically.

"Some of the men in the village talk about how they participated in killing Marines in Iraq during the war. Also of plane hijackings. They were even proud. My Hezbollah friends that are wives told me this as we shopped. I'm not sure why they bothered to tell me. They didn't say if their particular husbands participated in such. I think they were just being honest. That they could trust our friendship. My friends weren't bragging, only relating. But that makes all this more personal now to me. My relationship with them, I mean. My affection for them. It bothers my conscience to like them when I hear this. Even knowing Hezbollah is a terrorist organization, I could almost live with myself knowing, or assuming, that none of our Hezbollah friends had anything to do with this stuff. But now I know for fact some of them did these things. And I'm sure they would again. I'm aware that both sides think they are defending their way of life and fighting against oppression. I understand that on the one hand, but don't see it that clearly at all on the other. I can picture my brother in Iraq, or my nephew. I know for fact they wouldn't want to be there per se, but would be responding to a growing jihadist menace. Like what happened with 911. But now it's so complicated to me. Not so black and white anymore. My Hezbollah friends see America as invaders. I know we're not, but twisted or not, naïve or not, Hezbollah does think this. Before I knew them I got to hate them outright, then came to love much about them later on. But now, I wrestle with trying to see what created this in them. Why they would attack my country. But I can't just condemn them anymore. I don't agree with how they see us in Iraq, but I somewhat understand it now, even though it's wrong. I agonize, Max."

"I have found I love my adopted country, America," Max answered. "And also my American wife, who loves her Marine brother, and soon to be Marine nephew. I resent colonial adventurism and how the Middle East was sold out by the Europeans. Europeans allied with America across the ocean. Americans that propped up the Shah. But America also pushed the British and French to withdraw troops allied with Israel out of the Suez in 1956. America is the world leader. People resent America for getting involved or for not getting involved. I see how America gets its hand forced so often. Then there was 911, but then there was Iraq. I do believe America thought Saddam Hussein had weapons of mass destruction. But they created a mess. But they also drove out Iraq from Kuwait before that. Yes, it is so complicated. Before I was an Arab nationalist. I still am. But I know there is much craziness in the Arab world also, and that America is the only hope at times. I also have troubled sleep from all that is going on."

"I wrestle with all this, Max, everyday. It especially comes out in me at night while I'm trying to relax and sleep. I have justifiably felt disloyal to my country even being in the area where Hezbollah lives. I've watched my own countrymen attacked in nearby countries and even in Beirut in the eighties when Hezbollah suicide bombers killed Marines, sent not as aggressors or occupiers, but as part of a NATO peace keeping force trying to stabilize a ravaged country in distress. I can never condone these actions by Hezbollah. But through their eyes, it was either sickness or death to them somehow. It is so complex now to me.

He rubbed my shoulder affectionately.

"I so want to understand," I continued. "I want to grow. Then as I struggle with all this, I get horrified when I hear stories of women I consider fools. Women who convert to Islam then become Jihad Janes and join the terrorists. Somehow these idiots traded one black and white scenario for another. But I want perspective. Not naïve, airhead, Jihad Jane perspective. I hope for a clear head of perspective. My moderate, educated, partially Westernized husband, meaning you, helps me deal with this. You try so hard to understand also. You defend the Arab side to redneck Americans on the one hand, and then defend America to jihadist Neanderthals on the other. We're trapped right now. The answers come so slowly."

"If they come at all," Max sighed.

"But how can anyone understand any of this?" I moaned. "These fanatic Hezbollah devotees feel no guilt because they consider their acts as those of military personnel. They feel they know what they are getting into. In their eyes these Marines and soldiers were getting paid to kill their people and it is just a job to them. They don't consider that people like my brother are there to begin with because of things like 911. Or to prevent acts of genocide at times. They don't see anyone like my brother as a patriot. But I damn sure do and a heroic one too. Raising my nephew to be such a hero. But Hezbollah has been convinced that these intruders are mercenaries and kill for money. They feel they must dehumanize American patriots in order to remain fanatics. Submissive fanatics. This disgusts me, even as I love many of these very people now."

Max nodded agreement at the complexity.

"Hezbollah would never intentionally go after civilians," I continued while I searched for meaning, "which is their saving grace in their eyes. These invaders that Hezbollah fights are getting paid to kill them, in their eyes, therefore anything goes in order to defeat these adversaries. They are protecting their way of life, they think. It sickens me to see them simplify, even dehumanize, so much. But the problem is, I also understand it in a crazy way. I just don't agree. I want to correct this horror. Not just as their enemy, but also as their friend. We can work this out. I want all this madness to end. I want my nephew to be safe. To be the hero he is. To find common ground enough to work things out."

"But will we?" Max asked. "It seems so hopeless, except that nothing is ever so hopeless."

"And just as I get disgusted with my protectors in Al-Habib," I mused further, "I see how Hezbollah puts their money where their mouth is. These Hezbollah fighters are intensely dedicated as they fight for their way of life no matter what the politics are. I see this and even though they are my enemy overall, I can't help but be touched by their dedication to their cause, their families, and their way of life. At times I beg myself not to see this. But I do see it and this I know. I feel a sympathy for them in that regard. More than you do, Max. You hate them politically and everything they stand for. They ally themselves with invaders to this country and are embarrassingly, in your eyes, fanatics. I agree, but it is more personal to you since you are of their culture."

Max studied me. A sympathy for what I was saying, or at least the soul searching inside me, seemed to appear in his eyes.

"This disgust you have for your own fanatics I can even identify with in my own way. To be compared with how I despise the Ku Klux Klan. The Klan aren't just terrorist, they are from my culture and history. It is personal to me because of it. An embarrassment even. This scorn of a culture I love. So, Max, you see Hezbollah as backward, while you want peace with the world where possible. A high priority to you. This is how you cope with things. To overcome backwardness with knowledge and compassion if possible. Which I think of as Christian."

"Olivia," he told me further that night in our talk, "we must settle issues with education and diplomacy. I'm a fighter. I accept that at times there must be war. I accept that as much as any Hezbollah. But I am not a fanatic, nor a fatalist, nor a nihilist. I am a modern man. Hezbollah and much of Islam must grow up. All that is happening now with Hezbollah is killing, killing, and more killing. They are not defenders to me, but aggressors. When killing and aggression are over what will be left? I fear for the future of all Shia because of the association with Hezbollah. I am horrified with the way things are going. There are many ways to settle things with our adversaries. War would be included at times. But the normal Shia is something to be proud of and we are easily misunderstood. Hezbollah bridges no gap of this misunderstanding, but perpetuates more misunderstanding. Especially in their affiliation with Iran."

He studied me as if to see if I understood the paradox he felt. I not only understood, I identified with things he was saying. I welcomed his words. We were bonding over them.

"I applaud their dedication and have empathy for the fighters on a one to one basis," he finally continued. "For now they are all that is keeping us from being slaughtered. I am grateful for that, and also for their friendship and respect to me, and most especially what they have for you. But I blame Hezbollah for most of Lebanon's problems. Yet they stand up for themselves and do not accept bullying. They fight for their families and lives. I identify with that. Just not this fanaticism and joining a standing army to be used like fodder. And if I may so. Just like your brother was used in Vietnam. Soon your nephew perhaps. I do not understand joining the military. It doesn't make any sense to me. Your brother is so intelligent and knowledgeable. The Vietnam war was lost and unpopular when he joined. Hezbollah soldiers are so brave and fierce. But evil. Mindless robots. I would never join. There is a better way."

"But if Hezbollah had not taken over southern Lebanon," I added, "we'd all be dead now. That's an irony, but also a fact."

"It is so complicated," he sighed. "I have many sleepless nights."

CHAPTER 21

Things got worse. Max began work for a company in Beirut. Daily he drove for an hour and a half each way through isolated, sniper ridden roads. But these roads were the safest ones to Beirut. To drive any other way encountered a Sunni barricade in a town half an hour outside of Beirut named Saida.

The problem in Saida began when a Sunni cleric started a riot to instigate the killing of the few Shia living there. These Shia were slaughtered for no other reason than they were Shia. Women, children, and old men mostly. The cleric dressed like a woman, then escaped the army after the killings. Hezbollah intervened by themselves killing Sunni. Soon, all was quiet, but various Sunni villages around the Bekaa Valley tried to retaliate. Thus the barricade, as well as the threat of snipers, causing the need of the route Max was now forced to take.

"We are going to live in Beirut hopefully next week," Max told my welcoming ears one day that autumn. "I talked with a Lebanese company owned by a Syrian Christian with Shia bodyguards." His smile turned cynical. "That's Lebanon for you," he chirped. "This Syrian Christian wants to expand and relocate eventually to Africa. He has vast holdings there and after a couple of months here we will relocate to somewhere in Africa. We will live in a Christian sector in Beirut alongside him. That is good for you, Olivia. It will be near the American embassy so I really am not worried."

I couldn't hold my joy. I could go to church again.

"He, by the way, is pro opposition," Max continued. "You know, opposition to Assad, both jihadist and rebel. It has nothing to do with hating Assad, however. I'm not sure he cares one way or the other politically. His billion dollar company money launders for Assad and he doesn't want to pay any of the money back. Pure capitalist greed in other words. Thus, he needs a business development director like me to further expand his holdings, which he hopes to eventually move to Africa. So he hopes Assad will fall. When I asked him if he worried about civil war in Lebanon, he laughed at me and said he felt we were all perfectly safe. He's sure there will be no civil war. But he still wants to relocate. I have heard and seen how the jihadist opposition is happily stating they want to eradicate all Christians. We are all heretics to them, Christian, Jews, and Shia. Only the fundamentalist Sunni would survive. So there is a paradox right there for him. Basically it boils down to money and greed. I actually like him a lot. He is very intelligent. The area where we will live is right on the Mediterranean. It is beautiful and safe, at least for now. This is a real opportunity for us. The job fits me perfectly. So there you have it. It is quite surreal, don't you think?"

My head couldn't keep up with all the bizarre details Max was throwing at me.

"Why would you want to work for someone like that?" I asked. "He seems immoral. Amoral might be a better word. Are you sure you can trust him?"

"Olivia," Max said to me condescendingly. "This is the Middle East. It's not that I don't care or that I fully trust him. This is how things are here. I would not want to launder money for terrorists or for drug cartels, but there are so many shady things going on I have to choose which appall me the most. But there is so much opportunity with this company. I don't mean the money aspect, though that too. I'm talking about living in Beirut on the ocean, and starting a company in Africa later on. So, I'm taking it. I'll maneuver the best I can. As usual."

For much of our time in the transition, while waiting for Africa to open up to us, we almost forgot about the Arab Spring in nearby Syria. There was still turmoil, but it seemed far away. Hezbollah, at least for our area, seemed in control of things. Strife always existed inside and out of the country, but for much of Lebanon, these were quiet days.

Indeed, our situation in Beirut was perfect. We had a glorious apartment overlooking the Mediterranean. It had Arab furniture just like before, Persian carpets just like before, tiled flooring just like before, though this time the walls were a lime colored green soothing to any mood I was ever in. And it was just blocks from the Catholic Church the Maronite woman directed me to the first time I was in Beirut years before.

The dining was marvelous while the walks in the sand were wonderful, and I finally took the time to visit some of the many museums in Beirut. Art, historic, religious, and anthropological. Next to my time in Zahlé, these were my happiest days yet. The church, especially, provided me with friends and social events that kept me fulfilled.

Within weeks we were on our way to Africa. Just like the owner said. Max was to do a feasibility study in Khartoum in the Sudan, a country just south of Egypt and across the Red Sea from Saudi Arabia. This company intended to start a branch office there with Max as the chief financial officer and manager. I loved Africa. This was glorious to me.

There was a huge Muslim Sufi population in Khartoum near where we lived. Sufis are the mystical branch of Islam, much like the Kabbalists are for Judaism. Strangely, it was my brother who first told me of the Sufis, so I was interested in them and made a point to find out more while I was there. I soon learned they were not at all like the Sufis he had read about and shared with me. Philosophers and poets like the great Rumi and Omar Khayyam. These Khartoum Sufis were much more 'earthy' forms, or at least the ones that I met.

Sudan was by far the most primitive of any country we lived. Much more so than in Ghana. Electricity was so expensive that most people did without. At least the locals. Expats couldn't live without the air conditioning and fans. Finding a place with electricity and air conditioning was a huge portion of our expat package offered by the company.

Our apartment was in a nice compound built for expats like us. Not only the luxuries of air conditioning and fans, but running hot water, solid wooden floors, spacious rooms, bright, white walls, and European furnishings. I felt like a tourist in a hotel suite.

But our encounters with the Sufis were as typical as any we had with Sunni populations in the Middle East. None seemed a fan of the Shia even though Sudan was being helped militarily by Hezbollah. The Sufi brother-owners of the new company branch were quite vocal in their disapproval of Shia and this did not sit well with Max. So, my best chance of learning more about this supposedly mystical religion was thwarted immediately.

We were invited to a company party held to welcome clients. As is tradition, the men were separated from the females. I happened to be the only wife from a Western country living in Sudan among any of these companies being hosted. So, I was the lone outsider amongst all the sisters, aunts, children, and wives of the men. The women were very outgoing, mischievously so, and very interested in everything. They particularly loved America. There apparently was constant competition and pettiness among these wives about who got to live in the States when their husbands were assigned there, as opposed to those who had to stay in Khartoum among the client companies. The wives didn't get along well with each other because of this competition, which required constant intervention from their husbands to keep them separated and at peace. I felt very unnerved by it the entire party and wanted to go home. Enough so, that I made excuses why I had to find my husband just to get away for awhile. It turns out the men were even worse.

"You are Shia," one of the Sufi owners said to Max just as I arrived. "In fact, you are the only Shia here. Doesn't it disturb you how Shia are ruining the world? Look at the mischief of Iran and Hezbollah in your own country. That is because the Shia are not true believers. All these problems now come from this. Don't you think?"

"Are you saying the terror going on in Syria and Iraq now is coming from the Shia?" the Christian owners of the poultry branch scoffed. They looked at Max supportively as they said it.

"If the Shia had not kicked out the Sunni in the Iraq coalition, then none of this mischief would have happened," the Sufi countered.

"Enjoy yourselves," Max said as he turned to leave. "I am a business man. I want new opportunities in Sudan." He glanced at his Christian allies appreciatively. "I hope we are successful," he said as he took my hand to leave.

Welcome to Khartoum.

It got even worse.

Soon afterwards, a US embassy employee was walking along the side of the road and shot dead by a Sudanese Sufi. The animosity for the differing nationalities was building up. This rocked all the expat communities.

"All foreigners should go home," a man shouted at Max and me at a restaurant near the UN compound one day soon after that. "You don't belong here. You are trouble makers."

The Sudan is split between Sudanese who want to improve their country while valuing the Western world's successes, and those that resent and envy the opulent looking foreigners. Poverty is so vast and grinding that the resentment being played out is understandable. Especially when the wealthy are seen treating the unfortunate like trash. The class system is brutal and no one seems to care people are dying. Most of the resentment directed towards Max and me, we felt, came from the fact that we, as expats, were getting huge benefit packages while the masses of countrymen were left jobless and starving. The cost of food is outrageously high and people are literally starving.

Once, Max and I sat at a hotel restaurant with a Sudanese friend of ours. A wealthy Sudanese family sat at the table next to us. They spoke loudly in Arabic. Max put his finger to his lips for us to be silent so he could listen.

"Foreigners are trash," the man said condescendingly. "They never understand how valuable and wonderful the traditions of Islam are. They invade our country in such a crude manner. In an infidel manner. Foreigners never understand the Sudanese. They should be expelled from the country."

Max said nothing to the insult. It was fact finding for him. Reinforcing what we already knew about our new, seemingly xenophobic environment. And these incidences kept coming.

There was a famous Lebanese singer in the Sudan while we were there. Since the Sudanese love anything Arab, his popularity was huge. He later returned to Lebanon and as Max and I watched him perform on television one night the interviewer asked him what nationality or country had the ugliest women. This seemed to be a delightful question to his Lebanese audience.

"By far it is the Sudanese," the singer said forthrightly. "They are the ugliest people of any population on earth."

Sudanese everywhere saw this, which caused riots. His CDs were thrown into the street and people openly burned them as well. An open forum appeared demanding his apology.

"I refuse to apologize for what I said," the singer said when he heard about the riots he started with his statement. "I spoke the truth. What am I supposed to say? Someone has to be the ugliest. You asked me, I told you. I will say it again. It is by far the Sudanese. The amount of money I get from Sudan is not enough to make me want to apologize."

Lebanese in Khartoum were now being assaulted because of this. Max and I were even more afraid to go out now.

So, I was back, as in my early days in the Middle East, to looking for anything I liked about my new home. Much like in the musical, *The King And I*, where the actress let her son know that whenever she felt afraid she would whistle a happy tune. I looked extra hard to appreciate things I knew were there as my chance to whistle a happy tune so to speak. And in fact, I loved where the Sudanese were gracious, friendly, and exotic in their mannerisms and dress. There it was. My happy tune to get me through.

The women's heads in the Sudan are covered, but in an African way. They wear their long dresses in bright, beautiful cloth of every color imaginable. Beautiful, wonderful prints with a matching hijab that is not tied around the face, but draped around the head. The men often wore white dishdashas with turbans and sandals. Breathtaking. Some of the professionals, however, such as lawyers and doctors, would wear either a suit or button down shirt with slacks, Western style.

The southern Sudanese are mostly black and Christian. They separated from the Arab north in a civil war to create their own country. Khartoum is mostly Arabic in culture and ethnicity. Because of that I saw mostly the Arabic Sudanese.

There is much consistency in the Arab culture in Khartoum. When Max and I first got there we had dinner with the Human Resources Director of the company, the one who originally found Max back in Beirut and recommended he be hired. He was a white South African and openly an apartheid supporter who missed the old days of white ruled South Africa. His Sudanese assistant helped him with the family visa process. She was married with children, but was having an open affair with him. So, I was shocked by her attitude as we all went out to dinner together.

"How could you marry a Westerner and Christian?" she asked Max in Arabic right in front of me. "She is too old for you. How could you marry someone that can't give you children?"

The white, married South African didn't speak Arabic and in that comfort zone she exempted herself in her mind somehow from being considered a colored by her racist companion while talking to Max. She was so proud of her looks and openly wanted Max, who by now was impatient with this line of questioning and thinking. We had not been confronted with such since our first days in Lebanon.

"You know," Max answered her in English so that both I and her boyfriend could hear. "That Lebanese singer was right. The Sudanese really are the ugliest people in Africa. The women especially. You're not really Arabs and you imitate our culture very poorly. But if you think you are special, good for you."

A harsh, pro-Islamic dictatorship began after Sudan obtained independence from Britain in 1956. Stories surfaced connecting Sudan with Hezbollah and Hamas, giving weight to claims that the regime of Omar el-Bashir was involved with terrorists around the world. The Sudan's genocidal escapades caused concern as well. Khartoum relished hopes to bring about an Arabized Sharia state, an Islamized Africa, and eventually, a worldwide Islamic Caliphate.

Hezbollah, it was rumored sent recruits to Sudan to train as suicide bombers. Southern Sudanese complained of terrorist training camps for years, displaying maps of the spots on Sudan's vast landscape where Islamist-based camps were located. Jihadists also were implicated in terror missions regarding Darfur nearby. Sudan's Hamas connection was revealed when Israelis struck bases in 2009 in the eastern Sudan desert. These air strikes northeast of Port Sudan wiped out large truck convoys of Sudanese Arab smugglers carrying Iranian weapons to Gaza for Hamas.

For business matters, Max found the Sudan too much like Ghana. American currency was almost nonexistent. Expats would never allow any company to pay them in local currency because the devaluation was so severe that thousands of dollars in conversion were lost. Our company had no offshore banking outlet to alleviate these problems. So every pay period we had to scurry for connections with people who exchanged money on the black market. The majority of these black market agents were made up of white South Africans.

Because of the conversion problems, we did not have a bank account. We would have to deposit in local currency, which was worthless. We could not wire US dollars in or out of Sudan. To wire money to Max's home we had to fly to the next African country to send it there.

For us then, the Sudan meant Middle Eastern style terrorism, bigotry, and intrigue mixed with Ghanaian type poverty and economic despair. I couldn't ever be sure of my safety. In spite of violence related to desperate poverty, most of the Sudanese were very warm, friendly people, so I was glad I came to Sudan overall. But I can't really say I enjoyed much of my stay except for the experience of experiencing.

It was time to leave. The Sudan didn't work out.

CHAPTER 22

There was a worsening Arab Spring situation in Syria we had to face again upon our return. The Middle East is so volatile that complacency about tragedies occurs easily. Middle Eastern countries let things happen to themselves as if lulled to sleep by events. Because something is always happening there. As an American I wanted to know what my country was doing about all this. And Europe is just up the Mediterranean? Why so much complacency there? Having a nice life are you?

In Western democracies complacency occurs for the exact opposite reasons. We did experience 911, but it seems nothing ever happens to Western democracies anymore. That would be nice except that the masses are allured to a need to be entertained in their snug, if not smug, sense of false security. Anything else is a distraction. A tragedy back home anymore is someone being outsourced by their employer. Or even not having their contraceptives paid by insurance or tax dollars. The democracies have had the great colossus America shield it from extreme poverty and bullying for so long everyone thinks they understand peace. They even debate the need for a large military, as if our military is the cause of wars, not the source of complacent peace.

Before the Western media ever heard of ISIS, atrocities occurred all around where I lived. As late as the winter of 2014 my President was telling the masses that the junior varsity, the JV team, of the supposedly decimated al-Qaeda A team, was nothing to worry about. ISIS had just taken Fallujah, then Ramadi, in Iraq when President Obama made that proclamation. It now dawned on my otherwise astute brother that ISIS was the group I warned him about when he was glad America was supporting the opposition to Assad in Syria. Even with a President and media in denial, I still couldn't understand where the CIA was. Surely, they had to know the real situation.

Meanwhile, I felt as though I was living a horrible, surreal, old World War II movie. By the time Jihad Johnnie beheaded the first American journalist and posted it on YouTube, the drama of terror had already unfolded on the border of Syria and Lebanon, even before the fall of Fallujah in Iraq. The Lebanese were getting hit hard by Daesh infiltrators on our home turf. Hezbollah was already involved because they were protecting Assad. There was an impending feeling of fear and doom that was being generated on our borders during the Syrian civil war. Except for my immediate friends inside of Hezbollah in Al-Habib, I could have cared less about Assad. For there was more than a civil war going on against a tyrant. There was horror and genocide all around me.

Everyone panicked when two of our checkpoints were taken over by Daesh. Army guards at these checkpoints were kidnapped at gunpoint and taken to an undisclosed location. Scores of others, including police officers and soldiers, were herded to a location still believed to be within the mountains of Lebanon as well. Army and Hezbollah intelligence were never able to figure out the location Daesh was taking them.

The local families of the kidnapped created roadblocks in Beirut, as well as on the road to Zahlé. They were determined to force the Lebanese government to negotiate the release of their loved ones. Daesh's demands were intentionally such that they could not be met. To do so would mean giving up an entire area by the Lebanese to them. Daesh then began beheading some of the kidnapped periodically to further force their demands.

In the past, Hezbollah negotiated well with the opposition to get prisoners released. The families of these poor soldiers recently kidnapped went to Hezbollah to ask its leader, Hassan Nasrallah, to intervene. The soldiers kidnapped were a mixture of Shia, Sunni, and Christians. Interestingly enough, the only ones that had been beheaded were Shia, except for one Christian. Nasrallah tried, but again ISIS demands were to give up a very important part of Lebanon so they would have free access between Syria, Lebanon, and Israel. This was considered non-negotiable by Hezbollah for which Nasrallah received much negative attention regarding his decision.

His response was, "My own son has also been martyred. I know the feeling of losing someone you love. But Lebanon will be lost if we negotiate. I cannot do this. I am sorry, but I must choose the bigger picture. Daesh will not back down on their demand for our land. They want a permanent base from which to make more mischief. We must pick our battles for the greater good."

The Lebanese government and army were unable to handle Daesh. They did not have the means, training, or wherewithal to dominate, much less defeat, Daesh.

Tripoli in the north had been a well-known stronghold for Sunni extremists. It was formerly an al-Qaeda stronghold and thus ostracized by most of Lebanon. Only Sunnis seemed to thrive there. Many skirmishes occurred during the last few years, but were ignored overall in hopes it wouldn't carry over or create a basis for a new civil war.

In fact, the big concern was to avoid civil war at all costs. Until the Arab Spring, such acts of terror were looked upon as just another secular threat which could be contained.

Everyday, as Max made his way back home from work through the hour and the half detour from Beirut, I was especially glad to see him. Not just a pleasant evening spent with my husband, but even for the simple fact, not to be taken for granted, that he made it home safely another day.

"Hello, sweetheart," I greeted him.

He responded with a kiss. An American response he learned gladly from me.

"How was your day?" I asked him as we walked to the couch in our living room.

"Things are so unstable here," he replied, "that it affects our business. Everyone is worried about civil war or about Daesh. Everyone is worried about the Arab Spring going on next to us in Syria. How long can we have a stable economy with all the uncertainties? But anymore, how long can we go on wondering if we are going to be killed at any time?"

"I know," I said while nodding agreement. He sank back into the couch in deep thought. "Would you like some tea?" I asked him. "I just made some."

Max didn't answer. He always had so much on his mind. Was there something new worrying him or just the everyday worries encountered anymore?

"It's strange isn't it," I began as I poured him a cup of tea, "how the good old days now, seem to be when we only had a civil war as the problem. As deadly and horrible as it would be to have another civil war, at least we didn't have to fear Daesh before and worry about our friends and loved ones on every front. Daesh has united the different religious factions together, however."

Max leaned forward to take a sip of his tea, then sat back into the couch again.

"Things seem worse to me now than when I got here," I commented.

He nodded agreement.

"We fight a common enemy for now," he said in a subdued way. "This will not last. The hatred and fear of so many years, from all sides feeling oppressed, still exists among us. All the grievances of the past will never go away. So, our one relief is how united we are against a common enemy. But the reality is how all factions feel they are the ones being oppressed in our history. That still lingers within all Lebanese and is just waiting to come out again. We simply cannot forget how our way of life was lost with all the bloodshed and violence between us. Our loved ones and businesses that were destroyed by the past civil war. So, on one hand, we are determined to find a way to avoid civil war at all costs, but in other ways things have built up into a fear and hatred unprecedented. Daesh is just a distraction. A devastating, horrific distraction."

He sipped at his tea and thought some more.

"Lebanon is the worst it has been in years," he said with a sigh. "If you apply for a job, the first question asked is what religion are you. Or from what region. Unemployment is intolerable so the young are forced to migrate to other countries hoping for better opportunities. Crime is unprecedented because no one can make a living in a legitimate way. Countries are sick of taking us in now and deport all Lebanese no matter what religious faction they are. We have despicable reputations for money laundering and drug dealing. Why would anyone want us? A good honest individual that just wants to live with their families here are punished because there are absolutely no opportunities available for them now. Businesses go bankrupt. Banks are suspect. We basically have no government. How long can this go on? I suspect we cannot go on much longer."

"Now things are so bad we are grateful for the likes of Hezbollah," I added.

"This is why Hezbollah has taken such a strong hold," Max agreed. "They are the only opportunity the Lebanese Shia have. Since no country will take us, those of us that go abroad to get educated are prejudiced against. I experienced that myself. So, we come home to Lebanon where no opportunity exists. The really bright, intelligent individual has no better options than the uneducated individual."

"We're doing okay," I reminded him.

"I am highly skilled and educated, but also have a historic name that gains much respect. Even then we barely survive."

"But there is Hezbollah," I said. "Without having lived their history here, and their fight against my country far removed from me, all I see is their kindness to me, their respect for me, their support of me, and how they protect all of us. I really admire them now from what I do see about them. In this context. Not in their terrorist campaigns or adventurisms."

"Yes, Hezbollah has instilled a national pride in the oppressed and given them hope. I do not agree with their politics, but they have been good for us. I hate to admit it. I still am guarded in my respect for them, but I have grown to respect much about them."

"I can't and won't forget their history or their fanaticism," I continued, "but I am living the now with them. This is my personal relationship with them. And in that context, I admire these young men who are willing to give up their lives for their beliefs. In the context of what I live with them here, I support these people that I have grown to admire for their stamina and simple ways. Until it becomes an issue of whether or not they want to force me to believe as they do. That day may well come. I'm aware of it. That is the conflict. There may come a day when it is no longer 'live and let live' regarding how I live my life among them. But they have accepted me graciously, Christian that I am, American that I am."

"I understand that, Olivia. And even with me knowing their history and their adventurism, I have some of that same respect. But I have seen too much of them to have such a cherished perspective as you. But I understand you and know what you mean. I won't be petty at your expense. You have a level head about it. But remember. Hezbollah demands total submission and I can only support them for so long as they freely and bravely choose to defend mine and ours. But when I am forced to make a choice I will not choose them. For now I will accept our differences and be grateful for the protection they provide. As much as I hate to admit it, they have saved Lebanon from the abyss, puppets of Iran that they are. By pure coincidence of them being here after maliciously taking over. But circumstances form an appreciation in me how they have given their lives to protect their country and values, and in the meantime, ours also."

"I'm not making excuses for them," I came in, "but I see how you can get sucked into the illusion and passion of Hezbollah. I've studied them. It's not that I agree, but I see how it happened. Especially if they save families from starvation. But it's at a huge personal cost to give allegiance to them even for those reasons."

"Al Capone had his soup kitchens in Chicago during the depression," Max commented. "The drug cartels supposedly help the needy too. So did Osama Bin Laden. But somewhere you pay the fiddler. I will give them at least some grudging respect and even form a needed alliance with them just as America did with Stalin in the Second World War. But somewhere it comes back to haunt you, Olivia. Don't lose sight of that. Somewhere, sometime, the bill comes due. There are things to appreciate and survival is required. Just never lose sight of the entire picture."

"I know, Max. I know you're right. But I do appreciate what I've seen of them. I won't forget the rest of the story, but they do have a very human side. I am weary of the daily mourning and sadness for all the young martyrs and I am weary of grieving with their families. Hezbollah doesn't seem to have an exit plan and I fear for them because of it. They are fighting daily just to survive in this horrid, hostile land. I am grateful for their existence at this moment in time. If not for Hezbollah, Lebanon would be Syria run by Daesh. I would be more than dead. I would be grateful for death probably."

"That is why so many Christian factions have joined Hezbollah in this fight," Max added. "It has united so many of us when there was division before. ISIS is truly evil and there is absolutely nothing redeeming in anything they do."

"In America," I sighed, "the only decision an American teenager seems to have these days is what kind of car to buy, or if their girlfriend or boyfriend is cheating on them. Probably their parents don't understand them either. I can't stand that. I hate such shallowness. A sixteen year old Shia goes to war and fights jihad for his country against the worst enemy in history. You cannot help but admire their spirit. The Lebanese Army has joined with Hezbollah in the Daesh fight because they have openly stated that if left to their own devices Lebanon would be lost. These Shia fighters trained by Iran are so incredibly tough because they grew up in these mountains. They are used to little food, no heat, adverse conditions, and just go until they die. This is normal to them. I admire this and for the moment they are my ally. The ones here are my friends."

Cells of ISIS agents were discovered in our area and along the borders between Syria and Lebanon. Hezbollah remained fierce and strong in their pursuit and managed to push ISIS back to Syria.

I know I owe our teenagers in America an apology. My nephews that I love and admire especially. But the heat of the moment also brings out disgusting truths. Too much of what I released in my tantrum was too close to home not to pout over. My heart is on fire. America, world, quit living in shelter. In a bubble. In denial. Wake up.

CHAPTER 23

For months rockets hit the areas where I lived. Daesh bombed Christian villages, as well as Shia, in their attempt to create an Islamic country like the Taliban had done before in Afghanistan, the country that harbored Bin Laden and inspired 911. Some of the rockets were a mere three miles from our house. We heard them daily. We heard them in our sleep. Once, a rocket came so close the repercussion knocked me out of bed as I slept.

The road to Beirut remained arduous and long because the Sunni town in the more direct route remained sealed off. In one day, three people were killed by snipers including a fellow Sunni. But Hezbollah remained our protector as it did for the Christians in Lebanon who were all the more feeling a bond with them. Every faction seemed more supportive of Hezbollah daily, in fact, except for fundamentalist Sunni.

"Olivia," Khadija, my Hezbollah friend in Al-Habib, said to me in her daily visit to check on my mother-in-law and me. "I must warn you. Things are getting worse. You must be prepared for more disaster. Daesh soldiers were caught planting a bomb in our town's mosque."

I was surprised at how well I took the news. Was I becoming acclimated to all of this? This mosque of which she spoke was only a block away from our house. If Daesh had infiltrated Al-Habib so readily, an American like myself is especially vulnerable to attempts of being kidnapped. And if this mosque had been successfully blown up, it would have taken out the center of our town and the entire block in front of us would have been eradicated. Our view from the veranda would have been entirely different.

"Hezbollah has heightened security in our town because of the increased interest by Daesh in the area," she continued. "Hezbollah intelligence successfully thwarted the attack on this mosque and avoided disaster. Allah be praised."

"Walk with me," I beckoned her. "I was ready to walk my cat. He needs fresh air, but so do I. I do this every morning. I'd feel safer if you were with me after all this news. Do you mind?"

"It is my pleasure, Olivia, my friend."

Explosions all around kept both me and the cat jumpy. My friend showed no sign of fear, but only concern for me. Was she really not afraid? Is this yet another Hezbollah quality? Or was she simply trying to keep me calm by not displaying her own fear. *Will I ever get used to this*, I wondered to myself?

The entire walk I kept hearing explosions in the distance. One caused the earth to move.

"Do not be alarmed at these, Olivia," my friend assured. "These bombs now are from our men in retaliation. They are bombing in Syria now to drive away the opposition."

I stroked the fur of my jittery cat and shook my head in disbelief.

"This is surreal," I said with a forced smile.

Max stayed with me for a couple of days instead of going to work. Perhaps the road to Beirut was too dangerous to risk, but mostly he worried about me and his mother.

Nearby, Zahlé seemed calm when we visited friends there the next day. It was as if they had not a care in the world. Damascus is less than an hour away. One serious sweep by opposition forces and Zahlé, as well as Al-Habib for that matter, could be overrun and destroyed even if Hezbollah successfully drove them out again later. I wanted to stay, just to live in what seemed their denial. But we had to get back to our life in Al-Habib.

What are these people going through? I asked myself while looking out from our balcony towards the border as I inspected the origins of a new series of explosions around. I knew I could never tell anyone back home any of this. Maybe my brother.

If I have to run away somewhere fast, I rehearsed to myself as in a mental drill, *I can go to Cyprus, which is paradise to me, and safe, or to Cairo. Both are quick flights from Beirut. What is happening to this world?* I wondered in horror.

ISIS kept trying to take over the border towns of Syria and Lebanon. Meaning right next to us the fighting was fierce. Hezbollah, through its protection of Assad, successfully drove ISIS out of the majority of Syria for awhile. This encouraged me. I wanted ISIS so far away from me.

More hostages were taken from the checkpoints along the Syrian-Lebanese border, however. I couldn't conceive of the torment for the families of these victims. It all happened so close to me. This somehow made it more personal than hearing about people being harmed half a world away.

Thousands of ISIS fighters came pouring over the mountains trying to overtake the Shia town not twenty miles away from us one day. Most of the family of Mahmoud's former wife and daughter live in this town. But Hezbollah saved the day and within ten minutes drove them back across the border.

Every Christian in Lebanon now, it seemed, considered Hezbollah as Lebanon's saviors. With the Lebanese Army so inadequate, and with ISIS so tough, I knew that only Hezbollah, or perhaps the Russians who based in Syria, were as tough. Everyday I lived renewed awareness how Hezbollah was the only thing between us and ISIS. How these young fighters lose their lives fighting for their country. Though I constantly reminded myself, for discipline and perspective, how I despised their politics, I can tell you I cherished my Hezbollah friends. They became my heroes. They protect Christians, Sunnis, and Shia alike. They do not kidnap, rape, or behead.

In moments of reflection, the realization still dawned on me, nevertheless, of the almost certain inevitability that we would be enemies at some future date. But as Max and I often discussed, I cherished their friendship dearly anyway. If only we could live and let live and savor mutual respect in the broad perspective as well.

ISIS does not single out educated women, or Christians, or Shia. They execute everyone in their path, showing no mercy from the torture. Daily, it seemed, beheadings, rapes, being burnt alive, stonings, drownings, and dismemberment occurred. It happened for months on end all around Al-Habib and seemingly everywhere else. For eternity. Just for the show of power. For intimidation. For psychotic, demonic pleasure.

Daesh's presence kept growing daily along the Lebanese border because of Hezbollah. For confrontations. Winter is very harsh and Daesh runs out of food and shelter causing the need to raid small villages from desperation. So, Hezbollah doubled, even tripled, their fighters along the Syrian border. No one was ever safe. Executing Westerners makes for good publicity, but for every Westerner executed, five or more Arabs and Muslim are executed.

For a while I moved back to Zahlé to be among my own. To share my fears with my Christian friends, while Max stationed himself in Beirut in order to go to work and avoid the perilous and arduous commute. Zahlé seemed safe and I wanted to take advantage of it while I could. I was surrounded by wealthy Christians who had vigilant intelligence and protection of their own. I was watched after as if I was family. My building was astonishingly solid and safe with metal shutters on the doors and windows. The community was still supported by Hezbollah, who was always watching.

"Be aware," Abdul kept telling Max in their many conversations. "Our friends in Hezbollah tell us things. Zahlé is infiltrated. It is less safe than Al-Habib. I'm not sure how long your wife can remain there without you while you are in Beirut."

A nice distraction occurred one day upon the arrival of Khadija and her husband.

"Come with us to Beirut," she said. "You can stay at your husband's apartment there. Many Hezbollah are in Beirut now to help with security. Some from Al-Habib are part of the training there. My husband is an advisor for this. Daesh infiltrators are on the increase there. I am just going until the weekend. You can join us, then return with me to Zahlé where I will continue on to Al-Habib. Khalil is expecting you. We will meet him at the mosque in Burj al-Barajneh. He lives in this suburb near the mosque. Do you know this place, Olivia?"

"Yes, of course, I do," I replied. "I can't believe you're here and taking me with you to see my husband. What a treat for me. I miss Beirut. Especially Burj al-Barajneh. I've gone to the mosque there. It's Shia. The whole suburb is Shia. I suppose anyway."

"We will have a happy reunion then," she said smiling. "Then we will leave our men to themselves in Beirut. We have a car and driver for going, but you and I must take the bus for our return."

I appreciated Max's devotion all the more as we drove on the highway detour he had to travel to Beirut. It's long, winding, narrow lanes. At times, we felt like sitting ducks for any would be snipers in the hills overlooking. The security roadblocks were annoying also, even if for our own good. He endured all this just to see me.

It was dark by the time we arrived. Max was to meet us at a coffee shop he and I often patronized that was near the mosque.

"Are the streets always so crowded, Olivia?" Khadija's husband asked as he drove along looking for a place to park.

"It must be that services in the mosque are ready to begin," I explained. "I want to go to them. The four of us."

"Yes, that would be nice," she replied. "Perhaps there is still time. If we could just find a place to park and then find Khalil."

Suddenly, like a Biblical thief in the night, I heard a horrific explosion at the same time as feeling a massive impact. I remember absolutely nothing after that.

"Olivia," I vaguely heard Max say as I struggled to open my eyes and gather my thoughts. "Are you all right?" I felt the tender grip of his hand embracing mine. Slowly, consciousness seeped in. "Are you all right?" Max repeated as he stroked my forehand.

I opened my eyes ever so slowly and looked the direction of his voice.

"Where am I?" I asked only managing a raspy whisper.

"You're in a hospital ward," he explained.

I closed my eyes again and tried to make sense of what he said, but I barely had the energy to think.

"There was a suicide bomber," he explained patiently. "Two of them actually. You arrived just in time to nearly be killed."

I squeezed my eyes tightly, the only reaction I could manage.

"You will be okay. You're suffering a brain concussion from the trauma of the blast. The car saved you. Some of the people in the street near your car were killed from the impact. Many more were injured. Everyone in your car is okay, but recovering. All had concussions. There was shattered glass also, but you only received cuts. Nothing severe."

I listened to his words, trying to picture all he was saying.

"I don't see how you didn't have wounds from this," Max continued. "None in the car did. But over thirty were killed in the two bombings that occurred. Your car had chunks of body pieces splattered on it from some of the victims at the mosque. It was just outside the mosque. I heard the blast from the coffee shop and ran to see what happened. It was several minutes before I saw your car."

I squeezed his hand. I didn't want to hear anymore. All of us from Al-Habib had concussions. No severe wounds. That means everyone I was with survived. I needed to hold on to that. I couldn't cope with hearing about all the deaths and body chunks.

We were in the hospital for observation for three days. By the time I was able to sit up and watch the news on TV, all the details emerged of what I had been a part of on my arrival to Burj al-Barajneh. Thirty-seven killed and one hundred eighty-one injured from two suicide bombings set off at the same time in the same area. One at the mosque and one at a nearby bakery. ISIS claimed responsibility. There was a third suicide bomber as well, but he was standing so close to one of the bombers that he was killed from the blast. Small consolation, but something.

Max took off work to stay with us the entire time we were in the hospital, and then babied us at his apartment. We said very little, but kept to ourselves to heal our minds as much as our bodies. We read or watched the news only enough to try to understand what we never would grasp. Understand that more insanity in Lebanon just happened.

In my thoughts I began to imagine how the Jews must have felt during World War II. I never dreamed I would see the day it would seem so real to me. It was bad enough through the years to see the pictures and films of the Nazi holocaust from so long ago. Now I began to feel I was living something of it on my own. Not to compare, except to begin to identify.

"Is this the end of days?" I asked my brother in a frantic email days after returning to Zahlé. I would not share with him my encounter with the suicide bombing. But I needed to talk about my fears. My now apocalyptic fears.

Soon thereafter news came about mass shootings in Paris. Over a hundred murdered there. Shortly afterwards, scores killed at a Christmas party in San Bernardino, California. All by suicide jihadists. All related in some way to Daesh.

I was religious and loved Christianity, but I also decided long ago that many of the stories and traditions in church were sensational. Beautiful and sometimes dramatic traditions and beliefs, but not necessarily historical fact as much as spiritually fulfilling.

Even before the Beirut suicide bombings, fears were getting to me in the most profound way. Maybe Revelations was right. Even though written in code, maybe there was more to it than I gave credence. They say foxholes contain no atheists. I was more ready than ever to believe the most horrific and threatening apocalyptic scenarios in the Bible.

Meanwhile, after I moved back yet again to Al-Habib from Zahlé, the bombings by ISIS got nearer, while the beheading stories grew more gruesome and common. Hezbollah faced setbacks. Max had not ventured home from Beirut for a week due to sniper attacks on the highway. I was the most scared and paranoid I had ever been in my life.

Atrocities like in Hitler's Germany were happening all around me. Right where I was. Everytime horrors such as this happen people ask if this is the end of days. That's exactly what I was doing now and meant it. In fact, I was certain of it.

That's when I wrote my brother. I needed him now. He was religious, but also level headed. He had historical perspective for everything. I felt I could trust him. If he believed in end of days, then I absolutely did. But I needed to hear more about it. I was living the apocalypse somehow. Was it really happening? I needed to know. I demanded to know. If he saw this differently then maybe it would settle me down. But I needed my big brother.

I stared at the computer screen, thinking about how to put things. But soon I didn't care anymore. Honesty was the best policy. That's what brothers are for. He had to understand. So, just talk. Let it all come out.

"Cotton, help me. Don't breathe a word of this to mother. I don't want to alarm anyone. I know y'all know some of what's happening, but it's so much worse. The bombings, beheadings, the infiltrations, and invasions are all around. My friends in Hezbollah lose their sons in the tens of thousands. Cotton, don't you dare laugh at me, but is this the end of days? I don't know how anyone will recover from this. The Lebanese civil war wasn't this bad, even though families still reel from the atrocities. This is even worse. So much worse. People are out of their minds from grief and fear. Daesh, you know it as ISIS, has no conscience. It is worse than the camps Hitler created. I never thought any time in history could be as bad as then, but this may be. The brutality is unreal. There are so many things Americans and Europeans haven't heard. The slaughter of innocents is beyond the beheadings you hear about. Some get their heads blown off. ISIS is being innovative. The frivolous, psychotic joy they seem to derive. I see them as cowardly. That's what everyone says when expressing contempt. But it's true. They see no accountability, as if they'll never get caught in their unleashed and unashamed evil. But there is accountability and they will pay someday. The next generations will also pay in Lebanon, however. Undoubtedly, we will be a mentally ill nation because how can you possibly cope with this? If this is not Satan then what is? What do you think? You surely must have a clearer head than me now. That's what I need, a clear head. I wish I did not know what I have seen with my own eyes. Do they have predictions or wisdom about this in the Bible? Beyond the preacher stuff. Help me."

CHAPTER 24

The endless war against ISIS continued. The one oasis in it all was the email from my brother about the impending apocalypse I feared. Fears that would not go away. Fears that haunted from every crevice of my upbringing in the church prophesying how I was seeing the end of times. I waited impatiently on Cotton's reply. I even nagged him. My fears of seeming silly and superstitious were minimal compared to the horror around me inspiring my Biblical dark visions. Finally, his email arrived.

"Olivia, I don't consider you paranoid or superstitious. I'm glad you're talking about this. I love how you keep me informed of events and your coping of it. I can't believe how the administration and media seem to want us out of the loop. So much so it makes one wonder if they are in the loop themselves. To not want to be dragged into another war so badly, if that's the issue, that al-Qaeda must be considered decimated even though it isn't, and ISIS is JV, even though it isn't. That drone strikes and goodwill are enough. How this will all go away. I hope there is another way out than war. But just as alarming as war is a false peace. Why is it an either/or to us? As if we're bipolar. Not being on top of reality causes this. We seem so shallow as a society. I can't blame the government so much if it is society demanding to be lied to. Nothing works while stuck with a lying media and an out of the loop society. But back to your fear of the end of times. Remember growing up how every crisis seemed the end of times. That's where the Biblical end of times came from actually. It predated Jesus, in fact. The Jews created the imagery of the apocalypse. They lived in horrific times. It affected their psyche. Horrors predating Roman horror created apocalyptic fears. Then came the Romans themselves. The Romans did more than conquer and introduce the aqueduct. They ruled ruthlessly and demanded subservience. Any specter of rebellion and the Romans squashed it mercilessly. Then in the daily norm, they taxed the people beyond oblivion, even the poor. No peace at all in any aspect. The Romans crucified anyone that even looked like a rebel. That's how Jesus got crucified. Not because he was king of another kingdom as much as he had a following. One bringing hope to the impoverished, harassed masses. Nothing mattered to the Romans. Even some of the Jewish priesthood were corrupt. There was nowhere to turn. The Temple even got razed. In their day, both Jesus and Paul seemed to think the end of times was imminent. Some who believed in the apocalypse decided not to have children they thought it so near. Destruction, then renewal with God was the theme. The renewal of God's kingdom meant hope. Glorious hope. A vision to believe. To not give in to the doomsday staring them in the face. Many false end of times occurred in history. It isn't always bad to believe such. It keeps people focused. But also controls the masses. That's not happening with you. Your focus is good, but these are not end of times. They seem it for good reason. I'm glad it got your attention. You and I are sickened by the me-mindset of our generation. Of party mode America. Everyone wants to be left alone and it seems a plot against humanity for real life events to get in the way of false hope. Shallow false hope. Not the glory of God hope, but shallow, sensational hope. We have been secure for so long, prosperous for so long, that we don't mind destroying the goose that lays the golden egg since we've lost the connection of where security and prosperity occur. Better to lose connection and cling to false, shallow hopes. Things should be peaceful or prosperous on their own. Owed to us. Laid in our lap. No problems we should solve ourselves. We shouldn't have to earn security much less lose any sleep. You've got more guts than anyone I ever met. I'm glad Max is there for you. Islam has its virtues, but also some not so virtuous. Not just in its followers, but also the religion itself. Guys like Max feed off the virtues. Like you do off of Christianity. Keep me informed. America doesn't. I love you, Sis."

Cotton's assurances calmed me down and put my feet back squarely on the ground. Yes, things were horrible here. Beyond horrible. But there was hope. Hope we make for ourselves. But by solving problems, not by denying terror. I believe in Jesus. He is the core of hope inside me. But not falsely so. He created the me that can deal with this. I would indeed deal with this.

Hezbollah began making great progress against ISIS. The bombing was so close to us that buildings shook. But people adapted and began laughing again and acting happy. Happy because it was our bombs being dropped on ISIS.

It was reported that Hezbollah used chemical warfare on ISIS as well. Part of me quit caring. There were major battles, but ISIS was pushed back. Battles all around us. But victorious ones for us.

I was outside cleaning the balcony of our kitchen with the bombing so close. I first thought it was in our village, but it wasn't. It was in the mountains nearby and I loved to hear the bombings. To me it was a good sound. Sounds of us bombing them and driving them away from us. But five of our village's fighters were killed in a horrendous battle. The youngest was sixteen while the oldest was twenty-three. Max knew them and became depressed.

We also heard political analysts in this part of the world say Assad's Syria would not fall. It would not thrive or be what it once was, but it would not fall. Only time will tell. The Russians insisted they would not allow Assad to fall. What that meant to me wasn't that Assad would still be around as much as ISIS won't be someday.

"Olivia," one of the Hezbollah fighters told me one day as I made my rounds of greetings to my network of protectors and friends, "Daesh is the hardest fight we ever had. They are insane. Like zombies. We fight for our beliefs and our families, but ISIS just kills to kill. The toll on us is so heavy. We have lost so many fighters, but not near as many as they have. But they keep coming. As if they have nothing to lose. But how do they kill in the name of Islam? Muslims truly don't believe in this way. Nowhere in the Quran is it justified. In fact, the Quran speaks of how they will go to the worst hell if they kill fellow Muslims just for the killing."

The Mayor of our town lived next to us. I went to his house once when Max was home. This man seemingly knew everything going on. Who needs a newspaper? Especially a lying one?

"We have drones for surveillance," the mayor said. "In my basement I have access to cameras and satellite photos. Also the internet. I can watch and direct where our fighters should go. I never sleep anymore. Never. I have no time, but mostly I have no nerves remaining. One misstep by me and my fighters get killed. Then we lose ground."

"You have been successful," Max praised him. "We are safe because of you. Thank you for being so vigilant."

"Ah, well, thank you, Khalil. I feel your respect and it keeps me going. But take this with the respect I have for you. I know you are appreciative of Hezbollah, but you still have problems about us. But Khalil, so many complain about us and our beliefs, but the reason our fighters are so fierce is because this is all they have. You and others get to go abroad and get an education. This life is all our fighters know. They have nowhere to go. This is who they are. They will live and die fighting for their right to believe as they wish and for their family and tribe and for Hezbollah. This is all they have. This is what makes them such fierce fighters. They are making progress against Daesh and everyone is feeling better. Give them at least some credit. I don't hear so much bombing these days, so that is a sign it is moving away from us. Wish them well, Khalil."

Intense fighting between Hezbollah and ISIS lasted for days in a town nearby. An ISIS controlled town six kilometers from Al-Habib. Russia advised Assad to hit ISIS harder with more help from Hezbollah, the remains of the Syrian Army, and Russia itself. Iran also promised more support and wanted the war intensified so as to do as much damage as possible before the agreement with the US completed concerning nuclear proliferation in Iran.

The bombing near Al-Habib was part of that support. Our house shook at times from the explosions. It sounded right next door. But everyone was happy because it was Hezbollah kicking ISIS ass.

The town bombed was surrounded and Assad stated he would kill every man, woman, and child. ISIS uses civilians for human shields. This seems their favorite thing to do. In the past this town refused to give up its ISIS fighters. There has been so much hatred building up and directed towards this town. There were believed to be fifteen hundred ISIS fighters there. Finally, they were being slaughtered by every faction in support of Hezbollah and Assad. It could have been us being slaughtered. Or might be someday. Hezbollah saved this particular pocket for last so they could surround and corner them.

Seventeen Hezbollah fighters were listed as killed in this battle. Every day over the loudspeaker they announced the death of martyrs and it was more than seventeen. But Hezbollah killed over five hundred Daesh fighters. The town sympathetic to ISIS was completely wiped out. I can't say that I have no compassion for innocent women and children, but I'm so glad we are alive.

CHAPTER 25

It amazed me more each day when I saw our heroes in Al-Habib come in from fighting ISIS. Their ability to endure stark, cold elements and live primitively without a thought. This is what makes Hezbollah one of the few forces that can deal with ISIS one on one, toe to toe. The fighters grew up in demanding conditions and know the mountains better than anyone, so their ability to sustain themselves in the harshest of environments is unsurpassed. I have also heard this about the Kurds. The fighters I witnessed in Lebanon do not have all the winter gear we take for granted. They live frugally as a matter of course. They are a strong and fearsome force to contend with. What I call deprivation is what they call ordinary.

The Iranians that train Hezbollah fighters are some of the toughest on earth. Holdovers from ancient Persia perhaps. Or perhaps it comes from being Shia with their surviving, chip on the shoulder, underdog attitude. The Shia like to think so. The Shia have been so oppressed and brutalized by the world so long, they became tough in dealing with the worst of conditions with astonishing voracity. For now, even as disgusted as I am with the Mullahs in Iran, thank God I'm alive.

My knowledge of how the Lebanese Army cannot handle ISIS, and how the rest of the world refuses to, accompanies me everywhere I go. Whether from poor training, lack of money, lack of pride, lack of caring, or too much division, the Lebanese Army is little better than a second rate police force.

In the past, young Lebanese soldiers continually got slaughtered in conflict after conflict before Hezbollah. Long before ISIS reared its ugly head. The Lebanese Army is interesting because it is a combination of all factions. A great many are Shia, a great many are Sunni, and many are Christian. There is no social cohesion or identity in their army. This creates a problem. In the event of a civil war, martial law is out of the question because the Shia soldiers are loyal to their tribes first. If they must choose between protecting their own people against other factions in the event of major clashes, they will abandon their army duties and return to their own people. With the Sunni also, tribe comes first. Other countries have diversity of ethnicity, but Lebanon is not diverse as much as divided.

Such division in Lebanon, mixed with the fighting steel of Hezbollah, made the timing of the ISIS invasion noteworthy. Every Christian had to come to grips with sure, horrid death, or alliance with Iran's puppet Hezbollah. Hunger is the best cook goes the saying. So the odds are when the common enemy is gone, the alliance will not last.

Eighty thousand Iranian fighters became involved in some capacity in the fight against ISIS that was scattered along the Syrian borders all the way to Turkey. Then the Russians brought more troops. Hezbollah kills ISIS fighters in the thousands. All this was needed. For among the captured ISIS soldiers are Pakistanis,

Afghanis, and Saudi Arabians. ISIS just keeps coming. Wave after wave of mindless onslaught coming at these brave Hezbollah soldiers.

"We fight until we cannot fight anymore," a Hezbollah fighter told me. "But we keep fighting because it is the curse of the Shia to be oppressed by absolutely everyone, including by fellow Muslims. So, we know we have to be even more relentless than Daesh."

But in my world I fought my own battles. Just as I dealt with the complexity of living amongst the enemy, who is fighting my worst enemy for my protection, and though I all but hero worship some of the soldiers I've seen, I constantly get reminded who I am and where I came from. I still needed such to keep my feet on the ground even now. For it never failed to devastate me upon meeting men who admittedly harmed some of my fellow countrymen in other wars and were happy about it. My blood boiled. I wanted to ask them pointedly and hatefully why. How can you tell me of your oppression and then cause so much harm? Mindless harm that my Shiite husband despises himself. I will be working on this complexity forever, I sometimes think.

But in that complexity, watching my friends fight ISIS was awe inspiring. They have put their lives on the line for a Lebanon that despises them. Hezbollah has saved Lebanon when the helpless Lebanese Army could not and the rest of the world would not.

CHAPTER 26

One minute I felt numb from all the horrors, the routine of horrors, then became even more horrified somehow. I couldn't believe Daesh beheaded even the Japanese. They are out of their minds. *World, believe me, believe this horror, stop this horror*, I pleaded inside.

There was also the Jordanian pilot burned alive. Muslims abhor burning at the stake. For a fellow Sunni to do this to another Sunni, even an adversary, is just incomprehensible to them. It is very telling that ISIS chose to burn him as opposed to hanging or beheading. Burning at the stake is the worst crime you can commit against humanity. But ISIS did it. It was a statement by them.

The bombing in Beirut that landed me in the hospital as one of its victims was soon after these events. There is never time to recover in a world at war. My concussion healed, but my mind remained overwhelmed. A few months later two female suicide bombers killed and maimed hundreds of refugees in Nigeria. Refugees. The most downtrodden. Sitting ducks. This suicide attack barely made the news. I heard it through my Hezbollah friends. Were we so acclimated or so calloused to the worsening horrors?

Then came bombings in Baghdad spread out over a few days. Over two hundred killed, mostly Shia. Max was there on business for one of the bombings and heard the explosion.

The world seemed collapsing. Part of me still believed this was the apocalypse. These jihadists believed it to be such and things became a self-fulfilled prophecy with them. *We will get out of this someday*, I convinced myself. *I can just take the next plane out*, I assured myself further. Though I was horror filled, I was still confident I could survive it. And my husband needed me.

With Hezbollah fighting on so many fronts, Iran sent fighters by the thousands to bolster them. Iran had seemingly endless resources to devote to matters, in spite of economic sanctions against them. Many in Lebanon began to feel hopeful again. I allowed it to encourage myself as well at times, and used this optimism to once again move back to Zahlé, my personal paradise.

But not to be.

"You must move back to Al-Habib with your family for safety's sake," Abdul told Max and me yet again within weeks of moving there. He drove all the way from Beirut to tell us this. "There are again sleeper cells of Daesh discovered by Hezbollah in Christian villages nearby. The US consul said they cannot guarantee the safety of any American citizen in Lebanon, but especially in Bekaa. This means the both of you. They have banned travel to Lebanon for American citizens, but there are thousands of Americans already living here. No one pays attention to such warnings. But I'm warning you myself. You must live again among the Hezbollah in Al-Habib. Just like before. I had to tell you then, I must tell you now. I do not relish being the messenger of bad news."

"I understand," Max said in frustration. "But it has been safe here. The Christians protect themselves well here. It is better for us to be here. I have so far to travel to get to Beirut and it is closer from here than Al-Habib."

"Listen to me, Khalil. Daesh sleeper cells were discovered as part of a network of sleeper cells throughout many Christian villages, including Zahlé. You simply cannot leave Olivia alone anymore. It is worse than the situation before. These sleeper cells seem invisible and unpredictable. It is true, both Hezbollah and the Lebanese Army are doing a giant push against Daesh even as we speak, along the Syrian and Lebanese border that should clean out thousands of Daesh fighters. It should save us, I think. It is these sleeper cells that are the problem for you. Hezbollah is telling us that we should feel safe to go out and be normal again in a month or two. So, be optimistic, but wise. But I must say, America is not making friends. They still are bombing indiscriminately trying to get rid of Daesh and also Assad at the same time. Many people here are angry about this. You must take care, since you are Americans, that no one takes out there anger on you. You have respect in Al-Habib. That is no guarantee for your safety, but I feel you will be well received since they know you so well. But some of your politicians back home are talking about dividing Iraq up into Shia and Sunni factions. This is not setting well at all with anyone. I do not understand your country's intelligence network nor your politicians. Just be aware of this. Take care."

Between safety, caring for Max's mother, and missing my Hezbollah friends, we went back as suggested. The welcome and affection given us was so strong that I knew we made the right decision. And they showed no fear in telling us events of the war. This showed how they still accepted us.

"Have you seen the highway?" Khadija asked me the day after our return. "I have pictures to show you of it. Of the names and portraits of our beloved martyrs we have lost. Olivia, it is beyond despair all that we feel in our hearts. They are so young. The martyrs' pictures line the entire highway for miles. Hezbollah has lost more fighters than we are told. But they are making a difference in the war. We must be grateful."

Hezbollah had mounted an offensive of over two hundred thousand fighters against ISIS. Elsewhere, Egypt's new military government sentenced a thousand of the radical jihadists in the Muslim Brotherhood there to death as they began to clean up their country and protect their expats as well.

Still, the complexity of the war became even more complex. Hezbollah supported Assad because he is Alowite, which is a Shia offshoot, and because Syria has so many Shia shrines and holy places. They feel it is their duty to protect them. But Hezbollah eventually lessened that support because their fighters could not trust their Syrian counterparts. These soldiers would sell their own co-fighters down the river for money. As a result, Hezbollah put themselves in charge of their own protection. Otherwise, they never knew who was the real enemy. They could only count on their fellow fighters. But this wreaked havoc on Lebanon's economy.

Hezbollah continually worried about Iran's deal with America. The Prime Minister of Iran stated how the Mullahs must protect their people and government no matter how it affected anyone else. Hezbollah interpreted that to mean them. I interpreted that by wondering if I would be slaughtered someday.

Daily, there were still explosions. But Hezbollah prevailed and killed a hundred insurgents shortly after I arrived back to Al-Habib. As I watched our Hezbollah soldiers form and go off to battle, it sometimes moved me to tears. They touched the Quran and vowed their belief, then went forward to either die or kill the other side. Either way they fought until the fight was finished. I also watched films of soldiers expressing their devotion to the cause. Even though I knew they were brainwashed, there was a great need to fight and they kept going forward at all costs. It is jihad for them and they truly believe.

The fighters in Al-Habib are young men that work regularly each day at their job. Electricians, grocers, doctors, butchers, farmers, and plumbers. They live their lives then go to their other job, which is to kill ISIS.

There were still the cultural differences between us, however. I am not always sympathetic with them, even if it makes me seem like a bigot.

When Shia celebrate or mourn they shoot machine guns into the air. The bullets come back to earth and strike people, sometimes killing them. You can't tell them not to do it. They won't listen. When Hassan Nasrallah speaks on TV, people come out of their houses and shoot their machine guns in the air. Or if there is a wedding, the entire wedding party shoots machine guns into the air. When a martyr is honored, both at the gravesite and the funeral, people shoot machine guns into the air. It sounds like gun battle. Little kids shoot fireworks in conjunction to their family members firing their machine guns into the air. Sometimes these same children get hit by a stray bullet as it comes back to earth. But the adults still shoot their guns into the air. It is tradition and normal. No one pays attention to the firing of weapons most of the time because it is so normal. Even our cat, who cannot stand loud noises and so runs in fear, became so used to the gunfire that he sat on the balcony to watch the idiot humans wage mock war on each other.

One day the people next door began shooting their machine guns the most intensely I ever witnessed. Then fireworks began. This went on for hours. I thought at first it was a wedding, but then a beat-up pickup truck began driving around our alleyway on through town to the mosque a block away. A megaphone blasted for over an hour. This seemed unusual. Since it was in Arabic I couldn't understand what was said, but the tone was definitely solemn. I thought Hassan Nasrallah must be on TV again giving one of his inspirational speeches. I knew something dramatic must have happened. Finally, Khadija appeared and explained to me.

"A nineteen year old martyr," she began, "was killed in a battle against Daesh. His body was dismembered and they had to bring him back in pieces. This is particularly offensive to a Muslim, Olivia, as you know. We allow no autopsies, embalming, cremation, or anything that mutilates a body. Bodies are considered sacred and bathed by loved ones. He must be buried within three days because of decay and smell. To mutilate a body, especially of a fellow Muslim, is the worst offense. More than burning someone alive."

"Daesh is making another statement," I said in disgust. "It means more war. So much more war. Special war. They have to be annihilated. The very spirit of Islam was desecrated to our town. So there will be more intense warfare. Somehow this will never end."

A few days later Khadija returned with more news.

"The boy's mother lost her mind," she explained, referring to the boy that was dismembered. "She disappeared for days. No one could find her until she was seen in the next town wandering around looking for her son."

It was too painful to continue the story so my friend just stared at me breathlessly.

I could not take anymore. I collapsed on the floor and sobbed as if I was the one that had lost my child. I could not imagine anyone in hell so evil as ISIS and in my grief I prayed to God to let the grief I felt lessen that of the real mother's.

"I want out!" I screamed. "I want out so badly. Somewhere away. So far away. You won, God, or whoever it is that's testing me. I cannot take even one more horror. Ever."

CHAPTER 27

"I am not happy with my job," Max said to me after I related to him my reaction to the mother of the dismembered soldier. "We still have to worry about my mother. We cannot leave her here with Mahmoud. Maybe our friends in Hezbollah can take care of her, but they have their own problems. The war intensifies. But I will look for work in Addis Ababa. I can subcontract my services there. I checked on it. There is demand for consultants there in the financial sphere. The problem is getting clients, but I am ready to try and now is the time. Civil war may happen here at any time."

"I can stay," I said as bravely as possible. "I don't want to desert your mother."

"We will find a solution, Olivia," Max promised.

I felt as if I was deserting my friends just thinking of leaving. They were so brave. They were so good to me. I admired them in so many ways.

But the differences between me and my Hezbollah friends were so great. I knew I didn't want to be different like that. Different like them. In their manner of different. I wasn't trying to judge them, but I wanted to remain different from them in significant ways. Surely, I was as good an influence to them as they were to me, but the gaps left between us were probably insurmountable. At least for a long time to come.

I don't believe in fate or omens, at least I tell myself that, but when things happen that seem to fit some cosmic order, I don't argue. I leave it open. I even believe it possible.

One day as Max and I visited our friends in Zahlé, Abdul found us.

"How did you know we were here?" I asked him incredulously.

"I'll tell you," he said solemnly. "That's even why I'm here." This sounded serious. As usual. He turned to Max. "Khalil. I have some bad news for you. I was called by the mayor of Al-Habib. Daesh successfully made a gas attack in the area. Many people have died. But most were prepared and had gas masks. But your mother. She was alone in the house. By the time help came to see about her she was dead. In her bed. Her face blue. I am sorry to tell you this. Your worthless brother survived because he was in another town."

As strange as it sounds, I felt compassion, even love, for Max's mother. Somehow she could not help herself. As much as she taunted me, she also openly loved and appreciated me. It dawned on her that this infidel, American wife of her son was the one person who cared for her. Who was there for her. I felt loved by her.

Why did this happen now, I wondered? *Why did all of this happen now?*

Her death occurred not even a week after Max and I decided we wanted to leave. Was it a sign? I didn't want to believe this because it seemed disrespectful to his mother. Like a fate I wanted was brought forth by her death.

Our friends from Hezbollah showed her great respect as we buried her. They were family with us as they shared our grief.

We left Al-Habib and Lebanon feeling great affection for our friends there. They were of me now. Wondering how things would be with them after the war I put out of my mind. I refused to think of them as my enemy even though the probability is that we would become enemies one day for political and cultural reasons. They added so much to my life and that was how I was going to feel about them until my dying days.

Part of me wanted to go back to my home in Texas. Not just to be with my family again, but to open up people there about the realities of the world around us. I hadn't the slightest idea how to do that. My brother had not changed anyone's minds all these years, so how could I? I was a different person now. I didn't belong anywhere.

But now, as I relate these things to you, I know I belong here. Where I am now, in Addis Ababa, Ethiopia. They are a beautiful people. I feel more at home with them than in any home I've had. But I think it is because I needed to experience new things in new ways from the person I've become. I have so much more to experience in my life. Just what, I don't know.

It is a volatile world to be a consultant and constantly find new clients, but Max is the best and we've had more stability than we ever had before. He also is happy here. I could never be anywhere without my husband. We were meant to be. However anything else works in my life, this I know. We were meant to be.

www.ingramcontent.com/pod-product-compliance
Lightning Source LLC
Chambersburg PA
CBHW070312260626
47160CB00003B/819